T0106160

Sinsee Why Me

Destinies

Roxanne I Bohnow

iUniverse, Inc.
New York   Bloomington

Sinsee Why Me
Destinies

This is a work of fiction. All of the characters, names, incidents,
organizations, and dialogue in this novel are either the products
of the author's imagination or are used fictitiously.

iUniverse books may be ordered through booksellers or by contacting:

iUniverse
1663 Liberty Drive
Bloomington, IN 47403
www.iuniverse.com
1-800-Authors (1-800-288-4677)

Because of the dynamic nature of the Internet, any Web addresses or
links contained in this book may have changed since publication and
may no longer be valid. The views expressed in this work are solely those
of the author and do not necessarily reflect the views of the publisher,
and the publisher hereby disclaims any responsibility for them.

ISBN: 978-1-4502-6048-0 (pbk)
ISBN: 978-1-4502-6049-7 (ebk)

Printed in the United States of America

iUniverse rev. date: 9/9/2010

Chapter One

Sinsee had not wasted any time in taking control of Homestation. Looking back she could hardly believe that the battle for Homestation had taken place just four and a half weeks ago. With all the changes that Homestation was undergoing. Sinsee shocked Roeman yet again by adding one more statement of reality to the long list of changes that were already underway. As Sinsee looked across the desk at Roeman, she could almost predict his reaction even before she finished speaking. "I see no reason to restrict space travel from the colony worlds any longer. With the gravity fields that are now on the ships any norm can now travel in relative comfort. We control the ships and because of that we are actually the largest company to exist. We will need a new title to go with the magnitude of the volume of new business we will be doing." Sinsee smiled at Roeman, the look he gave her was not one of approval. "Really Roeman, I wish you would lighten up just a little."

"Just how light do you want me!" he asked in a snappish tone of voice. "Do you really believe that the ships crews are going to go along with you on this one? I for one don't believe they are going to like having some of those grounders on their ships." Sinsee knew that he was thinking of the past when the Millally were slaves on those very ships that they now controlled.

"Roeman no Millally living today outside of Millally herself was alive during the time of the space slaves. There is new law and that law is what we say it is. Plus I see only a small difference between transporting cargo and transporting passengers. We can make more profit from living cargo as well." Sinsee turned her monitor screen so that Roeman could see the figures she had projected for just the first year of full operation.

Roeman whistled. "Are you sure these figures are right? What about the cost of renovating the ships not to mention the cost of transporting people up to the ships. We can't just land those big ships on every world with out sustaining damage sooner or later."

"Renovating the ships is just another part of doing business. As far as landing on any planet goes, we won't have to do that. All we have to do is convince each planetary government to finance their own orbiting space station transfer platform. It would be in essence a hotel in space. The one compromise that we will have to make is that planetary control must be given their own space shuttles to transport passengers to the platforms prior to the arrival of any ship heading to the next planet of destination." said Sinsee with a smile.

"That is another point that will not go over well. Giving shuttles to any planetary government would break our hold on the control of space." Roeman shook his head. Sinsee realized that he was right on that point. She gave that one more thought and came up with a solution. With the number of Terra Two pure bloods on the increase we could train enough shuttle pilots to handle each space port." That seemed to satisfy Roeman to a point. "There is still the matter of Security on the stations themselves." he pointed out.

Sinsee tapped away on her keyboard and a diagram of the

station ring came up on the screen. "The station can stockpile cargo when no ship is due to arrive. That will also limit the number of personal needed on any given station. Almost every Terra Two telepath so far has a Lion counter part. So I really don't think that security is going to be a problem. Just the same I think we can come up with a reasonable solution to on station security before the first station even comes on line."

"We also have to keep in mind the lag time. Setting up any kind of set schedule is going to have a window of two weeks either way of an appointed ship arrival time." said Roeman. "We can give our exact time of arrival only once we have drop out of light change over. That way the port authority can notify any scheduled passengers to report to the space port for transfer to the space station hotel. Do we get any profit from the hotel?"

Sinsee had to laugh at Roeman's sudden interest in profit. "If you want to invest your own time and credits into the Hotel business, be my guest. For myself, I'm more then willing to let each planet make a little profit. Besides, the hotel will only be up and running when there is a ship due in. The rest of the time it will be empty. Where is the profit in that?"

"You know, the number of stations that are going to be needed are going to have to be made out of hull grade materials, and we have restricted production of those on the mining colonies." said Roeman as he leaned closer to Sinsee's screen to have a better look at her idea as to what the stations would look like. Just then there was a knock at the door to Sinsee's temporary office, it opened and in walked Patrick along with Jewbee .

"I thought you would like to know, the last of the med units have been cleared. If it hadn't been for the ships and their units I don't know how we would have handled the overflow in the hospital wing." said Jewbee as she sat down heavily in the only other unoccupied chair.

"What are the two of you up to?" asked Patrick as he moved

to have a look at what was on the screen. Sinsee explained her plain one more time and Roeman voiced his disappointment that the hotels would not be as profitable as he had hoped. "What are you talking about? Any planet bound person would give a years wage to spend a week in space. Forget about the passengers; think about all the Honeymooners who can brag to their friends that they made love in zero gravity."

"There won't be zero gravity on these stations." said Sinsee. "Too many norms become sick in zero gees. The point is to make them as comfortable as possible." she pointed out. Sinsee turned to Roeman. "How close is the nearest mining colony from here?" She asked.

"What do you mean close? You have got to be kidding? The nearest mining world is six months form here!" laughed Roeman. "You are going to have to stop thinking in terms of distance and start thinking in terms of the time it takes to get from one point to another, and remember, ship time is different from stationary time. Three months on ship time is three years on station or planet time."

"Then the sooner we get started the better." smiled Sinsee. "Have any of the on system station ships, that didn't join us, reply to our last message transmission?"

"Communications is getting swamped with personal requests for individual family information from those ships. They have been doing their best to get that information back to the ships, but cross-referencing ships personal with station dead is taking a lot of time." said Jewbee.

"Then transmit the full list of casualties to each ship. Let them see for themselves what happened here, make sure that you give station date of death so they know who died under the rule of the High Council and who died in the fight to retake Home Station." said Patrick. "The hardest part will be listing the children who died, remember to list their ages as well. I know that it is a hard pill to take for all of you, but that point must be made clear for every one."

"Patrick is right about that. I wish that there had been a different outcome for all those children. The fact that they were all descendents of ship personal will make it even harder for those on the ships." A tear rolled down Sinsee's cheek and she reached to wipe it away.

"I'll have those ships make contact with the colony worlds they are monitoring to set up a meeting with their ruling governments to legislate the construction of their space stations. We can also save time by sending them a copy of your station diagram." said Roeman as he punched in the command to copy to hard disk, then taking that disk with him to the communication office.

Jewbee rose to her feet slowly, she was not looking forward to sending a full list of the casualties to the ships, let alone having to compile that list. As she headed for the door she stopped and turned around to look at Sinsee. "I just thought I would mention this, I have decided to leave the ship and work at the hospital here on Homestation. That way I can be with Kreeote." With that said she turned to leave but before she reached the door Sinsee was beside her, placing a comforting hand on her shoulder.

"In that case I am going to miss you." said Sinsee, for it was her intention to go with Roeman to the Mining worlds.

Before Roeman took Sinsee's planes to communications he took them to the boys in fabrication and designs to have them double check her designs. The lead designer went over her blueprints with an eye for detail and was surprised to see that she had managed to make very few mistakes, and that he had to make only miner changes to her design.

"Our new Chandler is very well educated. I would not want her to know that I have made these changes to her design. No telling what she would do to me." the man said.

"On the contrary, I think she would be flattered that she managed to do so well on her first try. You might want to talk to her about her design and let her know what the changes were that you made. Just don't take up all of her time or should I say don't let her take up all of your time." smiled Roeman as he accepted the revised blueprints and made his way to the communication office. That done he returned to Sinsee's office where he found her going over the teaching files on ships navigation.

"What do you think you are doing?" he asked her as he looked over her shoulder.

"Hopefully learning how to pilot a spaceship, but this doesn't seem right to me." She showed him the plot she had tried to program onto the test screen. "I wanted the ship to go to Wallis Colony but I ended up over here instead. What did I do wrong?"

"That is simple. You forgot to compensate for the gravity pull of the white dwarf at turn over. Don't worry about that though, everyone gets that one wrong their first time out. Wait, your not thinking of making this trip to the mining world with us are you? No. It is out of the question. You are the Chandler, your place is here on Home Station."

"My place is where I say it is, not you. I am going to the mining world and just so that the trip is not a total waste, you can start teaching me how to captain a ship right now." Sinsee didn't raise her voice, she didn't get angry, and she just stated the facts.

"You don't give up do you?" She shook her head. "All right, before we leave I guess I can start you out on a shuttle. But no funny business, you do what I tell you when I tell you. Is it a deal?" Sinsee nodded her head in agreement. "I'll have Tiny get out a couple of AECS's. I am not going out there with you at the helm without protection. You could hit something and there goes our air supply."

"Oh you of little faith." she smiled at him and he smiled back.

"Faith has nothing to do with it. Just remember your little

collision with Henson in the passageway and then talk to me about faith." Roeman left her with that finale thought and went to find Tiny and the AECS's.

Her first lesson as a shuttle pilot left her shaking all over. Roeman remained calm as ice. He had let her make an attempt at landing the shuttle in the docking bay, but not before he had given the order for the bay to be completely evacuated of all personal. Roeman knew what to expect once the shuttle had past all the dampers but he deliberately said nothing to Sinsee. Once past the last of the dampers the shuttle picked up speed fast, Sinsee cut power and dropped the shuttle to the deck like a stone. Sparks flew out from the underbelly as the shuttle careened across the docking bay floor and came to rest just inches from the bulkhead. Sinsee turned to look at Roeman. "I hate you." was all she said as she unhooked her harness and got to her feet, heading for the hatch, Roeman caught her by the arm.

"You did good. In fact, you did better then I did my first time piloting a shuttle." He was smiling at her and that only infuriated her more.

"Is this how you train all of your pilots!" she snapped at him with fire in her eyes.

"As a matter of fact, yes it is." His smile became even bigger. "You're the first one who didn't crash on landing. Why do you think we are in full suits. Everyone crashes, everyone except you that is."

"Are you telling me that even you crashed a shuttle in training." This form of training made no séance at all to her, she became even more confused when Roeman began to chuckle.

"I think you should know that I crashed five shuttles before I was able to make a landing like the one you just made." Shrugging in an AECS made it dam near imposable but somehow Roeman managed to do it.

"What a waste of equipment. Why do you do It?" she asked him, her anger dissipating.

"It weeds out those who don't have the guts to be a good pilot. You reacted faster then anyone I have ever seen on their first run. I wouldn't be surprised if within a few work cycles you start landing this thing backwards."

"Right now I'm more interested in a long hot bath." She paused to look at him for a moment. "Have you ever thought that maybe you have lost more good pilots just because you wanted to scare the hell out of them just for the fun of it. There is a lot more to people then a blood and guts charge. Seems to me that you waste people in the same way that you waste equipment." Roeman watched as she left the shuttle and the docking bay. He got that sinking feeling that another one of their long traditions was on its way out the airlock. As Roeman made his own way across the docking bay he over heard someone demanding payment on a wager.

"She didn't hit the bulkhead so you pay me those credits."

"No way! The captain must have taken over the controls at the last moment."

"Well there he is. Why don't you ask Him?"

Without even looking back to see who it was who was arguing, Roeman said in a loud voice, " The Chandler herself set that shuttle down.

She is greater then any first pilot I have ever seen. Never doubt the powers of your Chandler. I am sure that I won't make that mistake again. I advise that you do the same." He continued to walk away from the two dock workers and made his way into the main corridor, he was hoping to catch up to Sinsee before she reached her quarters.

✳

As Sinsee entered her temporary quarters Kit raised his head and watched her as she crossed the room. {["Why are you so angry?"]}, his words came into her mind. {["And why are you wearing that suite? Has there been an accident some where on the station?"]} Kit didn't need to look at her body movements that were hidden under the AECS, he could feel her emotions as easily as his own.

{["I don't like waste."]} she snapped. {["I just don't get it. These people have so much knowledge and yet they waste equipment and man power on stupid games. There is so much good here and yet every time I turn around I find barbaric traditions that would make a sane person cringe."]}

{["Yes, I understand this feeling. But you are not like the others. Your mind thinks in a different way from them. You have taught them many new ways already, and they will learn more ways from you. They see and learn by watching you. As do my own people."]} Kit once again spread his massive frame out on the floor, his legs now stretched out into the room. It didn't take long and his even breathing indicated to Sinsee that Kit was once again fast asleep. Kit was doing a great deal of that lately, Sinsee wondered why it was that Kit and some of the other big Terra Two Lions were spending most of their time sleeping. She had better ask Patrick if he knew anything about this strange behavior in Kit and if it was a sign of some kind of sickness, but for right now she needed that bath so she headed for the bathroom, having to step over Kit's protruding legs that lay in her path.

As she drew her bath water she thought about what Kit had said, They see and learn, they see and learn. How could she show them that there was a better way and most importantly a safer way to train pilots if she didn't know how to pilot a shuttle to a safe landing with out scrapping the hull platting off the underside. The major problem was that coming from zero gravity into the full gravity of the docking bay was such a fast transition it was like falling out of bed in a sound sleep. It didn't help that no warning is given to the prospective pilot in training. Sinsee realized at that point that it wasn't a matter of landing as close to the buffing fields as possible. It was a matter of position, contact, and speed. She turned off the water, grabbed her gloves off the sink counter where she had left them and headed out of her quarters picking up her discarded helmet on her way.

Sinsee met with some resistance in the docking bay when she attempted to enter the shuttle she and Roeman had so recently disembarked from. With her anger mounting inside of her, she barked an order at the bay worker. "You will get out of my way or you will come with me, it is your choice." With that threat the man backed away from her and went to notify Captain Roeman as to what the Chandler was going to do, but by the time Roeman reached the docking bay Sinsee was already outside the station. Roeman rushed to the observation deck and the shuttle communication room.

Sinsee was picking points in space at random and moving the shuttle to each point with more and more accuracy. Now she wanted to see if this would work for contacting the under side of the shuttle to a point on the outside of the station. She moved the shuttle closer to the station. As she did this the com unit came to life, it was Roeman.

"Chandler, you are to close to the station. Move off now or you will ram the plating." warned Roeman.

Sinsee opened her com. "Hello Captain, where are you?" she smiled at the irritation in his voice.

"Observation. North of the docking port. Please return to the docking bay Chandler." From the tone of his voice this was not a request, it was an order.

"It is good to know where you are and I am flattered that you are so concerned for my safety, unlike earlier when you would have allowed me to crash this shuttle all over the bay. If you would please look out your port I would like to show you something." Sinsee maneuvered the shuttle away from where she had intended to make contact with the station and instead brought the shuttle around to observation. With the utmost accuracy Sinsee maneuvered the shuttle so that its nose began to inch closer and closer to the viewing port plexiform glass. She watched as those within the room scrambled for the exit. Roeman stood his ground standing just feet away from the port. The nose of the shuttle made contact with the glass and stayed there. "Do you like my game Captain?"

Roeman nodded slightly and stood there smiling at her. "I believe that your point is well taken. Will you be returning to the docking bay now or will you be staying out there for a little while longer."

"Now that I have made my point I think I will be returning to the bay. See you there no doubt." She moved the shuttle away from the port and headed it in the general direction of the docking bay.

Roeman cut the com to the shuttle. "No doubt Candler." he said to no one in particular. As he turned to leave, the others were just returning, seeing that it was now safe. A few of the worker made it a point to not make eye contact with Captain Roeman, but when he had left the room it became filled with the sound of voices. Many of whom were speculating as to what, if anything, the Captain would do to the Chandler.

Roeman stood at the far end of the docking bay, where he waited for Sinsee to walk the distance across the bay to him. When she walked right past him without even acknowledging his presence his eyebrows went up. With a half smile on his face he turned to follow her. Only one person bothered to watch them as they left the docking bay, a young man who had failed the pilot program, once the Chandler and the Captain had left the bay he turned to look at the shuttle, a twisted smile formed on his face.

With no one to hear him Roeman lit into Sinsee. "Don't ever pull a stunt like that again, at least not without me or one of the other captains with you." He reached out and took her arm and wrapped his around it. "You had those boys running for cover so fast I'll bet a few of them had to change their pants."

Sinsee tried her best to repress the laughter that was welling up and threatening to come to the surface. "I noticed that you stood your ground." she said.

"More like frozen in place." He stopped and made her look at him. "You have a lot of guts and I really don't want to see them splattered all over the outside of this station, promise me you won't do a stupid stunt like that again."

"That I can do Roeman, mainly because now there is no reason for me to do something like that again. I don't think it will take long before the pilot training program has more students then it can handle, and we are going to need every one of those new shuttle pilots in the near future." she tilted her head just so and that charm of hers hit its mark.

"There are so many different levels in you that it is darn right spooky." Roeman could not help himself so he started to laugh as they again moved on, heading for Sinsee's quarters. "You never got that bath that you wanted, did you?"

"I'm going to now." she said. "That is if I can get past Kit. I can't wait until the work is done on the inner sphere so Kit can have his own room. As it is he can just make it through the main door and into the living room."

"Why doesn't he stay in the converted cargo dome with the other lions that chose to stay on station?" asked Roeman as they neared her quarters. Sinsee didn't know the answer to that question but she intended to find out. As they entered her quarters they found Kit still asleep. "Does he do this a lot?" asked Roeman.

"Yes, more then I would like. I was going to ask Patrick if he knows any reason why Kit and some of the other Terry Two lions are sleeping so much, but I got distracted." replied Sinsee.

"You call that a distraction." laughed Roeman. His laughter woke Kit from his sleep and the big cat stretched and yawned. Standing up on his front legs he looked at one then the other of the humans.

{["You are still in that suit. Have I missed something?"]} Kit asked. That sent Sinsee into a fit of uncontrolled laughter. When she finally got control of herself she told Kit what she had done. {["You should have told me what you were going to do. I would have been more then happy to join you. It would have been the perfect opportunity to get away from some of these females who keep hounding me."]}

So that was why Kit spent most of his time sleeping. When asleep the big cat did not hear the mental thoughts of his fellow cats. There were a number of females on the station but very few males. Kit was the biggest of all the males so it would be natural for the females to seek him out for a mate.

"You won't have to worry about that." said Sinsee. "We leave soon for the mining colony. Those girls will just have to find some other buck to bother for a while." Sinsee reassured Kit.

{["That will prove difficult for them, being that no other male on this station is of mating age as yet."]} Kit yawned again, and lied back down to once again fall asleep.

"That was fast." said Roeman as he scratched his chin. "Is he alright?" Between giggles Sinsee explained what Kit's problem was. "Well if you think it is crowded in here wait until you have to spend months at a time onboard ship with that big cat stretched out in one of those small cabins."

"I didn't think about that. Maybe we had better convert an area in the shuttle bay for him. He can use the waist units that you and I use with some maneuvering, but I think he should have a unit of his own." she said.

"I'll get on that right now." Roeman had to step over one of Kit's hind legs to reach the door. "He sure is a sound sleeper."

✱

With every one busy working on preparations for the trip Sinsee soon found that she had nothing to do herself. She was board so she decided to take another trip in one of the Shuttles. This time she took Kit with her. Along with Kit she had the boys in the bay fix up a little surprise package. This time she let Roeman know that she was going out and asked him to join her in a different Shuttle. When he asked her what she was up to she would only say that he had to come out and see.

A short time later, Roeman, suited up, was in his own shuttle and lifting off the docking bay floor, as soon as he cleared the bay a number of the workers made their way to observation.

The moment Roeman cleared the station he began to look for Sinsee's shuttle. It didn't take him long to find her. He opened his com. "OK Chandler, You got me out here, now what?"

"Hi Roeman. Have you come to join me in a little shuttle dancing. It's fun. Watch this!" She put her shuttle into an axes spin and then countered it with a back thrust, bringing the shuttle to a full stop. "It is similar to a dance back home." Roeman gave it a try and wobbled for only a moment then regained control. "Not bad. How about we spice it up a bit." Sinsee put a music disk into the playback and began a series of maneuvers in time with the music. Roeman followed her lead and stayed right on her tail. When the music stopped Roeman took his shuttle to the right and Sinsee went left in a circle pattern until the two shuttles were nose to nose at the end of a half circle. "Now What?" Roeman asked with a smile.

"How about a little game of ball?" said Sinsee, she hit the switch that released a large orange ball from her bottom air lock.

Roeman looked at the ball and shook his head. " Just what am I going to do with that?" he asked her. He heard Sinsee call for the two other shuttles that had been off to one side watching their little show. These shuttles widened the distance between each other and when Sinsee gave the signal they dropped open cargo crates from their airlocks. Sinsee hit a switch and out from those crates expanded two rings, one for each crate. One ring was red and the other one was yellow. "You have got to be kidding."

"Not at all. The rule is that you can only use one thruster at a time and only at level 2. We start with the ball between our two shuttles, I want to get it into your red ring. You have to try to get it into my yellow ring. Are you ready?" she asked.

"Bring it on." Roeman moved his shuttle into place. "Who gives the signal to start?"

"I do." It was Patrick in Observation. "You two ready, good. On my mark, set, go!"

Sinsee let Roeman nudge the ball out closer to the playing field. He was having trouble keeping contact with the ball and the moment it got away from him Sinsee went for it, unfortunately for her she had no better luck keeping contact with the ball then Roeman had. Soon Roeman swept in and took the ball from her. This back and forth maneuvering went on for some time. Unknown to the two contestants they were being cheered on by a number of spectators in observation.

Roeman saw his chance and made a move that sent the ball heading straight for the yellow ring and through it. When Sinsee suggested that they go again she was interrupted buy Patrick, "Chandler, you have Kit with you don't you?" When she said that yes she did, Patrick said that she had better call it a day. "Kit uses up a lot of O2. When was the last time you checked your levels?"

"I see what you mean. Sorry Roeman, looks like I have to call it a day for now." said Sinsee. "I'll tell the boys to pack it up."

"Don't do that just yet. I want to get in some practice." One of the other shuttle pilots offered to play a game of ring ball with Roeman and he accepted. "See you inside after a while Chandler."

Ring ball turned out to be a good training tool for the new shuttle pilots, only they worked with a single ring and were timed on how long it took them to get the ball into the ring. Only the best pilots were allowed to challenge each other to a two ring game. Everyone had their favorite pilot and betting on that pilot became the pass time of almost everyone on the station, including Sinsee.

Sinsee worked out the new contract agreements for the Colony Worlds. There were still a number of restrictions that the Millally refused to give up, and the one thing that Roeman insisted on was that any Ships Captain had the right to restrain any passenger that got out of hand, but if the offence was bad enough, then his or her home world would be fined and further restrictions could be implemented against that world. It was suggested that cargo could be expanded for some of the colony worlds, but when Sinsee wanted to know why only for some and not for all, she was told that there were some worlds that still had a war like mentality, and it would not be wise to provide them with anything which they could use against the Millally at a later date.

Roeman set a departure time for the Antiack and the ship was provisioned for a two year voyage. A large supply of meat was added to the regular store of supplies. The last thing Roeman wanted on his ship was a hungry Lion even though he knew that Kit would eat grains and vegetables as well.

One of the things that Roeman had done was to convert a number of small cabins into a larger accommodation for Sinsee's uses. "But why go to all this trouble for me? I never minded bunking with the other crewmembers before." she said.

"You are forgetting that you are the Chandler now. We can't have you climbing in and out of a crew bunk in crew's quarters any more. If you will notice also, that fabrication has enlarged the doorway to accommodate Kit as well. This isn't the only improvements that have been made. Medical now has its own gravity containment field. They can now go to zero gravity without affecting the rest of the ship." Roeman walked over and opened another door for Sinsee. "This is your bedroom. The door to the left is your bathroom and I'm sorry but the shower is still a sonic vibration cleanse. Can't have running water in case we loose gravity. If someone were to be in a water shower at that time they could drown."

Sinsee returned to the main room and sat down in one of the overstuffed chairs. "It's not fair Roeman, I'm not the only Chandler anymore."

"True, but you are THE CHANDLER." he said as he sat down in the other chair that was beside hers. They sat there for some time in silence. Roeman could see that it bothered Sinsee to be separated from other people by her rank as Chandler. Here she was, a young women who had saved the Catsman race, the Millally Homestation, and she had even given the Millally a Home World. True, she was making changes willy nilly, but all of those changes have turned out to be good for everyone all the way around. Now here she was sitting here feeling cut off from the very people she saved. "You know, you could start thinking about who you want on your board of advisers. People you could be close to. People you can trust."

"I trust you and Jewbee. I'm sorry she is not coming on this trip with us. I miss her already." Sinsee said as she pulled at a loose thread on her blouse.

"Do you want to send her a com message and ask her if she wants to be on your Board of Advisers? You know, it just might be a good thing that we will be gone for a few years. Jewbee is going to need that time to get over having a swollen head." Roeman chuckled under his breath.

"What about you, Roeman. We need someone who can deal with the ships and knows how to get things done. Just look at what you did with your own ship. You want the job?" Sinsee smiled at him. Roeman laughed even harder until he realized that she was serious.

"I'll have to think about that one for a while. You see, the thing is, I like being a ships captain. I am not sure that I can just give that up." he confided .

Sinsee leaned forward to look deeply into his eyes. "Why can't you do both? I'm not going to spend the rest of my life on Homestation. I want to visit the colony worlds."

"All of them?" Roeman scratched at his chin in thought. "That could take a whole life time."

"Good." said Sinsee. "That means that you can take your time teaching me how to captain a ship. I'll have plenty of time over the years to watch and learn from one of the best." Now it was both of them who laughed. Roeman was glad that they were the only ones in the room. He didn't let go of his emotions very often, and never in front of the crew, well almost never.

"Isn't it lucky for you that it is going to take us a while before we reach our first destination then. You can start your training in navigation. You already have a head start in that field as it is. You can learn just where all those colony worlds are that you are so anxious to see. That way you might just change your mind about visiting all of them." said Roeman.

"So it is back to school for me, is it. Or are you using this to keep me out from under your feet?" she asked him in a jokingly manner.

"Unfortunately, this is going to put you right under my foot as you put it. Navigation is on the bridge, and that is where I should be right now. You can join me there when you are ready. Oh yes, you might want to check in on Kit before you come to the bridge." smiled Roeman. "The boys from fabrication had some fun with his accommodations as well. I wouldn't mind playing around in there myself." He rose to his feet and let himself out.

Before Sinsee went to see Kit she stopped in at communications and sent a message to Jewbee. Not waiting for a reply she headed down ship to have a look at what fabrications had set up for Kit.

Kit's room was half the size of the shuttle bay and all the free standing structural supports were wrapped with reinforced rope. These supports led to upper platforms that were carpeted with what looked like grass. There were hanging nets from over head made from the same type of reinforced rope on the supports. There was even a sonic cleanse shower, and that was where Kit was right at the moment. He was wiggling his body and purring rather loudly.

{["You might not want to spend all your time in there. You could lose all your fur if you over use that thing you know."]} she said as she reached in to scratch his head.

{["Never happen. But you are right, I have been in here long enough."]} Kit moved out of the shower and pounced up onto one of the rope covered supports and climbed up it to leap over to the upper platform. {["I hope that your room is as nice as this. Would you like a drink of water?"]}

{["Sure."]} Sinsee looked around for some other way to reach the platform. Off to the side there was a ladder frame that protruded from the bulkhead. She went to it and started to climb, at the top she stepped easily onto the platform. She was surprised to find that there were many human conveniences on this lofty platform. Someone had done their homework as well, for there was a mural of the forest where she had found Kit, on the back wall. {["Wow! I think I'll move in with you. This is great."]}

{["Yes. I feel right at home here. You will find drinking cups and things in that cabinet in the corner at the back. Just stand on the floor plate and the water will flow."]} Kit indicated the floor plate with his paw. Sinsee got a cup and a bowl but when she stood on the floor plate nothing happened.

{["I must be too light to activate it. You're going to have to stand on it for me."]} she said.

{["It works for the big man."]} said Kit as he came over to put his paw on the plate. The water flowed and Sinsee filled the cup and bowl.

{["You must mean Tiny. He is big even for a human. I'll ask him to adjust the plate for me the next time I see him."]} She carried the cup and bowl out to the center of the platform setting the bowl on the floor. Instead of taking one of the human chairs Sinsee sat down on the floor. Kit lay down before her.

{["Is something on your mind?"]} asked Kit. He felt that she was troubled about something.

{["Roeman suggested that I form a board of advisers. That sounds good but I really don't know many of the Millally. Most of them look at me as unapproachable. That's not what I want."]} she said.

{["Sometimes what we want and what is right are two different things. You can achieve one through the other but only in the right order. Think about all the things that make up your world right now. There is our home world. That means your people and mine. There are the Catsman. And there are the Millally themselves. Each group will have their own wants, but if you see to their needs the wants will take care of themselves."]}

{["You make it sound so simple when you put it that way but I will be dealing with humans and no human is simple."]} she said.

{["True, but you have done well for yourself so far. Have you been thinking about yourself all this time or have you been thinking about others?"]} He let her think about that for a little while. {["You can not change what you are. You can only do your best. For you that is perfect."]}

On her way back through the ship Sinsee stopped in at communications again. This time she asked Jewbee to find her representatives from every aspect of the station. These people would form a secondary board. She also asked her to see if Preegar would be willing to serve on the main board as representative for his people. Jewbee had a good feel for people and with Preegar at her side Sinsee felt that she would have no trouble finding just the right board members for her. She also asked that a message be forwarded to Terra Two, asking that a representative be found who would be willing to live at Homestation. With that out of the way she made her way to the bridge and her lessons in navigation.

Four months into the trip Sinsee was plotting courses faster then anyone Roeman had ever seen before so he gave her the opportunity to do the real thing. He had her plot a course into an unclaimed system and placed the ship in orbit around the fifth planet out from the sun/star. What he did not tell her was that she was not using the mock training program. As always she had the course locked into the system in record time. "That's it, take her in Henson." said Roeman.

"What! This isn't a simulation?" asked Sinsee.

"Nope." said Roeman as he headed for the passageway. "Care to join me for a cup of coffee Chandler?" His use of her title told Sinsee that something was up. It had been a long time séance anyone had called her Chandler. She rose from her seat and followed Roeman. Instead of going to the galley he led the way to her quarters.

Once inside Sinsee snapped at him. "Why did you do that on the bridge? Do you know how long it took me to get everyone to treat me as one of the crew and stop bowing to me every time I entered a room!"

"Yes I do know, and I am sorry that I have to put a stop to it. In two months we will be arriving at the Mining World of some of the stuffiest government officials you may ever meet. I know it is a mining world but these people do everything by the book. They are so stuck into rules and regulations that they even have a manual that tells them how to make love." said Roeman.

"You're joking, right." she said, but from the look on his face he was not joking. He was dead serious. "But why do I have to give up my friendships on the ship just because the miners are a bunch of stuffed shirts?"

"Because you now represent the Millally. We have managed to maintain a hard line with these people. You have to be the one in control and you can't do that if one of the crew slips up and calls you by your name. Remember what I told you about the Chandler. Knowing her name gives power to the one that uses it." he said.

"That was before, this is different." she said.

"No it is not. Only in that you are dealing with Millally, these people are not Millally. The planet leaders are expecting the new leader of the Millally and right now you don't look like a leader to me. So, I'm going to be sending you two girls who are going to help you look like a lady. You know, hair, makeup, clothes, that sort of thing. In the mean time I am going to make sure that every one on this ship starts calling you Chandler again so they can get into the habit."

Sinsee started to chuckle. She had learned from the best teacher on her planet how to use the wiles of her feminine side. She could tell Roeman this fact but she thought it would be more fun to play along with him. "I hope those girls know what they are doing." Just then there was a knock at the door and Roeman answered it, he stepped aside to allow two women to enter. These women could never be mistaken for girls. They bowed slightly to Sinsee with respect, Roeman introduced them to Sinsee. There names were Abby and Tessa, along with them came four medium suit cases, which they opened at once. While the women were fussing with the cases Roeman took his leave.

Sinsee was amazed to discover that there were shampoos and conditioners among their supplies along with a generous supply of makeup.

"The Captain has given permission for you to use water to clean your hair. The sonic cleaners do a good job but there is no replacing a good conditioner. But then the Captain does not understand these things. It took Tessa some time to explain the importance of maintaining healthy hair to the Captain." Abby was rambling on and at the same time she was busy unbraiding Sinsee's long hair. Tessa was looking at Sinsee's hands and nails, making clicking sounds the whole time.

Sinsee was pampered in a way that not even Nika could have found fault in it. Abby talked none stop and Sinsee was brought up to date on just about all of the gossip onboard the ship. Sinsee had spent so much time on the bridge and with Kit in his quarters that she had almost forgot that there were more then two hundred crew members onboard. Each one with their own unique set of everyday problems, some more pronounced then others.

Still all that talking reminded her that instead of being a part of the crew she had actually isolated herself from them, other then those on the bridge. The bridge personal treated her as an equal, but then the bridge crew's were at the top of chain as personnel went. Sinsee finally began to understand why Roeman was so concerned about her wanting to associate with the rest of the crew. Then a thought came to her. What if it wasn't so much that the bridge crew treated her as an equal but rather that she was treating them as her equal. Maybe it was that old status thing coming into play. "I'm damned if I do, and I'm damned if I don't." she said aloud.

"I beg your pardon Chandler?" asked Abby.

"I was merely talking to myself." Sinsee recovered. "I thank you for providing me with all of these wonderful personal care items. I have been so busy and I have so much more to do. I seem to have neglected my own personal care."

"Yes," said Abby. "I can see that. I mean with all that you have to do, where would you find the time to look after yourself. What you need is a personal dresser, to look after your things as it were, someone to see to your appearance. I understand that your predecessor had an entire team to see to her needs."

"Yes, well I don't know about a team, but you may be right about a personal dresser. I will need someone who knows what she is doing, someone who can blend in with the people and keep me informed as to what the people really think. Someone who can alert me to any problems that I can deal with directly. Do you know anyone like that Abby?" smiled Sinsee.

Tessa started to laugh. "She found you out Abby. I told you she would." Abby started to blush as she attempted to apologize to Sinsee.

"Enough of that Abby. You have the job, but only under one condition. You will never gossip about any government affairs you may over hear. Anything else, I leave to your good judgment." Sinsee turned to Tessa. "You are also welcome to join Abby, Tessa."

"Thank you Chandler. I promise that I will keep Abby under control." teased Tessa as she pinched Abby's arm. A loud thump at the door prevented Abby from complaining. Tessa went to see who it was. Both women were shocked when Kit pushed his way past them to make his way to Sinsee. He stopped and sat down on his rump, tilting his head one way then the next as if he were trying to decide weather or not he liked her new look.

{["Well, what do you think. Do I look presentable?"]} she asked him.

{["As far as humans go, I would have to say yes."]} Then with his hind paw Kit began to scratch his neck. Some of his mane came out in his claws.

"Oh Kit, it seems that I have not only over looked my own grooming but I have over looked yours as well." Sinsee picked up a brush and started to brush out his long mane.

"No, no, Chandler. You will ruin all our fine work on your nails. Let us care for your mind brother." said Abby as she took the brush from her. "Oh my, your hair is so thick. You have a lot of mates as well. Tessa would you please hand me those clippers."

Sinsee intervened at that point. "You can not cut his mane off. It is a symbol of his rank."

"Well in that case it will take a long time to pick out these mates." she tried to use a comb but it broke. "Well this won't work. I need to talk to Jerry down in the machine shop." Abby picked up another comb from her case. "I'll be back in a short while." With that she left.

"Will your brother be going with you when you go to talk to the leaders of the mining world?" asked Tessa "I for one would like to see their reaction when they see him walk into their halls. You could ride in on his back as you did when you first came to Homestation. I didn't get to see that one myself. I'm not saying that I would have wanted to see that. From all I have heard that was a hard fight."

Sinsee had to laugh. She could see why these two women were close friends. "You do understand that there will be people who will try to get close to you because of your working directly for me don't you."

"I never really thought about it, but it could happen." said Tessa. "At my age I think I can tell when someone is trying to use me. Abby may seem like a flighty airhead at times but she is very much aware of people and their intentions. So if you are thinking that we might use our positions for some type of advantage, just let me assure you that the advantage will be yours." Tessa bowed lightly to Sinsee.

"In that case, I think that you and Abby should join me on the planet." smiled Sinsee. "The two of you can be my eyes and ears behind the seines. I can tell that you have a way of getting people to open up to you. I want you to use that knack to find out how the general population thinks about the new changes that will happen, and what they think of their own government. I want all the gossip you can dig up."

"Abby is going to love this. She was right about you. You can see talent in anyone. Only one thing though, in order to get people to talk to us about the juicy stuff we have to give them little tidbits ourselves." Tessa waited for Sinsee to say something.

"I know that you would never do anything to harm the cause of your own people. That said, you know what you can and can not say." Sinsee looked at her with raised eyebrows.

"Yes Chandler, I understand." Tessa returned to the job of packing up all her tools.

Over the next two months Sinsee became more accustom to the unique qualities of her new helpers. Abby could find anything, anywhere. She knew just where to go on the ship and who to talk with to get what she wanted. Tessa was a gem with thread and needle. She put together a small wardrobe for Sinsee that did not get in the way of Sinsee's body Movements and yet showed her attributes to her advantage.

Roeman was more then pleased with the way that Sinsee now carried herself. When he thanked Abby and Tessa for the way they were teaching Sinsee how to behave like a lady the women put him straight.

"Captain, the only thing we have done is to see to her personal appearance. In no way have we showed her how to walk or talk or handle herself in the company of men. These things she already understood. Your problem is that you are looking at her as a little girl, try looking at her as The Chandler." Both women walked away from him in a huff.

Sinsee's plan to ride Kit was topped off by Roeman's own plan. There were six Catsman onboard who would serve as Sinsee's personal guard, complete with matching uniforms. Even the saddle that Kit was to wear matched the uniforms. When Sinsee mentioned that she thought it was a little over kill with all the glitter, Roeman explained his reasoning behind all the pomp.

"It's not over kill as much as it is to show that you are in complete control. The fact that you can mind talk with the Catsman and Kit will be to our advantage. Right now the

Mining Leaders think that they have the upper hand because of the shift in power within the Millally. It's Best to show them that they are wrong right from the start. You will be the first Millally leader to personally make an appearance on any world. The fact that you have chosen their world actually does give them an advantage. Our advantage is that they don't know about the Catsman. Showing them that there are other beings in the universe besides humans is a good way of getting their attention." said Roeman.

"Then there is just one more thing I want to know. Why is the saddle a side saddle?" asked Sinsee. "And why do I need a saddle at all? I never used one when we took back Homestation."

"That was Tessa's idea. She has made you a dress to wear that won't allow you to straddle your legs over Kit's back. I have seen the dress and I agree with Tessa." Roeman formed an hourglass figure with his hands to give her an idea of what she was in for. "We will be in orbit in two hours so I'll be on the bridge. You should go to your quarters. Abby and Tessa are waiting for you. Oh, and don't let on that I told you anything about the dress. The girls wanted to surprise you."

Three shuttles transported everyone to the surface of the planet. This was Sinsee's First trip into an atmosphere riding in a shuttle. It was completely different from riding down in a full scale ship. The moment the shuttle hit the atmosphere it began to shake and buck. Sinsee looked behind her to see Tessa and Abby hanging onto each other in a death grip. This was their first time riding into an atmosphere as well. Then Sinsee remembered Allison's reaction to standing under an open sky. "Listen to me," she said to them. "When we land I don't want either of you to look any where but at ground level, do you hear me. Never take your eyes off the ground. You have never been on a planet before and I don't want either of you showing any weakness to these people. Do you understand me?" The two women nodded their understanding. Sinsee didn't like being gruff with anyone, it just had to be done sometimes. She could see that their fear of the shuttle entering the atmosphere was lessening as they now focused on what she was saying to them. "Stay close to each other, if you have to, hold each others hands. Talk to each other to take your minds off of anything that might cause you fear. Most of all try to remember that what you don't see can not harm you."

Roeman felt a twinge of pride in the way Sinsee handled Abby and Tessa. He knew that this was her first trip down in a shuttle as well and first timers were prone to flipping out because they always thought the shuttle was breaking apart. He brought the shuttles in over the port and set them down as far away from the port buildings as he could. He had been in contact with their man at the port who told him that the mining guild had been preparing for their arrival, when he didn't offer any details Roeman suspected that the Guild may have taken over the port.

"We'll just sit here for a while. Lets see how long it takes them to figure out that we are not just going to walk into their little trap."

"How can you be so sure that it is a trap?" asked Sinsee.

"Because that is what I would do if I were them." he answered.

"And if they don't come out to greet us, what then?" she wanted to know.

Roeman turned in his seat to look at her. "The old contracts are still in place." He saw the look that she gave him. "Don't worry. I wont hurt anyone. I'll just open up a pit in front of that building. Shake things up just a little."

"I would really rather that you not do that Captain. Please open a link to the port manager for me, if you will." said Sinsee with that same authority she used when she was taking over in a serious situation.

"What are you going to do?" asked Roeman as he raised an

eyebrow at her. When she did not answer him but just sat there with a half smile on her face Roeman became very interested in seeing just how she was going to handle this so he opened the link to the port. The voice on the other end was not the port manager. Sinsee leaned forward and spoke as clearly as she could.

"I am the New Chandler of the Millally Spacing Guild. You will refer to me as Chandler. I have come to you through the blood of my own people. Must I now spill your blood as well. The old laws have not yet changed. There is a great war ship in orbit around your world. Release those you now hold against their will or die with them." Sinsee motioned for the link to be severed.

"Well that was blunt and effective. Here come our people now." He was right, the port manager and his staff were making their way to the shuttles. Sinsee felt that something was not right. The group coming this way is to close together. Almost as if ......

"Roeman! Put a shuttle between those people and that building now! Full shields!" Even as Sinsee gave the order Roeman was hitting the thrusters to put their own shuttle between the building and the Millally on the ground. Just as he reached them a huge blast exploded from within the main building. Roeman had to tilt the shuttle so that its shields covered those on the ground from flying debris. Tessa and Abby were screaming in total fear. Roeman set the shuttle down and opened the hatch, grabbing his sidearm as he exited.

Sinsee unhooked her harness and went to Tessa and Abby to make sure that neither of them was hurt. Fast maneuvers in space were one thing but doing them in full gravity put a great deal of strain on the human body. Tessa was having trouble breathing. Sinsee put her ear against Tessa's chest, she then felt very gently around where Tessa's harness had rested against her body. Tessa screamed in pain. Sinsee opened the emergency panel med unit. She took out the pure O2 line and placed it over Tessa's nose and mouth. Roeman came back into the shuttle and seeing what Sinsee was doing he moved to help.

"There are more injuries out there. I've got five people looking through the debris of that building, just in case someone survived that. How bad is Tessa?" he asked.

"I think she has two broken ribs, one for sure has punctured her lung. We have got to get the wounded up to the ships medical. And Captain, if there are any survivors in that building, they go too. This wasn't our doing but we can damn well help." Sinsee went outside to see what she could do out there. Roeman linked up to the ship to let them know what had happened, at least what he knew so far. Two more shuttles were sent to the surface along with medical teams and supplies.

As it turned out, the Mining Guild had nothing to do with what had happened at the port. A small group of rebels had taken over the port with the hope of using the Millally Leader as a bargaining chip with their own leaders. Before Roeman had this information he wanted to take out one of their cities. Sinsee was forced to counter his order to the ship in that regard. "Well at least let me take out one of their refineries."

"No. We are going to need all those refineries, or have you forgotten why we are here?" After the truth came out Roeman was a little bit more subdued, but not by much.

They stayed at the port until a representative of the Mining Guild finally showed up, along with their own ambulances, rescue workers, and medical teams. When they saw how the Millally were treating spacers and grounders alike in medical care it resulted in immediate cooperation from the Mining Guild.

Poor Abby was torn between going with her life long friend back up to the ship or staying by her Chandler's side. Sinsee had to order her back to the ship. "You can come back down when you are sure that Tessa is improving."

"Thank you." said Abby with tears in her eyes.

Sinsee walked over to where Roeman and the Mining Guild representative stood looking over the damage. She spoke to Roeman as if the representative were not even there.

"I will say it again Captain Roeman. I do not like waste, be it food, equipment, or lives. This should not have happened." She was playing a role and she hoped that Roeman would catch on. He did.

"Yes, Chandler. I agree." He turned to the man standing next to him. "My I introduce you to a member of the Mining Guild. His name is Lin Ray. Lin Ray, this is our Chandler." The man reached out to shake Sinsee's hand and quickly withdrew it when he saw Roeman reach for his sidearm. "No one touches The Chandler. It is death to do so."

"Sorry, I did not mean to offend the Chandler." said Lin.

"YOU misunderstand. Our Chandler can enter your mind. If you are untrue, YOU DIE!" Roeman nodded his head slightly.

"I see." said Lin. "Thank you for preventing me from making that mistake. I will let the others know of this to prevent any personal contact." Lin bowed deeply to Sinsee and left to pass the word.

"Still fostering the old legend, Roeman." she said.

"Seems a good way to keeping you safe right now." he replied. "Lin told me that they were expecting us to land at the capital building instead of here at the port. They were unaware of a rebel take over here at the port.

"So the Mining Guild has its own problems. I hope our new contracts can solve that for them. Did any of the rebels survive the blast?" she asked him.

"One, but he may not survive the trip up to the ship. It might help us if we knew what was wrong here." said Roeman as they moved away from what was left of the port building.

"We'll get some answers as soon as Abby gets back." said Sinsee. Roeman stopped walking and looked at her retreating back. He wondered what Abby had to do with anything.

✳

The meeting with the Mining Guild went rather well. The Leaders were grateful for the new orders of hull grade metals and very surprised to learn that it was the Chandlers intention to once again permit travel between the colony worlds. When Sinsee explained that the Guild would have its own space station but that the station itself would remain under the control of the Spacing Guild and would be under the security of the Catsman race there were no objections.

The Mining Guild Station Ring would be the first station to be constructed. They could learn by doing. That way they would know how to fabricate and construct the next station with greater speed.

They spent hours going over the new contracts. It was more mundane then anything else. Things like, would you clarify this point for us, or, will we have free rain on this or will you want one of your own people to oversee this on our end. She was starting to understand what Roeman had meant when he said they had rules for everything. She wondered if they had to ask someone for permission to go to the bathroom. Sinsee yawned, and that started a chin reaction. Kit let out a low roar. Sinsee was pleased at the Guild Leaders reaction to him.

"Yes, my Brother, I know. I am hungry as well." She turned to the others at the conference table. "I do beg your understanding Guild Members. It has been a very long day and as you just heard, my Brother wants his dinner as do I. Shall we continue this meeting midday next." To Sinsee's shock the Guild Members wanted to put her request for the meeting to come to an end to a vote. This time Kit let out a loud roar. That did it, members started to pickup their papers and make their way to the nearest exit. It was all Sinsee could do to fight the need to laugh.

Abby was waiting for Sinsee in a well furnished apartment. There was also a table set with ample food and drinks. Fresh meat, still dripping with worm blood was on a platter set on a small sideboard for Kit. Sinsee gave Abby a hug and asked about Tessa. "She will be alright in a few days. If we are still here by then she can join us or stay on the ship. I'm not lacking for help around here, but I have to tell everyone what to do and when to do it. These poor folks don't seem to be able to think for themselves."

"I know what you mean. Other then that, what have you learned so far?" Sinsee poured herself a glass of what looked like wine and sat down at the table while Abby served her by filling her plate for her and talking none stop. Sinsee listened while she ate. By the end of the meal Sinsee knew that she had to find out more about this mining law.

"Abby, do you think you can get me a copy of their mining laws. There has to be a way around what they are doing." said Sinsee.

"Yes, you would think so, but so far no one has found a loop hole big enough to break their hold over the little guys. That is if anyone has bothering to try to find it." Abby sighed, showing her disapproval. "They have more red tape around here, it is a wonder that the whole planet isn't drowning in it. Maybe I should talk to that nice Mr. Lin, no, I think it should be his aid. There is a bit of the adventurer in that one's eyes."

"I don't want to know how you get it for me, just get it." said Sinsee.

"Yes, Chandler." Abby left the room, weather or not she left the apartment, Sinsee did not know, but one hour later Abby was back and directing a young man who was pushing a terminal cart into the room. "Right here should be just fine. Yes, yes. That is just right. I don't know what I would do without you. Your mother must be so proud of you. How long have you been working for Mr. Lin again." he whispered his answer so Sinsee missed it. "And yet look at all you have accomplished for such a young man. Why, I'll bet that within three, no, two years, you will have Mr. Lin's job." The man said something again. "Yes, that is Her. Would you like to meet her? No. Oh well, if you must, you must. Do come back and visit with me tomorrow." She followed the man out of the room and was back after making sure that the young man had left the apartment.

"Here is that information you asked for." said Abby as she handed Sinsee a small 4 by 4 box. Within it were a number of reader disks. Sinsee thought Abby was kidding, the memory on one disk alone would have been enough to fill a small room with books. "Like I said, RED TAPE." Abby left the room again, this time so that Sinsee could work uninterrupted. Sinsee's long day turned into a long night. It was only one hour before the sun would come up that Abby came back into the room. "Chandler, you need to get at least some sleep. You have to deal with these people again this afternoon."

"Thank you Abby." Sinsee turned off the terminal and pushed herself away from the cart.

"Have you found anything that can help yet?" asked Abby as she followed Sinsee into her bedroom, she started to help Sinsee undress and get into bed. She pulled the covers up and tucked them in around Sinsee.

"It is no wonder this place is in such a mess. They even have laws for the laws. How does that happen?" Sinsee yawned and yawned again.

"For now I think you should put that out of your mind and get some sleep. That is what you need right now." said Abby.

"Yes, what I need right now." Even as she spoke the last word Sinsee was falling asleep. Abby quietly left the room, closing the door behind her.

Just before noon Roeman showed up to escort Sinsee to her meeting with the Mining Guild Leaders. Sinsee came out of her room dressed in black pants and white blouse with a blue vest, form fitting. For her foot ware she had on knee high boots, also black. Even though she looked striking in that outfit, Roeman didn't think that it was appropriate for a meeting and he said so.

"That would be true if I was going to a meeting, but I am not. I asked permission to visit some of the actual mines today and the Guild Members were pleased that I would take such interest in mining itself." said Sinsee.

"I find that rather hard to believe." smiled Roeman.

"I thought you would. The truth is they didn't want me to go to the mines at all. They said the mines were filthy and filled with vulgar workers who wouldn't understand proper manners. They were concerned that someone may insult me." She waited for him to say something and when he didn't she continued. "This is an oppressive Government that works under a jumble of laws that have been added onto over the years so much so that the original founding laws of this world have been buried in obscurity. Those laws have never been revoked, only buried under so many other laws that it would take a lifetime to uncover them. That is for a person with a normal mind."

"Are you saying you found the loop hole?" he asked.

"I think so. Those rebels at the port weren't after me. They wanted to talk to me before the so called guild leaders. The mines once belonged to free miners, the government confiscated those mines from their original owners without compensation. The mine workers are now forced laborers with mounting debt to the government." Abby came in at this point carrying a blue over coat for Sinsee. She thanked her and asked Abby to tell Roeman what she had learned about the port.

"The rebels didn't blow themselves up. There have always been explosive charges under the port buildings. In fact every important building on this world has them. They have been used in the past to detour any form of protest. These very rooms were wired for sound and yes there were explosives here as well. Oh, don't worry about them. I took care of them even before the Chandler entered the building." She pointed to small cubes around the room. "I have given them something to listen to as well."

"How did they know to blow the port?" he asked.

"That was my fault. They were listening in when I made my demand. Lucky for our people who ever was on the other end must have had to get permission from someone higher up in order to blow the port. It was that time that saved our people." she said.

"Then if the miners knew that the building was rigged to blow, Why did they stay in there?" asked Roeman. "Why not come out with the others?"

"I don't know. Maybe death was preferable to what their government would do to them. Did the one we send to the ship survive?" Roeman shook his head. "I wish he had lived. We could have gotten more information from him then we ever will from the Guild Leaders."

"But why do you want to go to the mines? From what you say, the Guild does not want you there." Roeman opened the door for her and she walked out of the apartment before him.

"At this point it is just to prove to the Guild that they can not control me. They reluctantly are providing us with transportation to visit two of the closest mines today. And here comes our ride now."

Two ground transports rolled up in front of the complex where the visitors were being housed. Four Catsman stood waiting at the bottom of the steps for Sinsee and Roeman and when they reached the bottom of the steps the Catsman took up guard posts in front and behind them. They walked out to the curb this way and once at the transport one of the Catsman opened the door and looked inside. He took from his belt a small scanner and ran it over the seats and the rest of the interior.

{["You are right Chandler. There are monitoring devices within. Should I have them removed?"]} he said.

{["No. I will need you to ride with us in this transport. I may need to say something to the Captain that other ears are not meant to hear. You can type it out on your wrist com for him. Tell him now about the monitoring device."]} The Catsman started to type and Roeman looked at his own wrist com and nodded his understanding.

Sinsee climbed in first then Roeman and then the Catsman entered. The other three Catsman entered the second transport and the transports drove off.

Abby was standing at the top of the steps watching as the transports and their occupants moved out of sight. She then reentered the complex. Now that the Chandler was gone she would return the monitoring devices back to their normal functions. She intended to spread some gossip of her own that would insure the safety and respect of her Chandler.

As promised, Mr. Lin's young assistant returned to visit with Abby. "Hello Mr. Cane. I was wondering if you had forgotten your promise." smiled Abby.

"Yes Mam, I mean No Mam. It is just that I had to do some work and couldn't get away until now." he said.

"Well what ever the reason you are here now. Have you had lunch yet? No. Then why don't you and I go into the kitchen and I will fix us something nice." Abby offered.

"I don't want to be any trouble Mam." said the young man.

"Please call me Abby and I will call you by your first name as well. You and I don't need to stand on all this protocol stuff. So Jeffery, would you like coffee, milk, or would you like something a little stronger?" she asked him with a twinkle in her eye.

"I am not so sure that I should. Mr. Lin has me on call around the clock." replied Jeffery.

"Then we will have coffee. I don't drink milk myself but our Chandler likes it so I make sure there is always fresh milk for her when I can get it. Which reminds me, I should see to the replenishing of our milk supply on the ship. In stasis milk can last for ever but it does get used up." Abby placed the coffee on the small table and started to fill a platter with an assortment of cooked meats and cheeses. She also cut slices of fresh baked bread and put that on another platter taking these to the table. Jeffery's eyes grew large as he eyed the food Abby was offering him. He reached for the bread and took a handful of meat rapping it in the bread. From the way he stuffed his mouth Abby figured that he rarely got to eat good food. That also explained why he was so skinny. "Easy boy, you will choke on it if you keep stuffing it in your mouth that way. Take your time. There is plenty more where this came from."

"Sorry." Jeffery said around a mouth full of food. He took a sip of the hot coffee. Abby decided to give him a glass of milk, which he downed in one gulp. She refilled the glass again and this time he sipped instead of gulping. Using the sleeve of his shirt he wiped his mouth. "I was wondering about your Chandler. She seems very young to be the leader of the Millally."

"Young! Why Boy, she is as old as time. Oh not in the way you think. The Chandler has the gift of mind speak. When she came to our Homestation to free us from our unjust rulers she used her mind speak to reach into every mind on the station. It was wonderful. The power that came from her was given to us for one glorious day. Some of that power still remains in each one of us. We serve Her because we want to, not because we have too. We share in everything we have with each other. I think she wants to give this to everyone. Don't get me wrong. There is still a chain of command and we follow that chain. The higher up you go on that chain the more responsibilities you have to those under you. Those under you must have every thing that they need to do their jobs and see to their own comfort. In turn each person works so that everyone can benefit."

"You mean that she doesn't take what she wants?" asked Jeffery.

"Surely you jest. She would climb down into a grease pit to retrieve a tool dropped by a worker if we let her. She would take no more then she needed for herself as well. She baulked at having to stay in special quarters on the ship. Why she actually wanted to stay with some of the regular crew. Can you believe that. But of coarse the Captain would not let her. There is one thing about our Chandler that can be unnerving to most people. If you make contact between your skin and hers, she automatically goes into your mind. She can kill you with only a touch of her hand if what she finds in your mind is not good or she can take away your fear. Even we Millally try to avoid contact with her skin. Not that we fear her touch so much as we do not want to intrude into her mind. And what a mind it is. Let me tell you something about that. The Chandler was able to read all of those disks you supplied me with the other day."

"All of them?" Jeffery asked in astonishment.

"Oh yes, and she can recall any part of them that she may need." Abby assured him.

"Then she found what she was looking for." he asked.

"If it was in there, she found it." said Abby. "If not, then not. She did not say. Now look at me, here I am doing all the talking when I was hoping to learn more about you. What does your Father do?"

"He is a crew leader in the mines. If it weren't for him I would be working in the mines still. Dad made sure that I received a good education. He and Mother did without a lot of things to get me into one of the best school systems we have. I may not have been at the top of my class but I wasn't that far under it. That's why I am working for Mr. Lin Ray. I just made the grade for a government job by a hair."

"Yes I can tell that you are a smart boy and you remind me so much of my own son. I wonder if your Mr. Lin will let me, I mean our Chandler borrow you while we are here. You could stay in one of the empty apartments down the hall and you could keep Mr. Lin informed as to any needs the Chandler may have, plus I rather like your company." she said. "I can tell you all about our Home Station and maybe some day you will come to visit me there."

"You mean I could go onto a spaceship?" Jeffery asked.

"Yes. If you would like I could arrange for you and Mr. Lin to ride up to our ship on the next shuttle. Would you like that?" she asked.

"Would I ever!" he rose from the table. "I've got to go tell Mr. Lin. He wont believe me, I know that. Is it alright if I bring him back here so he can hear it from you?"

"Yes, please do." she said. Abby knew that Mr. Lin would already have that information before Jeffery could reach his offices. She was sure that someone higher up then Mr. Lin was already on their way to that same office. "I will ask Mr. Lin myself if we can have the loan of your services. That way he wont think that you are trying to get out of your duties."

Later that day when Sinsee and Roeman returned form their trip to the mines, Abby told them what she had done. She also indicated that the monitoring devices were still on. Sinsee smiled at Roeman, and he nodded his head. "You should have cleared that with Me first." said Roeman. "I do have to admit that you have a good idea though." he turned to Sinsee. "Perhaps some of the Guild Members themselves would like the opportunity to see the ship. There is still the problem of selecting those workers who will function in zero gravity. As you know Chandler, very few planet bound people can handle zero gravity. We will have to teach them to work inside an AECS suit. I am afraid that our stay on this world may be extended far beyond what you were expecting."

"Not at all, I will send for two other ships to handle the work load here. By the time the first of the station ring fabrications are ready for transport top side we should have a trained construction crew. And Abby, I expect you to train this young man of yours in all his duties here. Perhaps he will have a calming effect on you. Give you someone to talk to other then myself." Sinsee winked at Abby.

"Yes Chandler." said Abby in a subdued voice but she was smiling the whole time. "Would The Chandler like her evening meal now?"

"Would you care to join me for dinner Captain?" she asked Roeman.

"I really should get back to my other duties, Chandler. But I thank you for the offer." What he meant was he was going to contact the ship and give them a heads up about their up and coming visitors.

The rest of the evening was uneventful so Sinsee retired early. In the early hours of the morning she was awaken by the horrible sound of sirens going off. She wiped the sleep from her eyes. As she left her bedroom she saw Abby standing at the open front door in her night robe and slippers, she was talking to someone. Sinsee walked up to her.

"What is it? What has happened?" she asked the young man standing in the doorway.

"There has been a massive cave in at the mine. Men are trapped, maybe even dying or dead." said the young man. "My Father is working this shift."

"Maybe we can help." she said. {["KIT! GET UP! I NEED YOU!"]} Sinsee called to her friend. Kit came out of his own room. "We may need those big paws of yours my friend."

"What can It do?" asked the young man.

"HE can find the trapped miners." she turned to Abby. "Go get the Catsman, they can dig through the rubble without bringing the rest of the tunnels down on top of them." She turned to the boy. "Do you know Where Captain Roeman is?" He nodded. "Good, go to him and tell him to get the shuttles ready to move. Tell him I said so. Now Go!" Sinsee returned to her room and got dressed. By the time she was dressed Roeman was at the door.

"The shuttles are on their way here. This is a hell of a way to wake up." he said.

"Tell me about it. Just think how those men in the mine feel. {["Come on Kit.']}, We have got work to do. By the way Roeman, did you sleep in those clothes?" They walked out of the building into the chill air of the pre-dawn hours just as the shuttles landed. The young man stood at the bottom of the stairs, fear for his father was written all over his face. The Catsman boarded first. "What are you waiting for boy, get in." said Sinsee. "You know where the mine is, so you sit up front and show the Captain where to go."

"Yes Mam!" he said as he scurried into the shuttle. He waited for Roeman to take his seat before he sat down. Roeman showed him how to strap in.

"We need a com link with the mine just so they don't panic when we drop in on them. Boy, what is your name?" He gave it. "OK Jeffery, do you know the com link numbers to the mine?"

"Yes Sir, 1001005, My Father is the crew leader for the number ten mine. It's one of the oldest mines on the planet." he said with pride.

"Don't worry Jeffery, we'll get your dad out of that mine. Hang on!" Roeman powered up and the shuttle shot up into the air. "JUST POINT THE WAY BOY!"

While Jeffery directed them in the right direction Sinsee made contact with the mines main office. The supervisor was unavailable at the moment but the man Sinsee talked to said he would let him know that they were coming. " And just in case no one thinks of it, thanks for the help." said the man and the line went dead.

As the mine came into sight they could see a plume of dust rising into the sky. Men and machines could be seen moving all over the grounds just outside the main entrance to the mine. Roeman set the shuttle down as close as he could to the entrance. Their ears were assailed with the noise of the men and machines the moment the hatch opened. The mine supervisor ran up to greet them. "Am I glad to see you." he said.

"How far down is the cave in?" asked Roeman.

"Come with me, I can show you on the map." He led the way to the line shack where tables were covered with maps. "Cane tried to tell me it was a bad idea to open a new tunnel off of line 180." he looked at the boy. "I'm sorry Jeffery. The main office gave the order even after I tried to tell them what your father said. I'm so sorry."

"Was it the old tunnel or the new one that caved in?" asked Sinsee.

"The old tunnel is impassable. I don't even know if the new one survived. The com lines were severed in the cave in. We have no way to know if anyone is alive down there or not." he said.

"What is this mark here?" asked Sinsee as she pointed to a line that someone had tried to erase but failed to remove it completely.

"That is one of the oldest lines in the mine. It has been closed off for most of my lifetime." said the supervisor.

"Does it run above or below the new tunnel section, because it crosses the new tunnel here. It's easer to dig down then it is to dig up." said Sinsee.

"How do you know so much about mining?" asked the supervisor.

"That my friend is why She Is The Chandler of The Millally." laughed Roeman.

"The Chandler of the Millally! No one told me the Chandler was coming." He backed away just enough to bowed at the waist.

"Find out where that tunnel is in conjunction with the new one." said Sinsee. "And while you're at it, stop all that machinery moving around out there before it weakens this system any further with all that vibration."

"Yes, right away Chandler!" he went out to send runners to stop all the equipment." After a short time he returned, "There is no record of how deep that old tunnel is so we wont know if it is above or below the new one. Sorry Chandler."

"That is alright. I think I just thought of a way we can do this." she turned to Roeman. "Captain, can the altimeter on the shuttle be made portable?" she asked him. He said he thought it could be. "Good, now all we need is to know the exact depth of the new tunnel. I can calculate the distance we will have to enter to reach this point where the two tunnels cross." said Sinsee as she stood over the map table.

"It is a very old tunnel." the supervisor said in a low voice. Sinsee looked at the man and could see that he was reluctant to go into the old tunnel.

"I am not asking you to go with Me." she said. She stepped outside the line shack and raised her hand, at the same time she mentally called for Kit and The Catsman to come out of the shuttle. The crowd around the line shack backed away. She went back inside and waited for the others to arrive. "I will need you to supply my people with the right equipment we will need. You better include medical supplies with that. Get me something to write on." Someone handed her a pen and paper. "Thank you." She started to work out just how far they had to enter the tunnel. The supervisor showed her just at which point he thought they could enter the old tunnel.

Roeman had retrieved the piece of equipment they would need from the ship. "The power pack one of the miners gave me seems to be working. You know that this thing was never meant to work under ground don't you."

"Yes, here let me see it. It doesn't read down to the level we are going. What if we reverse the leads. It would give us a reading in reverse wouldn't it?" she asked him. He didn't know so she went ahead and reversed them anyway. "Once we are in the mine and going down we will know if this thing works. Cross your fingers." Taking the map with her she headed for the mouth of the mine. Jeffery wanted to go with them, Roeman looked at the boy. He had more guts then the mine supervisor. He nodded and someone handed Jeffery a head lamp and wished him luck.

They headed into the mine and climbed onto the tunnel tram that would take them deep into the mine. Roeman kept his eye on the altimeter.

"Well I'll be damned, the thing is actually working." He showed it to Jeffery who smiled the biggest smile Roeman had yet seen on the boy.

When they reached the level where the old tunnel was, the air had a musty smell to it. Sinsee checked the map. "The entrance should be around here somewhere."

"Found it ." said Jeffery. "Mathinson was right, this tunnel hasn't been used in a long time. I don't even know if we can get this seal opened. It has corroded over time."

"Stand aside Jeffery." Try as he might, Roeman could not budge the old seals. One of the Catsman tapped him on the shoulder and Roeman stepped aside. "Be my guest." he said, then turned to Jeffery and winked.

To Jeffery's amazement a full set of what looked like blades sprang out of the Catsman's hands. Jeffery took a step backwards only to come up against Kit. A moment of panic came over his face until he saw the soft smile on Sinsee's face. He watched as this unique being ran those blades of his around the seal, then with one tug the old hatch opened. The stale air in the tunnel was no worse then what they had been breathing, at least not by much.

Roeman shined a light into the tunnel. "Looks clear to me. Who wants to go first?" Just then Kit growled. "I take it he wants to be first."

"No, he doesn't want to go in there at all." said Sinsee.

Jeffery was looking from Sinsee to Roeman and then at Kit, who was sniffing the air in the old tunnel.

"Gas!" said Jeffery. "He smells gas! One spark and we wont have to worry about anything anymore. We can't take the lights in there. Even their power cells could ignite the gas. We could use our breathing masks, but what good will that do us. We can't see in the dark."

"I can." said Sinsee. "Jeffery, I want you to go topside and get the supervisor to get some blowers down here. Take Kit with you, or better yet, Kit you take the boy. You can move faster then the tram. Come on Jeffery, get up on Kit's back. Hold onto his mane here, that's right."

{["The boy is frightened."]} said Kit. {["I know. Don't let the supervisor bully the boy. If you have to, you have my permission to bit him in the ass. Now get going."]} she patted Kit's side and he took off back the way they had come. Sinsee looked down the old tunnel. "Looks like I'm first in line. Leave anything that might make a spark behind. We'll do this hand to shoulder. Anyone falls off my train just give a shout and I'll give you a hand up."

"Lets do this before I lose my nerve." said Roeman. They all linked up like the good little train that could and Sinsee stepped into the old tunnel.

It didn't take long before they began to run into obstacles, but there was nothing big enough to stop their progress. Most of it was a matter of climbing over or ducking under. They made their way deeper into the tunnel, then all of a sudden a breeze came up from behind them. "Looks like Jeffery came through for us, but just to be on the safe side keep your breathers' on." said Roeman. Sinsee agreed and told the Catsman to keep the breathers on. They came to a point where the tunnel had partly caved in.

"It looks like we can get through this part. I'm going to go on by myself for a way to see if we can get to the other side in the clear." said Sinsee.

"Don't take all day." Roeman didn't like being underground. Sinsee was gone longer then Roeman would have liked and he was just about to try and follow her when he heard her returning.

"We're in luck, it is clear all the way to where the tunnels cross. The altimeter reads that the new tunnel should be ten meters beneath that point." It didn't take them long to reach the point where Sinsee said the two tunnels crossed.

"Well lets get digging. What do we do with the dirt we pull out of this hole?" he asked her.

"We'll have to shunt it farther down this tunnel." said Sinsee.

"I don't know if you have noticed this or not but I can't see my own hand in front of my face let alone see to carry dirt down this tunnel." said Roeman. "I have a small pen light with me, and the air has been moving for a while now. Do you think it would be safe to turn it on?"

"There is only one way to find out. But first I want everyone to lay down on the ground. If there is a flash it may pass over our heads." she said, passing the word to the Catsman. "OK Roeman, everyone is down, light it up."

"Did you have to put it that way? Ok, here we go." He turned the pen light on, nothing happened. Roeman breathed a sigh of relief as did the Catsman.

The Catsman took turns digging the connecting tunnel while Sinsee and Roeman moved the excavated dirt and rocks down the old tunnel. Working as hard as they were they didn't notice that the air was getting clearer, not until a light came from some where down the tunnel. It was Jeffery with a number of men along with Kit. Roeman greeted the boy, he wanted to know how they knew it was safe to enter the tunnel with the lights. Jeffery patted Kit on the shoulder. "When Kit entered the tunnel I knew it was safe so I just followed him. He had some trouble getting around that last part of the tunnel, he wouldn't give up though."

"You sure are handy aren't you Kit." Roeman scratched Kit behind his ear. Kit purred and Roeman laughed. "I know just how you feel." said Roeman.

The men who came with Jeffery took over hauling the dirt for Roeman and Sinsee while the Catsman continued to dig. As far as anyone could tell, the Catsman were making good progress. Sinsee had calculated an angle of descent that would allow for at least a little hand and foot stability. The work continued for some time then all of a sudden the Catsman in the hole stopped digging. {["Chandler."]}

{["What is the matter? You can't have broken through yet."]} Sinsee stuck her head down into the slanting hole. {["We have hit something. Not dirt and Not rock."]} Sinsee could feel the building excitement from the Catsman. "Really!" she said aloud. {["Let me have a look."]} One of the Catsman came out of the hole to make room for her. Sinsee tied a rope around her waist and handed the other end to the Catsman then she went into the hole head first. One of the other miners saw what she had just done and his mouth dropped. A little while later she came up with a fist size hunk of gold in her hand. "Well it's not rock, that's for sure." She tossed it over to Jeffery. "Put That in your pack Kid. It's yours now." She looked at the other miners. "If any of you have an objection to the boy getting the first of it, you can talk to my friend over there. Kit chose that moment to yawn.

"Chandler," one of the miners stepped forward. "They wont let the boy keep the gold. It belongs to the Guild."

"Not according to your laws. You see this old tunnel has been abandoned for many decades, see that pile of stones over there." she pointed to a small pile of stones she had put there earlier. "That is a new pile, it also verifies that I have staked my claim on this tunnel. It and anything in it of value now belongs to me and that gives me the right to give it to anyone I see fit too. Of coarse I will have to register my claim within two weeks. Then I can contract a work crew to mine what is here. My crew will have a twenty-five percent cut in what ever comes out of this tunnel. That is the way the Law is written and that is how I will do it."

Jeffery let out a yell. "She did it! She found a loop hole!" He turned to the other men. "Don't you see? We can use this law and take back what is rightfully ours. The Guild can't stop us."

"Is this true, Chandler?" asked the man who had spoken up earlier.

"Yes. Jeffery provided me with a copy of your mining laws and that law is still on the books. Once someone uses that law it can not be changed for at least one hundred years. I intend to use it when we get out of here."

All the miners started to talk among themselves. Roeman interrupted them and reminded them why they were there in the first place and they all got back to work.

The Catsman dug around the vain of gold and finally broke through to the other tunnel. They dropped a rope ladder down through the roof of the tunnel. Sinsee and Jeffery were the first to enter the tunnel. The air was really stale down there and air tanks were lowered down to them. At first there was no sign of any survivors in the tunnel.

"If any one is still alive they would be close to the 180 tunnel. That's where they would be expecting the rescue team to break through to them. They don't know that the whole tunnel caved in." said one of the miners.

Jeffery grabbed one of the air tanks and headed off down the tunnel at a dead run. Sinsee and her Catsman were right behind him. They found Jeffery's father and the others. Sinsee helped Jeffery put the face mask on his father then she checked him for injuries. He had a broken leg and maybe a broken or cracked rib. One man had a broken back and could not be moved until they got a back board down here for him. Sinsee was reluctant to give him something for the pain because he had to be fully aware when they tried to put him onto the board, only then would she give him the injection that would allow him to sleep.

With men pulling on the rope from above and Jeffery helping his father from behind, they managed to get him up into the old tunnel. All of the others were able to make it out under their own power except the man with the broken back. Because Sinsee had angled the entrance to the new tunnel they were able to slid the man up through the hole.

Four of the miners carried the man on the back board down the old tunnel. Jeffery's father was given the treat of riding out on Kit's back. He did have to get down once though, so that Kit could get around that one obstruction but he was put right back on once they reached the other side. When Jeffery's father came riding out of the mine on Kit's back there was a lot of yelling and whistling from the crowd that waited at the surface.

Sinsee said that the two injured men would be taken to the ship and receive medical treatment there. While Roeman was reinstalling the altimeter back into the shuttle Sinsee had a little talk with Mathinson. While they were talking the mine manager finally made his appearance at the mine. He pushed Mathinson aside and started to thank Sinsee for her help when Sinsee slugged him right on the jaw, sending him backwards on his ass. Mathinson had to put his hand over his mouth and turn away. Sinsee pointed her Finger at the man on the ground. "Never interrupt me when I am speaking to someone else. Go back where you came from, you are no longer needed here!" she took a step towards the man and he scrambled to get away from her. It wasn't until Mathinson saw the fire in her eyes that he realized just how close the mine manager had come to losing his life at the hands of this woman, for he recognized great power when he saw it and he saw it in her eyes. He bowed low to her.

"As you have said, Chandler. The old tunnel will be reinforced starting in three days. By that time the Guild will have already realized that they can not stop you. And Chandler, may I thank you for what you have done here today for all of us." Before she could walk away he spoke again. "There is something else Chandler, one of the men at the port, he was my eldest son. I thought you should know."

"You can be proud of your son. If it had not been for his sacrifice, I would never have involved myself in the political affairs of this world. I do not like waste nor corruption. Things will get better here. You will see."

"Thank you Chandler." he bowed once again, then went to talk to Jeffery. The second shuttle blasted off with the injured men onboard and headed for the ship. Everyone on the ground watched as the shuttle went higher and higher until it became a tiny speck in the sky, including Sinsee.

Sinsee entered their shuttle and there was Roeman laying on his back under the control consol. "Did you remember to reverse the leads again?" asked Sinsee. "Damn it." said Roeman. "Just a moment, OK, they are reversed now." He finished reconnecting everything. "We can leave anytime you say so."

Sinsee stuck her head outside and called for the others to get onboard. First Kit got in then the Catsman, they waited for Jeffery, who came running up to the shuttle and jumped inside. "Mathinson says that you should go the mines records office right now to file your claim before the mine manager has a chance to file his report. He is going to stall him as long as he can, but we have got to hurry." said Jeffery as he strapped himself down in his seat.

Roeman was lifting off just as Sinsee got the hatch closed. "Just point the way Kid. I'll get us there in record time." True to his word, Roeman got them to the records building in no time flat. Sinsee was just finishing the filing of her new claim when a heavy set man came stumbling into the office. Jeffery stepped between him and Sinsee.

"I am sorry Sir, but you are too late. Mining Guild

Member Chandler has already filed her claim in the name of the Millally Spacing Guild." smiled Jeffery. The man raised his hand to back slap Jeffery and found it in the grip of one of the Catsman beings instead.

Sinsee stepped forward. "This young man is my aid now. You will show him the same respect that you show me. Is that clear." The man nodded, and the Catsman released him, he then left the building.

At the next meeting with the Mining Guild, Sinsee was amazed that they didn't raise even one objection to the remaining points in the new contract. "You are sure that we are all in agreement on this. I would not want any bad feeling between us at a later date." she said. "No? Very well then. I will expect work to begin within the week. Is there anything else?"

"Yes." said one of the older members. "Why did you do it?"

"Because I do not believe in slavery, no matter what form it takes." she said. She saw a number of the members wince at her words. "You have an opportunity to change things around here. Make things better for everyone, not just for the few. I hope that you will take this opportunity. For those of you who do, I am sure that you will have the backing of the people. For those of you who don't, you will find that the power you hold will diminish over time. The choice is yours now. Sink or swim."

The meeting ended on that note and Sinsee returned to her apartment. There she drafted a contract between the Spacing Guild and Jeffery Cane. He now held all rights to the gold mine in the name of the Spacing Guild. One half of the profits were to be used to improve the living standards for the miners themselves. Twenty five percent went towards wages for the miners who worked the claim, and the last twenty five percent was for any equipment that the mine would need.

"What about your share?" asked Jeffery.

"We don't need any." said Sinsee.

"What did I tell you, Jeffery." said Abby. "Our Chandler is the finest human being to ever live. I hope you learn from her example."

"Yes, Mam. I sure will." he smiled.

"Your father will be out of our med unit in a few days. The other one will take longer I'm afraid. But until then I seem to recall that Abby promised you a trip to our ship. How about it Jeffery, you want to take that trip?" asked Roeman.

"Sure! When can we leave?" he asked with excitement.

"Just as soon as we are all packed." said Sinsee. "There is no other reason for me to stay here any longer. Any work I have left to do can be done from the ship." What she didn't say was that she didn't want to stay on the surface any longer then she had to, just incase someone had the desire to take action against her for what she had done at the records office.

Abby started to organize the servants to packing up the things they had brought with them and some of the things that people had been giving as gifts of gratitude for what the Chandler had done in the mine and after. There was so much that Abby said she would stay behind and see that everything was sent to the ship. Roeman promised her that he would send another shuttle right away. In the mean time one of the Catsman would stay with her.

It was a fun trip up to the ship, Sinsee watched Jeffery's reaction to zero gravity and was pleased that the boy had no ill effects. She was even more pleased when he wanted to try his hand at flouting around the cabin. Roeman said it was OK with him and Sinsee helped Jeffery move around. The next thing Roeman knew the two of them were playing at being spinning balls. "Hay! Watch it! Remember what happened the first time you tried that!"

"Sorry." said Sinsee. "I wish there was a place big enough for me to do this more often."

"There is. We have a training dome on Home Station where you can spin to your hearts content." said Roeman.

"Why didn't you tell me this before?" asked Sinsee as she moved up next to Roeman.

"It's where we train as children to handle zero gravity." Roeman looked at her. "I never thought to use it as a play room. Look out!" Jeffery was headed their way and it looked like he couldn't stop. Roeman reached out and grabbed him. "That's enough for now. Everyone back to your seats." he watched as Sinsee helped Jeffery back into his seat. "Tell you what, if you would like, when we get back to the ship I can cut the gravity and you can go play in Kit's room." Kit made a rumbling sound from deep in his chest. "Does that mean he likes the idea?" Sinsee just laughed.

The next three weeks were more fun and games then work for Sinsee. She had invited Jeffery and his Father, Mark, to stay with them onboard while they remained in orbit. Roeman arranged for Mark's wife to join them. Most of the time Roeman would find them cavorting around in Kit's room. The big cat was getting very good in zero gravity. Sinsee even managed to work out a dance using Kit as a platform. But all this fun and games had to come to an end sometime, and the day came for the Cane's to return to the planet.

Sinsee hugged each one of them as they entered the shuttle that would take them home. When she came to Jeffery, the boy had tears in his eyes. "Now, none of that. We may see each other again some day. You never know. Until then, you take care of things here for me." She handed him a folder. "This makes you our representative here, more so then just the mine. I know you will do what is right." Jeffery hugged her and kissed her hand, then he entered the shuttle. The seals closed and Sinsee and Roeman left the bay. They went to the bridge to monitor the shuttle as it made the decent to the surface.

"You know," said Roeman. "With all the injuries that happen in mining, it might be a good idea to set up a medical unit on the space ring. We could put our own medical teams in there along with a number of med units."

"I already thought of that." said Sinsee. "I sent a message to Jewbee the other day. She'll send a team and the specs for the Med Units on the next ship."

"Your always one step ahead of me, aren't you." He looked at the view screen. "I'm going to miss that boy."

"Me too." was all she said.

They made three more planetary stops before returning to Homestation. Sinsee had no trouble at all with two of the planets but the third one was a different story.

✱

"Last stop before we return Home." said Roeman as the view screen showed the planet that the Antiack was about to orbit. "Lets open a link to the port. No reason to come in unannounced. This world still has capabilities to blow a ship out of the sky. We tried to find their missal sites but they have them hidden real good."

"What is their export?" asked Sinsee.

"Meat and fine leather goods. Those boots of yours came from here." said Roeman. "They also have a wood product that is very rare."

"The link is open, Captain."

"Burner One Port. This is the Antiack. We are preparing to orbit Burner One. Please notify planetary defenders." Roeman waited for a reply.

"Antiack, this is Burner One port. We have been expecting someone to show up. We got a transmission about five months back. Is it true that we have a New Chandler?" asked the man on the other end. His voice said that he was very tired.

"You can ask Her yourself. She is coming down to have a talk with the locals." said Roeman as he turned to wink at Sinsee.

"Are you nuts!" said the man. "These people are crazy

down here. We try not to have anything to do with them, and you want to bring the new Chandler down here!"

Sinsee wanted to talk to the man. "Port, This is The Chandler. What is your situation down there?"

"Chandler, I am sorry. I didn't know you were listening. I mean I… Oh Hell. There is some weird shit goes on around here. I highly recommend that you not make planet fall." he said.

"You're a little sparing on your reasoning Port. I have come here to speak with the local government and that is what I intend to do unless you can come up with something more to tell me." she said in a tone that demanded an answer.

"OK. But you are not going to like this." he said.

"Get on with it PORT." she snapped.

"Two years ago we learned that the high ups around here have a thing for human flesh and I'm not talking about sex." He waited for an answer and when none came he asked if anyone was still there.

"Just how did you find out about this?" asked Sinsee.

"I was invited to one of their feasts. There was this little girl that they were showing off. She had these marks on her leg. Anyway, that night when we were eating I saw those very same marks on the roast they were passing around. I haven't touched a piece of meat sense that night. I also stopped all export of meat from this planet. The locals are pretty hopped up about that one. I know that I over stepped my authority on that one but it was a matter of principle." He waited for a reply.

"You did the right thing, and I want you to know that I agree with you on principle." she told him. "Get all your people together. We're pulling off this world." She turned to Roeman. "I want a sanction placed on this world. From this point on no ships will come to this world and nothing comes off it." She returned her attention to the man at the Port. "Do you have a shuttle that you can bring your people up to the ship in?"

"My shuttle isn't big enough for all of us. I have a crew of thirty people." he said.

"Forget your shuttle." said Roeman. "I'm bringing the Antiack down. Rig your shuttle to blow. No need in leaving it for the locals. I don't have room for it in my bay any way.

"I'll have to give the locals a reason for you bringing down your ship." said the man.

"Then tell them that the Leader of all the Millally is coming to see their fine world. Tell them that the Millally leader has heard of their fine leather crafts and is coming for a personal fitting. Tell them what ever the hell you want but get us cleared to land." snapped Sinsee.

"Easy there Chandler, it's not his fault that these people are a bunch of freaks." said Roeman.

"Just get my people out of there Captain!" she snapped at him. She turned and left the bridge. What is wrong with me she thought. Why am I shaking so hard. She heard Kit roaring from some where in the ship. Two of the Catsman were running towards her. What is this she thought and then she wasn't thinking any more. All she could see was red. Some one was trying to restrain her, then she was free. Free and mad as all hell. Something worm was going into her arm. Who's that? Who's there? Were am I? Then there was nothing.

The Catsman on the bridge was trying to explain what he had felt. He typed out what he and the others felt.<It was a very powerful mind.> <It seemed to know that The Chandler was going to do something that it did not want her to do.>

"Can you still feel it?" asked Roeman.

<Yes..> typed the Catsman. <It is still trying to get into her mind.>

"Where the hell is it coming from?" Roeman didn't expect an answer to his question and was surprised when the Catsman began Typing.

<It is coming from the surface of the planet.>

"Can you pinpoint the location?" Roeman asked him.

<Maybe if we were closer the mind would be stronger and we could find it.>

"When you say we, you mean all of the Catsman together, don't you."

<Yes.>

"If we do get closer and the mind gets stronger, it could control you."

<Yes. That is one possibility. It might be advisable that you restrain us as you have The Chandler.>

"That's a good idea. You wont mind being used as a homing device will you?"

<The mind must be stopped, for the sake of The Chandler. We will do this.>

"Fine, get the rest of your boys up here and would someone find me a lot of strong rope or something to tie these guys down with." said Roeman.

"Captain, if this mind thing is trying to get to the Chandler, couldn't we use her as a decoy for the mind while they search for it?" asked the navigator.

"That would be fine with me if she were able to give us her permission, but right now she is in sick bay under heavy sedation." He shook his head. "Right now I could really use her too. She always seems to know what to do."

"If she were here now she would tell you to do it." said Henson from behind Roeman.

"She would, wouldn't she." Roeman couldn't stand the thought of that thing getting into Sinsee's mind one more time. "No. We go with the Catsman's plain." He turned to his screen, then to the com officer. "Get me the Port again." The com officer nodded. "Burning One Port. Do we have that permission to land yet?"

"Conformation has just been given. Activity increase in preparation for arrival of Millally Leader. Flight pattern D2niner 7654. We will be ready for your approach. Port out."

"D2niner 7654, sounds like they have got some company." said Henson.

"We take out that mind first, then we worry about the Port after." said Roeman.

"You got it Captain." said the bridge crew in unison. Now that was freaky, thought Roeman.

Only one of the Catsman was aloud to have one hand free so he could type what they were all feeling. Henson stood by with more rope if it became necessary to restrain the Catsman's arm.

Roeman kept thinking about what the Port manager had said. "The higher ups. That's what he said."

"I beg your pardon Captain. Did you say something?" asked Henson.

"The Higher Ups! Henson! Do we know where the main government building and Leader housing is on this dirt ball of a world?" asked Roeman.

"No, but we can find out. Com, get the Port back on line. I hope they can still answer." said Henson. It took a while but they finally got through. "Port this is the Antiack again. Our Leader would like to do a fly by of the city and have a look at the government building from the air. We hear that they are quite a sight. Can you give us a fix?" said Henson.

"North northeast of the river." came a quick reply. "Shit! Back off butt face!" The connection went dead.

"Hang on! We're going in. Shields to full power! We're going to burn us some air!" said Roeman as he took the controls.

"Oh Shit!" said Henson as he hit the ships intercom. "All hands to your stations! Full suit! Repeat! All Hands to your stations in Full Suit!" Henson used his extra peace of rope to tie himself to the back of the seat the Catsman was seated in so that he could look over his shoulder at what he was typing. The ship began to shake as it hit atmosphere at speeds it was not designed for. "Captain." said Henson.

"Not now Henson." Roeman pitched the ship and started to come in on a curve. "OK Henson."

"The mind is growing. The mind is angry. Not one mind. Many minds. Minds are close… Closer… Closer…… Anger… Great.. Anger… Kill… Kill All… Pain… Joy In Pain…"

"Yaw, I figured that one out for myself." Roeman pitched the ship again and lined it up on the river. "Missals launch on my command, Full effect. If we have to take out the whole city so be it. FIRE!" The missals launched and Roeman pitched the ship and headed back towards the port. "Hang on! Shock wave headed our way. Six, five, four, three, two…" The ship bucked and almost ended up on it's nose. Roeman fought for control. Everyone was hanging onto something. The rope that held Henson in place broke and he found himself going head over tea kettle over the Catsman who reached out with his one free hand to grab Henson and hang onto him. Roeman started to get control as the shock wave passed by them.

"Is Every one OK?" asked Roeman as he looked around.

"A.O.K. Captain." said Henson. "Jess, help me untie these guys."

<The Minds are all gone.> typed the Catsman. Henson worked to untie the knots that had tightened from all the buffeting. He finally gave up and took out a knife and cut the ropes. <Thank You>

"You're welcome." said Henson.

Sinsee woke to the touch of someone holding her hand. She blinked in an attempt to focus her vision. She turned her head to see Roeman standing next to her.

"Welcome back." He reached to move a lock of her hair that had fallen across her face. "You gave me quite a scare. For a while there I thought I might loose you."

"Roeman. What happened to me?" She tried to sit up and felt a little light headed. Roeman helped her into a sitting position.

"Mind control. Seems a while back those fools on Burner One started playing around with genetics. The problem with that is they didn't know what they were doing. Those Higher Ups were genetically enhanced humans who controlled the minds of everyone else. Pure evil. What they did to their own people... I can't even say it. If your interested, there is a whole report from the investigation team I sent in after we blew half of the city apart. So far it looks like we got all their freaks, and I do mean Freaks." Roeman shook his head. "Even after we destroyed half of their city and killed half the population those who were left were grateful. It's all in the report." Sinsee saw a tear roll down Roeman's cheek, she also saw that he was sporting a black eye. She reached over and wiped the tear away.

"Who gave you this?" she asked.

"You did." He looked deeply into her eyes. "I almost lost you to those bastards!" He bent down and hugged her placing his head on her chest. She reached up and ran her fingers through his hair and the next thing she knew they were locked in a very passionate kiss. Roeman pulled away from her still holding onto her shoulders. "It took me almost loosing you to realize that I love. When you weren't by my side, it was like there was a big hole in me."

"Not any more." she said softly. "I have loved you for some time now. It's just being Chandler for everyone has gotten in the way. That and I thought you wouldn't want someone like me."

"Not want you! Girl, I can't live with out you." He pulled her to him and held her in his arms.

That night Roeman stayed with Sinsee in her quarters. No one talked about the fact that they would spend long hours together in her quarters on the long voyage home, not even Abby and Tessa.

Chapter Two

As the Antiack came into view of Home Station the bridge crew got a surprise and Roeman called Sinsee to the bridge. When she arrived, the main screen was displaying the magnificent sight of the Catsman ship, stationed just off from Homestation. "Now that is a sight!" she said. "Did you know about this, Roeman?"

"Not a clue. She rather looks like a little moon going around the station, doesn't she." Roeman was leaning forward in his seat as if that would give him a better view of the ship. "You want to tell our friends to come up and have a look?" asked Roeman as he looked at Sinsee, the smile on her face told him that she already had. He smiled back at her, it seemed that everyone on the ship was smiling these days.

The Catsman ship wasn't the only surprise that waited for them at Home Station. Dr. Brion was also there to greet them along with Pregger and Jewbee, who was holding a baby girl, half Catsman and half Human. Sinsee made a huge fuss over the baby, whose name was Reekee, and asked if she could hold her. Jewbee handed Reekee over to Sinsee, showing Sinsee just how to hold her.

Sinsee was so happy for her friend. She knew how much

this meant for Jewbee to have a child and it looked as if motherhood agreed with her for she seemed to glow with a loving radiance.

Sinsee looked over at Roeman, who was talking to Captain Tankfull, and wondered what a child of theirs would look like. The thought filled her with a worm feeling. She looked at Dr. Brion. "Brion, I need to talk to you later, in private, if you are not to busy."

"I'm never to busy for you Sinsee." He reached up to tickle Reekee under the chin. "This little girl is the best work I have ever done."

"What do you mean?" asked Sinsee.

"Catsman and Human's are not exactly compatible for mixing DNA's. It took a while before we got a viable embryo. I waited until I was sure of the growth before I implanted it into Jewbee." He took Reekee from Sinsee and cradled her in his arm. "Yes, you are my little darling, aren't you." he cooed to the child. Sinsee had never seen Brion act like this before. Then again, she had never seen him around a baby before.

Jewbee came back over from talking to Abby and Tessa. "We have another surprise for you. Your new quarters are finished and ready for you to move into them." She took Reekee from Brion, who seemed reluctant to give the child up. "I told Abby and Tessa to have your things brought to the center sphere." She turned to the others. "Come on you guys, we can't spend the rest of the day in the docking bay." Jewbee and Sinsee walked side by side and the others just filed in behind them.

Sinsee was amazed at the work that had been done in their absence. You couldn't tell that there had once been a bloody battle here. The corridors had been widened and there were small gathering nooks with over stuffed chairs and end tables. When she saw her new quarters she had to ask if her aunt Nika had designed them. Jewbee had to admit that Miss Nika had sent her some photographs of some of the more stylish homes on Terra Two. "There is also a private corridor that gives you access to any office in this complex. Just in case you don't want to go out into the main corridor. You have access into the Great Hall as well."

"This is all so wonderful. But do I really need all this." Sinsee swept her arm before her.

"Perhaps you don't need this, but as Chandler, you have no choice." said Roeman. "Jewbee, is there anything to drink around here? I feel like having at least one night where I don't to worry about cave-ins or mind freaks."

"Cave ins? Mind freaks? Just what have you two been up to while you were gone?" asked Jewbee.

"Pore me that drink and I'll tell you all about it." said Roeman.

They spent the rest of the afternoon and evening catching up on all the things that happened here on Home Station and other places. Sinsee spent most of the time with Jewbee and the baby. Though she didn't think that Roeman was telling the story about the mine cave-in right.

"Now Roeman, you make it sound like I did it all on my own. As I recall, I didn't go into that tunnel alone." she rebuked his story.

"You at least have to admit that you weren't afraid. I kept thinking that the whole damned planet was going to fall in on top of us at any moment." said Roeman as he put his arms over the top of his head in mock fear that something would fall on top of him right then.

"Well I'll never understand how anyone can deliberately go under ground." said Jewbee. "It sounds like back braking work."

"You're right on the mark there Jewbee. One of the men we pulled out of that mine had a broken back. If we had left him in the care of the mining medical staff he would have been paralyzed for the rest of his life." he told her.

Jewbee looked at Sinsee. "So that is why you want the

station ring to have med units. I wondered about that. Your message didn't give a reason."

It had been a wonderful home coming for Sinsee, but all to soon it was over and everyone started to say their good nights. Before Brion could leave, Sinsee pulled him off to the side and had a short talk with him. He told her to come to the hospital wing the next day.

Sinsee woke bright and early. Roeman was still sound asleep so she left him there knowing that he would sleep for at least a few more hours. He had more then just a few drinks the other night. Brion had marveled at the quantity of alcohol Roeman could consume. Sinsee herself was able to drink without it affecting her to much, but she could not drink at the rate that Roeman had the Night before. She dressed herself and left a note for Abby not to disturb Captain Roeman, leaving it on the door to the bedroom, then she headed for the hospital wing.

Dr. Brion was waiting for her in his own office. "I had a feeling that one day you would want this, so I brought it with me." He opened a small case and took out a hypodermic injection gun. He then picked up a vile filled with a blue liquid and snapped it in place on the gun. "This won't hurt to much so long as you don't tighten your muscles." She started to roll up her sleeve when Brion shook his head and she winced. "Just lean over my desk and I'll do the rest."

It all happened so fast, Sinsee wondered if Brion had done it right. "Is that all?" she asked turning to see that the vile was now empty.

"That's it." he said. "One more thing though. Now that you have this in your system you should start having your monthlies start up again in about a week, so you might want to prepare for that." She said that she would be ready and after thanking him she headed back to the center sphere and her quarters.

During the next few weeks Sinsee found herself occupied

with the reports from the ships that were starting to come in. Some of them were even on their way back while others were having trouble convincing planetary governments that the offer of renewed space travel was genuine.

A report came in from communications requesting a ship to go out and reset the relay satellites, they were starting to get delays in the relay time again. Sinsee went to communications herself to find out how long it would take to reset the satellites. She was told that it all depended on weather the satellites were still functional or not. But in either case it would be a good idea to have all the satellites checked. Perhaps she could order the ships to check the satellites in their sectors, the shift supervisor recommended. Sinsee asked if all the ships were capable of repairing or replacing the satellites, the supervisor didn't know, so Sinsee went in search of someone who would know. The corridor was getting crowded so she slipped through an empty office and into her private corridor. She entered Roeman's office through the back door. Roeman was going over the file work on the break down of the Catsman Ship, New Home. Tankfull had suggested that they use New Home as a model for a passenger liner.

Sinsee dropped down into the chair next the Him. "How is it going?" she asked.

"Not bad considering." he smiled at her as she looked at his screen and asked him, considering what. "Well from the looks of the information we have now, the Catsman went about building their ship in a very strange way."

Sinsee leaned closer to have a better look at what was on the screen. "Is that the drive or the power plant?" she asked him.

"It's the power plant. From what Tiny says they must have built the power plant first and then built the ship around that. The drive is part of the power plant through this shaft." he pointed it out for her.

"Did you say shaft! That thing looks like a cavern! What

is this?" she looked closer and pointed on the screen, her finger tracing the lines. Roeman was saying something about them trying to find a way in today. Something, memory nagged at the back of her mind and all of a sudden she knew what that chamber was. "Roeman! Get the work crews on the line right now. Don't let them open that Chamber!"

"What's wrong?" his hand flew to the com link on his desk.

"That is a giant freeze chamber. If they breach that hull without any protection they will all die instantly!" Sinsee couldn't wait for Roeman to relay the message, she reached out with her mind to the Catsman who were working with the investigation team on New Home, but it was to late.

PAIN! OH MY GOD! THE PAIN! NO!

Darkness reached up to enfold her mind and she sank down into it.

Sinsee woke to the sound of Jewbee's voice as she mocked Roeman. "No! Not YOU! OH this is rich. I can't believe it.!"

"Don't tease him so, Jewbee." said Sinsee in a weak voice. She tried to sit up and found herself being held in place by Roeman. Someone was telling her to rest, it was Brion. Sinsee tried to ask about the work crew. {["Still thinking about others."]} came the familiar touch of Kit's mind. She was told that her warning had saved a number of lives. They still didn't know what was inside the chamber. Sinsee managed to tell them what she had felt. The embryos as they died. Waves of death and pain.

"It's alright my love, you go right ahead and cry all you want to." Roeman lifted her into his arms and held her there. He rocked her as if she were a little child.

"Oh Roman, I don't want to be responsible any more. I can't take it." she buried her face in her hands and cried even harder.

"No one ever said that you had to do it all." He continued

to rock her until she fell back to sleep, only this time it was a natural sleep.

✳

Roeman and Dr. Brion had their hands full just trying to keep Sinsee from trying to do to much as she recovered from the backlash of mental anguish she suffered when the giant cryo chamber was breached. It was Jewbee who finally got through to her and forced her into two weeks of bed rest. "I know that this comes at a bad time right now, What with the find of a lifetime for Pregger and his people. But Chandler, you have to understand something. That shock you took could have done irreparable damage to the psyche of your unborn child. Right now I have no way to monitor for damage." Kit rumbled deep in his throat and Sinsee gasped. "What did he say?" demanded Jewbee.

"He says that he can sense no mind touch with the child." The fear in Sinsee's voice alarmed Roeman. In all this time Sinsee had never shown fear. Even in the battle for Home Station she had taken chances that had endeared her in the hearts of all Millally. Now fear had come to the surface. Roeman put his arm around her and held her close to him. He desperately wanted to protect her and the child she carried.

"That may be because you are only a few weeks along. My problem is that we have no reference for dealing with an expectant Chandler. In all my life there has only been one Chandler. Her own children were already grown when her powers manifested in her. So I am at a loss as to how to handle you and what now grows inside of you." Jewbee placed her hand gently on Sinsee's stomach.

Dr. Brion spoke up. "We actually do have an advantage in this instance." Everyone looked at him as he smiled and pointed at Kit. "Kit has been helpful in the past when it came to finding others like Sinsee on Terry Two, and sense he never seems to very far from Sinsee's side, I see no reason not to take advantage of this. I will insist on one thing though, that another rider and Lion be present." Jewbee wanted to know why he thought that was necessary. "I don't know about you, but I'm not telepathic. I want another human translator." He looked at Sinsee. "Not that I don't trust you to tell us what Kit says my dear, it's just that I am also thinking about your mental state. There are some tests that I would like to do, but I would prefer that you were a few more weeks along. So until then I don't want you doing anything that could put stress on you. That means no running around the station. You have a staff to do that. In a few weeks we will find out if the child is developing as it should."

"Brion is right. You need to relax and put your feet up. I wish there was some way to shield you from the other telepaths on the station." Jewbee knew that it was an impossible wish, but she could at least arrange for there to be as little direct contact as possible.

Sinsee reluctantly stayed in her quarters for about four days, But when Kit snitched on her when she had left them to stretch her legs, Jewbee ordered her into the Hospital where she could keep an eye on her wayward Chandler. Sinsee was livid with Kit and did not talk to him for two days. Oddly enough that did not seem to bother Kit at all. His comment was that all females with cub were prone to act strangely for a time, but that sooner or later they would get over it. The young rider who translated for Kit blushed beet red at the big cats candor about such a delicate subject. What was worse was that Dr. Jewbee agreed with Kit. By the end of the two week restriction on Sinsee the young rider was asking to be transferred to one of the ships. It didn't matter which one as long as it was scheduled for departure from Home Station soonest. Roeman granted the young rider's request and the next day the boy and his Lioness were on their way to take up a posting on a system satellite platform. They would replace the security team that had been on duty for the past two years.

All of Dr. Brion's tests showed that the child was developing normally and even Kit was beginning to sense the beginnings of a mind within the child. Everyone was pleased with the results. With all the tests behind her, Sinsee was more then ready to get back to work.

Dr. Brion thought that now would be a good time to fill Sinsee in on the plans for the wedding. He called everyone together who he thought would be of any help to him and set up a dinner party where they would break the news to Sinsee.

The dinner went quite well. Sinsee seemed to have a good appetite and tried a sample of everything that had been prepared, except for the food that had been meant for Kit. While she was cutting into a rather thick cut of meat she stopped and took a real good look at it. "This meat didn't come from Burner One, did it?"

"Not likely." said Jewbee. "After what you told us I had all the meat we had in storage checked, anything from Burner One is being tested for human DNA." Jewbee shivered visibly.

"This meat comes from Terra Two." said Patrick. "Nika had a private supply sent here just for your use."

"What a relief!" said Sinsee as she stuffed the meat into her mouth. "Oh yum. This is good. This alone makes having to put up with all this Chandler special treatment worth while." She reached for a glass of wine and Jewbee took it away from her. "That's not fair Jewbee."

"Fair for you, not fair for your child. You know that." Jewbee replaced the wine glass with a glass of milk. Sinsee made a pouting face at Jewbee but she drank the milk.

After dinner everyone went into the living room where they sat and had coffee, starting up one conversation after the other. After a while Sinsee felt that they were skirting around something. "Roeman, what is going on here?"

Roeman held her hand, and looked at Brion. "Well Doctor, this was your idea. You tell her."

"Sinsee, you are going to get married." He held up his

hand to forestall any objection. "Here me out. You come from a world were a woman marries, then has a child. You are also going to be a roll model for so many people now being born on Terra Two. You know our laws. And yes, I know that you want to change those laws. If you had only heard the way Jayson chewed my ass out for this. Any way, You and Roeman are going to be married right here on Homestation.

Sinsee was more then just surprised, she was enraged. How dare they make such a decision for her without asking her first. She looked at Roeman who was listening to Brion and what he was telling Roeman at that moment. How could Roeman understand what this would mean for him. He was about to say something when Sinsee stood up. "**NO**!" She looked at the shocked faces around the room, then turned to Jewbee. "You just let him walk into communications and decide what I am going to do with my life." She turned her anger on Roeman. "In all this time have you ever given a damn what a grounder thought?" Roeman reached out for her hand and pulled her back down next to him.

"In the past, no. But then I never thought that I would fall in love with a grounder. I like the thought of being joined in the way of your people." He smiled at her and when she tried to pull her hand away from his, he held on the stronger. "I know how you feel about this, for the first time a woman of your world has full freedom. You don't want to give that freedom up. I would like to remind you that I am not a man of your world. I am a Millally male and you my love, are the Chandler of all the Millally. Any time you want to put me aside, you can." Sinsee saw that Roeman meant what he was saying.

Dr. Brion would have said something at this point had it not been for Jewbee who shook her head at him. She motioned for everyone to leave the room, giving Roeman and Sinsee the time alone that they needed. The others followed her into another room.

Once the others had left the room Sinsee took both of

Roeman's hands in hers. "Roeman, you don't understand what they are asking us to do." she spoke in a normal voice now that it was just the two of them.

"Sure I do. This is a contract between the two of us that means we are paired. What is the big deal? Millally men and women have been pairing off for thousands of years." It was plain to Sinsee that he really didn't understand.

"Roeman, when a man and women enter into this type of contract on my world, it is for life. There is no putting aside."

Roeman chuckled for a moment until he saw that Sinsee was not smiling. She was serious about this. A life contract was not something the Millally ever did. Pairing was done for the purpose of producing a child. A man paired with a number of women and the same was true for the women. There had been those who did a double pairing, but that was for a desired trait from their first pairing. He had not thought that this would be a life pairing, even though he had studied her world, as much as one could from the cold depth of space, he never knew that they paired for life. He was now beginning to understand why she was so upset.

They sat there for sometime, not saying anything. If they went through with this contract it would set precedence for other Millally to do the same. The first time chosen pairings would end, and the first time girls could choose who they wanted. Well maybe that might not be so bad, thought Roeman. "Well, you did say that our ways would have to change. Would it be all that bad to grow old with me, I know that I am older then you, but, does that really make a difference?" He asked her.

"Roeman are you asking me to marry you?" She tilted her head just right and let the overhead light reflect in her eyes the way Nika had taught her to do.

Roeman smiled at her. "That doesn't work on me and you know it. As to this thing, Yes. Will you take me for the rest of your life, in the way of your people?"

"You know what this will mean for all of the Millally. I so

love you Roeman, I only hope that in Fifty Years from now you still love me. I know how much you hate change."

Jewbee, who had been listening at the door from the other room, silently closed the door all the way. She turned to the others who waited for her at the other side of the room. The smile on her face told them what they wanted to know.

"Well that went well." said Brion as he rubbed his hands together in triumph. "Now, where should we hold the ceremony? I was thinking about one of the central docking bays. We can shift the ships to the other bays. There is plenty of room with half of the fleet out running planetary errand's for Sinsee."

"And just what would you know about that, Doctor?" accused Jewbee.

"Get used to that Jewbee." laughed Patrick. "My Uncle has always had his nose in other folks business." Patrick ducked just as Brion brought his hand up to smack him in the back of his head.

"Don't be so smug you little runt. I have half a mind to send you home." Patrick was laughing as he took cover behind Jewbee. Ignoring Patrick now, Brion asked how long it would be before the ship with Jayson and Nika onboard would arrive. Someone said in seven cycles. Terry Two was the closest system to Homestation. The lap's time would be closer to normal. It had already been two weeks from the last time Brion had talked to Jayson. He wondered if he would ever get used to the time difference between ship time and ground time. Maybe not.

Jayson had informed Brion that Nika was trying to bring half the planet with her. Department Heads were fighting over who had more right to go with them. Jayson finally had to step in and settle the argument by setting up a lottery, after all someone had to stay behind and keep the place running.

"She has no idea that Jayson and Nika are on their way here, does she?" asked Patrick.

"No she doesn't, and I want to keep it that way. Jayson said he was bringing her family with him. That will make a nice distraction for her. She shouldn't be working so hard in her condition." said Brion. Jewbee wanted to know what was wrong with her condition. "Well for one thing, she is pregnant. That mental blast she took when the Catsman cryo chamber blew really could have hurt her. Yes, I know that you have every Catsman on this station listening in on her and the child and that Kit has been keeping in contact with the developing mind of the child. By the way, does she know that she is never left alone?"

"Doctor, she is The Chandler, of course she knows. I did try to stop them from contacting her directly and allow her the time she needed to recover." said Jewbee as if he should already know this.

Brion looked at Jewbee's Catsman mate, he wondered how a telepathic race could keep any secrets. Jewbee knew what Brion was thinking when he looked at Pregger that way. She had already had numerous conversations with him on this topic. "Don't worry Doctor, Pregger's people know how to control their thoughts, unlike you."

"Good god woman, are you becoming telepathic now?" Brion was shocked that she knew just what he was thinking.

"If I were, I wouldn't need this." she held up her wrist to show him the small translator. "You always get that same look on your face when ever you look at any Catsman. That means only one thing, you're wondering about their telepathic abilities.

Brion cocked his head and looked at Jewbee for a moment. "What your saying is that I am becoming predictable, is that it?"

"You know," said Patrick. "I was thinking that maybe we should wait for Nika to get here, she can decide where the wedding should take place. Knowing Nika, she will any way. You know she will too, if you stop to think about it."

Brion did know just how Nika was, strong willed, bull headed, her way or no way. She and Sinsee had that in common and there was no wonder in that. Nika had had quite an influence on Sinsee from the first day she arrived at the Foundation. It wasn't so much that Nika was given a free hand as much as it was that Nika had more free will then any woman on Terra Two. Brion had always been fascinated with Nika sense he was a child. He remembered the first time his father had taken him and his brother Parry to a function at Jayson's home. Nika walked among the men as if she belonged there. If someone made a comment about her not knowing her place, she would put them in there place and then show them to the door. The sight of her escorting one man to the front door and then closing that door in his face stayed with Brion all these years. Brion could remember hanging onto every word that Nika had spoken that first day, and he had fallen madly in love with Nika as a young boy. She of course was a full grown woman and he knew that she would never look twice at him, being only a child at the time. He had never married because he could never find anyone his own age that was like her. He never told anyone the reason why he never took a wife, but now he found himself surrounded by women Just like Nika. He was still in good health and did not consider himself to be all that old, and there was that Lab Tec in the hospital that showed interest in him.

"Uncle, Uncle!" Patrick's insistence broke his daydreaming and he realized that the others had been carrying on the conversation without him.

"I'm sorry, what did you say?"

"I said it won't be easy to keep the Chandler from wanting to be involved in the every day aspect of running this station. It was hard enough keeping her quiet while we ran those tests in the hospital." Patrick winced at the memory of just how difficult Sinsee had been and wondered where the little girl had gone who had always done as she was told.

"Patrick is right. From the time Sinsee came here she has worked none stop. She's been sending ships all over the place. Just today she has ordered instructors and equipment sent to three worlds that have reverted to Non Tec societies. She wants them brought back up to speed so they can contribute. And that is just sense we released her from the hospital." said Brion.

"I don't see why we have to limit what she does. After all, it's not as if she is actually doing any hard labor." said Jewbee. "Pregger will let me know if she becomes tired or weak. Until the ship arrives from Terra Two it might be a good idea for her to go about her work. There have been a number of petitions from people who want to see her. Not all of them are for disputes. Most are just those who want to be reassured that all the changes are really good for us."

"You make it sound as if they are requesting an audience with a Queen." laughed Patrick. Jewbee shot him a look that put a catch in his throat. "You're not kidding, they really do think of her as a Queen."

Jewbee had to think about that for a moment. She knew what a Queen was, but it wasn't the same thing for the Millally. "No. Not a Queen. Our Chandler keeps the law, she judges between right and wrong. With one touch she can know who is faults and who is just. If a person harbors evil within them, that evil is reflected back at them many fold. Some go mad at seeing their true self and some just drop dead. When our Chandler stands in judgment there is no escaping what is true." Jewbee let that sink in before she continued. "In that respect, Sinsee has been laps in her duties. She should see some of the petitioners and settle their disputes."

"No." said Brion. "What you are talking about is her telepathic talents. The last thing we want is for her to expose herself and the child to more backlash and frantic emotions from someone being judged as you call it."

Pregger was tapping on his translator. Jewbee read it aloud

for everyone to hear. "You are worrying too much. Let Roeman deal with his mate. He is not about to let her over do anything. Nor will Sinsee put the child at risk." He paused for a moment with his eyes closed. "Sinsee wants us to join them now." He headed for the door drawing Jewbee along beside him.

✴

Sinsee continued to work as she had been doing with one exception, she no longer exercised in the heavy gravity gym. Even Millally women who were with child had their limitations.

She checked on the progress of the work being done on the Catsman ship in person. When she wanted to suit up and have a look inside the massive cryo tank, everyone objected. But the strongest objection came from Kit. So much so that Kit put himself between Sinsee and the rack of suits that hung just outside the new access chamber. His angry growl surprised everyone including Sinsee.

When Brion heard what Kit had done he stopped worrying about Sinsee and started to concentrate on a certain Medical Tec. In the mean time Jewbee and Patrick started to set up a neonatal care unit for the Catsman embryos. Gestation tanks were being dismantled one peace at a time and documented to make sure that they would go back together in the right order the first time. It was young Halley from Tankfull's ship who was in charge of the dismantling of the units. The young man had chosen to stay on Home Station and raise his younger sister himself. Tankfull was sorry to lose the boy but Patrick was overjoyed to have him, which is when he could get him. The break down crews were always trying to monopolize his time. His popularity was growing with leaps and bounds, but his ego remained the same.

Patrick and Halley were attempting a rather tricky fitting when word came that the ship from Terra Two was getting ready to dock in bay 98, all the way on the other side of the central docking ring.

"You better go." said Halley. "They'll be docked and unloading by the time you get there. I think I can handle this last part without your help. Go! Or you will miss all the fun."

"Thanks Halley, I owe you one!" said Patrick as he jumped to his feet, grabbing a rag to wipe his hands off as he made his way out of the medical wing. It had been a long time sense he had seen anyone from home. He half hoped that his father had made the trip with the others. From what his Uncle had told him, there had been a large number of people trying to join Jayson and Nika on this trip, if only to get a chance to say that they had been to space. What he remembered of his own trip to Homestation, he hoped they liked looking at bulkheads.

Jewbee and Roeman had decided that Sinsee should hear those who had petitioned for an audience with her. They arranged it so that the event would coincide with the arrival of the ship from Terra Two. That way Jayson and Nika could make their entrance into the Great Hall as a surprise for Sinsee.

The central Hall in the sanctuary sphere had been cleaned and draped in white brocade. A plain unadorned bench was brought into the Hall and placed on a small raised platform in the center of the Hall. Sinsee was expected to stand on this platform or sit on the bench if she grew tired. For the first time Sinsee was going to learn what it really meant to be a Chandler of the Millally. She was more then willing to do this duty when she learned that Allison had done this once every five years.

What she didn't like was the group of people who came into her quarters to help her dress for this event. Abby had to explain that this was part of the ceremony. Sinsee was appalled at the number of layers of fabric that she was expected to wear. "You will be thankful for all this fabric in the Hall of Truth, believe me." said Abby. "The temperature in the Hall is being lowered to the point that you can see your own breath." Sinsee shivered at the thought of spending hours in that much cold.

She asked why they would do that. "It is a reminder to all of us that our lives are spent in the cold of space. Truth is the cold hard fact of our lives. Besides, while everyone else is shivering in the cold they will see that the cold has no effect on their Chandler."

So it was just another myth of the Chandler. Sinsee would do it this time, but she made it clear that this was one of the things she was going to change. She new that Allison had done this to add to the deep mystery of the Chandler, it may have been another way for her to protect herself. Sinsee didn't think that Allison would have used this as a way to control the people. What ever she did this for, Sinsee didn't like it.

The finial layer of fabric was white with gold thread embroidery done in an elaborate yet delicate design. The drape of this last garment concealed the many layers underneath. Sinsee looked at her reflection in the mirror. She didn't look like she was wrapped in a cocoon but she sure felt like she was.

"It looks alright, but I am starting to sweat." She was rushed into her private corridor and down to a waiting chamber that lead directly into the Great Hall. There were other women there, all of them dressed in white robes, none of them were as elaborate as Sinsee's. At the moment Sinsee entered the room all talking stopped and as one they lowered their heads.

At the tone of a bell they all lined up in two rows. Four in front of Sinsee and Four in back. At the door on the other side of the room there waited two men dressed in black and silver. They wore short shoulder capes, also black, and hanging from their belts were old stile swards. Sinsee just caught the glint of silver on the backs of their boots. Sinsee thought that they were spurs, but she didn't have time to look again as the men went through the now open door.

✳

Patrick had just made it to the docking bay in time to see the ship's ramp lowering to the decking plates. The first person he saw was his father, Dr. Parry Nathin. His father looked the same to Patrick even though he knew that more time had passed for his father then for him. Next out of the ship was Jayson, his sister Nika was by his side with her hand resting on his offered arm for support. As they moved down the ramp Patrick made his way through the dockworkers who had gathered to get a look at the grandson of Tenco Dee, who had risen up through the ranks on Terra Two to become it's ruler and passing that privilege on to his grandson, Jayson. But it was the elegance of Nika that everyone was enthralled with. As Patrick made his way forward he heard some of the comments that were being made in whispers here and there. He had to smile to himself, no one who ever met Nika, came away as the same person.

"Welcome to Homestation Sir." said a guard dressed in black and silver. The guard motioned for them to follow him.

"Where is my Grand daughter?" asked Jayson of the man who's back was before him. Patrick reached them just then and answered for the guard.

"The Chandler is hearing petitions in the Great Hall. That is where this man is leading you now. She doesn't know that you are coming."

"Patrick! How are you my boy?" Jayson took in the way the boy looked. His clothes were dirty and there was a dark smear of some kind of lubricant across his chin. "You look like you've been working hard."

"Yes Sir, there is more then enough work to go around." He turned to see the expression on his father's face. "I've been working on the gestation tanks that we hope will act as naturally as the womb for all the Catsman embryos that are in cryo-freeze. We had to expand part of the medical wing to accommodate the units, but it will take years to bring all the embryos to life. We just don't have enough room for all the units, not to mention the room that the young Catsman will need." He had perked his father's interest. Parry wanted to know more, in fact, he very much wanted to see one of these gestation tanks.

Nika looked back at the two Doctors. "Go ahead Parry, I will give Sinsee your regards." She looked at Patrick. "Don't you ever look in a mirror?" She asked him as she took in his state. "Only when I have the time." he said as his father lightly shoved him out of the procession line.

"Let us go see what you have been working on." said Parry as he followed his son in the opposite direction.

Jayson was chuckling to himself. "They never change, do they?" "No" said Nika at his side. "They never do."

✱

After two hours of listening to petty squabbles, Sinsee began to think that this whole show was a huge waste of time. Just then a young man came running into the Hall with three guards right on his heels. He ran up to Sinsee, tripped and fell at her feet, tears streaked his face.

"Help Me! I can't find her any where! She wont answer my calls!" Sinsee held up her hand at the guards who were reaching for the young man, They backed away.

"Who is it you can't find?" she asked him as she knelt to help him to his feet.

"Missy, My Lioness. She has disappeared." he wiped the tears from his eyes, but they were replaced with new ones.

"When was the last time you saw her?" The young man was reluctant to say and Sinsee placed her hands on his face. Everything he had ever done she instantly knew about. She made him look at her. "It's not your fault." she said in a soft whisper. Turning away from the boy she called for Kit. Kit was beside her in a flash. She mentally called to Pregger as well. Pregger enter the Hall from the door in the back, followed by Jewbee.

"We Need your help." she said mentally and vocally. "There is a Lioness somewhere on this station who needs our help. Be careful, if you find her, don't move her. Send for Jewbee right away." She turned to Jewbee. "Get your staff from O.B. together." Jewbee nodded and ran out of the Hall. Sinsee turned to everyone else and had to raise her voice to be heard over the confused conversations. "I am sorry for the interruption. You must understand, this is the first birth of a Terra Two Lion on the station, and there may be complications." Sinsee tried to find Roeman's face in the sea of faces. "Roeman! Where are You!" There was an edge of fear in her voice that everyone picked up on. Somehow Roeman was at her side, lending her his support. "Roeman, I can't hear the Lioness, she must be unconscious. No wonder the boy is in such a state. Have someone take him to our quarters." Roeman signaled for one of the guards, told him what to do and told him to be kind to the boy. They would be along shortly.

Patrick and his father arrived at the hospital only to find it in a state of Chaos. Halley came running up to them. "Am I glad to see you!" He said, almost out of breath.

"What is going on around here?" asked Dr. Parry, as someone bumped into him in the crowed corridor. They never even bothered to apologize, and Parry frowned at the persons back.

"There is a Lioness giving birth somewhere on the station and she is not answering any telepathic calls. The Lion Riders are dispersing all over the station in the hopes of finding Her." He motioned them to follow him into a side office. "The Chandler is coordinating the search telepathically with all the Catsman and Lion Riders heading up individual search teams."

"Where are they searching?" asked Dr. Parry. Halley tossed up his hands and said everywhere. "That won't do." said Dr. Perry. "A birthing Lioness seeks out a den when it is her time. Are there places on the station that might resemble a cave or tunnel?"

"Shit!" said Halley as he opened a com. "Send the Lion

Riders into the maintenance tunnels. Dr. Parry says that the Lioness would have been looking for some kind of den!" Halley looked at Dr. Parry who nodded once. "I sure hope you are right about this."

Patrick smiled, "If there is one thing about my father, it is that He is never wrong."

"If you say so." said Halley. A few moments later a Female Catsman showed up at the office door and informed them that The Chandler wanted them in Her quarters NOW! "She must be having fits by now. We better get there as fast as we can. Come on." said Halley. "There is a rail tube not to far from here. It is the fastest way to reach the center sphere." Halley was leading the way.

"I thought those tubes were only used for cargo?" said Patrick as he and his father followed Halley out of the office.

"They are." said Halley. "But they are also a real gasser to ride!"

"Why is it that I don't like the sound of this?" said Dr. Parry as he followed the young man down the corridor to a half size hatchway.

"Don't worry Doc. I've done this hundreds of times. I promise you it's safe so long as you keep your hands on the strapping bar at all times. Jewbee had a fit when I came in that one time I lost my fingers." Dr. Parry looked at the young mans hands as he held them up for inspection. "A short stay in the Med Unit and their as good as new" Even knowing that a med Unit could rejuvenate limbs was no comfort to Parry as he watched his son climb into a cargo pod. Halley tapped the bar in front of Patrick, who grabbed onto it. When he was ready for take off Halley hit the switch and Patrick's cargo pod took off with a swishing sound and in the blink of an eye was out of sight as it went into the tube like tunnel. Dr. Parry could hear his son somewhere down the tube. "WHAHOO!" Halley laughed. "You're next Doc. Keep your hands on the bar at all times." Parry climbed into his pod and then took a death grip on the strapping bar. "See you on the other side Doc." Halley hit the switch. Dr. Parry's reaction was the same as his sons, only just a little higher in pitch.

Hitting the gravity field of the next sphere was like having your stomach go from your throat to your feet instantaneously. For the first time Parry wondered how he was going to stop this thing. Another gravity field hit him, "How many more of those things are there?" he wondered and lost count after the ninth field. Finally His pod started to meet with a series of shield buffers and began to slow down. It actually felt like going through a thick fluid. The pod neared a bend in the tube, once around the bend Parry could see Patrick and two other men waiting for him. The two men were there because they heard the proximity alarms alerting the arrival of cargo pods. They weren't very amused when Patrick's pod came around the last bend. Patrick explained why they were using the rail tube and that there were two more pods coming in, one of which was occupied by an important Doctor from Terra Two. Patrick didn't bother to tell them that he was also his father.

The handlers reached out to grab the pod and slow its forward motion even more. "We've got you Doctor." said one of the cargo handlers. He helped Dr. Parry to disembark from the pod. While Parry was trying to get his legs to stay under him Halley's pod came into sight. "I might have known." said the cargo handler. "You just don't give up, do you Halley!"

Halley jumped out of the pod, "No time to talk, the Chandler wants the Doctor and us in her quarters right now. This was the fastest way to get here from the medical wing. You wont have to make a report on this one." Patrick was leading the way through stacked cases of cargo crates. "This way Doctor Nathin." Halley opened a door at the far end of the cargo storage, it opened onto the main corridor in the center sphere.

Patrick could hear the handlers behind them. "That boy is going to get someone killed one of these days." "Leave off

Tanner. You know You've been dying to try it yourself." "Not me! I like my fingers just where there are, Thank You." Their conversation was cut off when Halley closed the door.

Parry was impressed with this new corridor, it was nothing like the others he had seen on the station. There was art work on the walls and nook seating here and there. It was really rather nice.

They turned down another corridor and passed a number of guards. Half way down the corridor Patrick knocked on the door to Sinsee's personal quarters. Roeman opened the door, surprised to see them there so soon. Halley explained about his little short cut. "No wonder you got here so soon. Maybe you should design a personal carrier for those tubes. It would save on the time it takes to get from one place to another around here."

"I don't think that the Handlers would appreciate the extra work load." said Halley as they walked into the main room.

"Not their call. We will talk more about this later, right now we have another problem" Roeman pointed to Sinsee and Pregger sitting on the couch. Jewbee was keeping an eye on Sinsee's blood pressure while Pregger was trying to lend his telepathic support.

Jewbee looked up at Dr. Parry, and shook her head. Parry walked over to Sinsee and placed his hand on her forehead. "She is hot and sweating like crazy. She is using a great deal of higher brain functions right now, but that doesn't explain why she is burning up though."

"The gowns! I forgot about the gowns!" Jewbee began to remove the many layers of gowns from Sinsee and the men turned their eyes away.

"She will need to eat to replenish the calories she is burning through." said Parry. "She doesn't need to use her mouth to communicate with the other telepaths."

Some one went to see about food and the rest of them settled down in various seats around the room. Parry changed places with Jewbee and continued to monitor Sinsee. Soon the serving staff came in with the Food. Sinsee began to wolf it down like she was starving. Parry told her to slow down or she could end up chocking on her food.

Pregger was also making short work of vegetables and grains that had been brought for him. His race was vegetarians despite their appearance. When introduced to dairy products they became ill. They had no problem with fermented drinks. In fact they could drink four times the amount that humans could drink with no side effects what so ever. A trait that Patrick had come to envy. No one bothered to ask the Catsman how they felt about the Humans eating meat, and the Catsman never made any comments one way or the other.

Half way though her forth helping there was another knock at the door. This time it was Patrick who got up to answer it. The look on Jayson's face was one of mild irritation. "How did you get here before us? I thought you and your father were going to the hospital."

"Been there, done that." laughed Patrick. "Dad's inside with the rest of them. I'll tell you how we got here, but right now we are having a bit of a problem."

"So I heard." said Jayson as he moved past Patrick. As Jayson made his way into the main room he saw that Sinsee was being looked after by Dr. Parry. His attention went from her to Roeman and he made his way across the room over to Roeman. Roeman stood up and extended his hand in greeting.

"Not exactly the way we planned this Sir, I am sorry about all this." said Roeman.

"Quite alright son. We have been told of the situation. Has there been any news?" Jayson sat down next to Roeman.

"Nothing yet. The search teams have been in the maintenance tunnels only a short time now." said Roeman as he sat back down in his chair. "If a person wanted to, they could stay lost in those tunnels for months at a time. That is how our people avoided being caught."

"Fortunately we are not dealing with a human. Are the Lions with their Riders in those tunnels now?" He got an affirmative. "Good. Those Cats should pickup her scent soon. Even a scent that is days old will still be detectable to them. Which one of the spheres did she live in?"

"Damn it!" said Sinsee. "I am sending all search teams into the third sphere. I should have thought of this sooner. Thank you Jayson." "My pleasure." was all he said. Ten minutes later Sinsee got the message that they had picked up the scent and it was strong. Jewbee left to join her team and Dr. Parry went with her, but not before contacting the ship they had come in on. Parry ordered his personal medical bags and cases to be brought to the search area.

Once the Lions got the scent it didn't take them long to find the unconscious Lioness. Beside her were two cubs. Parry moved in next to the Lioness and moved his hands over her still swollen belly. "We've got a problem here. She has a cub stuck in the passage. Jewbee, open that small case and get the injection ready for me. No, not that one, this one." he pointed to the right vile. Opening the second case he selected a scalpel.

"What are you going to do with that?" asked a shocked Jewbee.

"I am going to save this Lionesses life and that of her unborn cubs. Watch and learn, Girl. You have been relying on your Med Units far to long. Now see how a real doctor works. You do what I tell you when I tell you the first time and we wont lose a single life, you got that!" Jewbee said that she understood.

Even though Jewbee thought that Parry was killing the Lioness, she was amazed when the first of the four remaining cubs was removed from the cesarean incision. She was even more amazed when Dr. Parry removed the last cub along with the birth sacks and began to delicately sew the incision closed. His hands worked as if he were repairing a delicate flower to its original state. He bound up the abdomen with yards of medical strapping. Only when he had given the Lioness a complete physical would he let the rest of the medical team members move her onto the cargo gravity lift. He walked beside her, monitoring her the whole way back to the Hospital.

Sinsee had been monitoring the entire time through the mind link with one of the Lion Riders who had been in the search party. When she announced the birth of six healthy cubs and the expected full recovery of the Lioness, everyone in the room cheered, but the young rider fainted.

Hours later, Jewbee joined the others in Sinsee's quarters, along with a few of her medical staff who were now busy monitoring Sinsee's recovery from her prolonged mental link. Jayson was explaining about the new find of pure bloods.

"There is no doubt what so ever, the integration was so complete that we never took the possibility into consideration until more pure bloods started popping up then we could account for." Jayson looked around the room trying to read the different reactions of all those present.

"Let me get this straight," said Jewbee. "What you are saying is that about one eighth of your population was Millally, even before you started to change the genetic make up?"

Jayson smiled at her. "That's right Doctor. Our ancestors have been escaping space ever sense the first cryo chamber was placed on a ship. Not all replacements were from faulty chambers. Some of those chambers were purposely turned off without the revival boards functioning. You know as well as I do what that means for the occupant."

Roeman ran his fingers through his hair. "I had heard the old stories, but I thought that that sort of thing was only done if a chamber malfunctioned. This kind of information could start another war."

"Yes it could, if that were the story I am about to break to the rest of the universe." said Jayson.

"Just what are you going to tell them to explain a planet populated by Millally. You can't tell them that it was a freak of nature. Who in their right mind would believe a story like that?" said Jewbee.

"Sinsee speaks highly of you, so I can only imagine that you have a really good cover story. How about sharing it with us." said Roeman as he leaned forward in his seat with anticipation.

"Our ancestors have already provided us with part of the story. They must have made good their escapes to more then just Terra Two. That means that there are Millally decedents on every colony world. A natural evolutionary selection." Jayson waited for their reaction.

"Jeffery! I knew that boy was special. Remind me to send a message to the Captain of the Claw. I want them to test Jeffery for trace lines of Millally DNA." Roeman said to Jewbee.

"You think the boy is one of us?" she asked.

"He has got to be. No grounder that young has that much courage." said Roeman. "That kid has Balls."

"Speaking of Ball's, " said Nika. "We are going to have a Ball here to celebrate Your marriage to Sinsee. So for right now lets deal with one thing at a time, and the first thing on the list, is the list."

The conversation turned to the up-coming wedding. After a time the men retreated to another room to let the women do their thing, what ever that was.

Sinsee sat in the nursery unit of the hospital holding one of the cubs in her lap. The young rider beamed with pride as his Lioness rested her head in his lap on the floor, her stomach bound in fresh bandaging. Jewbee entered the room and looked down at the pair. "You know, we are going to have to find a way to modify some of our med units to handle the Lions. As it is they don't work on the Lions or the Catsman and I am not a mechanic. With so many things going on at the same time I never got around to having it done." she came over to Sinsee and rubbed the tips of her fingers under the chin of the cub in Sinsee's lap. "They are cute little things aren't they."

"What I don't understand," said Sinsee. "Is how she had six cubs. Kit assures me that they only have two at the most. A normal birth is only one cub." Sinsee put the cub down on the floor with her other siblings.

"Maybe it is because the gravity on the station is different then that of the planet." said Jewbee. "If that is the case, I want every Lioness on the station in here for a scan. They breed in a set cycle don't they?"

"Oh No, not again." Sinsee put the word out, right then and there. Telepathy came in handy and this time she didn't mind the link. Sinsee put her hand on her own stomach. "You don't think I could possibly be... " she left the sentence unfinished.

"Not this time." said Jewbee. "But I wouldn't put it past Roeman."

Sinsee didn't know which way Jewbee meant that, but it fit both ways and she just had to laugh. "Jewbee, I love you for your sense of humor." She managed to get the words out between bouts of laughter as she almost fell off her seat.

Chapter Three

ROEMAN AND JAYSON WERE in Sinsee's main office when word came that there was an incoming transmission from Terra Two for President Bane from Captain Henson. Roeman said that they would be right there and he and Jayson headed for the communication office. When they got there the shift manager apologize to them and explained that another satellite was out of sink again and that there would be a delay in the relay. "It's going to take the ship some time even before it reaches the first relay. So for now we have to put up with the delays."

Jayson said that he understood, and that he could put up with it if she could. She asked if he wanted the room cleared and he said no. "There will be no secrets here." said Jayson. "If I can't trust you and your staff, then you are in the wrong job." It was a complement and a warning all in one. She nodded her head in agreement and signaled the operator to begin the transmission.

"Home Station to Terra Two, You may begin transmission now." There was a span of silence. "Mr. President, I'm sorry, but we have got a bit of a situation here. It's my fault. I never told my crew not to talk about the wedding around the ground workers. I've had news crews climbing up my back side for days now. One of them shoved a microphone in my face while I was on the sitter in the port building. He is not doing any reporting at the moment because his jaw is wired shut. Sorry about that. I have also got Regional Directors, City Managers, and even some religious Leaders demanding transport to Home Station. Right now my crew is hold up in the ship. Security has its hands full here at the port. I have been tempted to turn on the ships shields, one news crew actually got onboard the ship. I should have contacted you before this, but I thought I could handle it. I was wrong. What do you want me to do?"

[Over]

"For the moment I want you to contact the Foundation and have them send every available security officer they can spare to the Port. Then I want the planetary guard sent in as soon as they can to lock dawn that Port. I'll you give my personal codes so they know the orders come from me. That should give you and your crew some breathing room for now. As to the rest of it, I'll have to get back to you. Now write down this code, memorize it, then burn that piece of paper." He gave the code to Henson.

[Over]

"Thank You Sir. I guess I can stop pulling my hair out now. One more thing, Is it true that a Lioness had six cubs? You know how the grapevine is."

[Over]

Jayson offered Roeman this one. "Hi Henson, Roeman here, To answer your question, Yes. And we have got Eleven more Females expecting multi births as well. Jewbee is having fits because our med units wont work on the Lions or the Catsman. She is having to do things the old fashion way. Luck is with her in one respect, she has all three Doctor Nathan's helping her.

[Over]

"And here I thought she was the Goddess of Medicine.

Are the Females producing enough milk for the cubs? We can always load up on dairy if they need it.

[Over]

'Good point Henson. I'll talk to Jewbee and find out. Open a link again in about twelve hours from now. We should have something for you by then."

[Over and Out]

[Over and Out]

Jayson thanked the shift manager and she thanked him. Roeman was certain that the moment they left she would remind her staff that they were to forget anything that was not their business.

On the way back to the office they talked about what could be done to get things under control on Terra Two.

"I really didn't know that your people would take this marriage thing so seriously." said Roeman. "It seems to be a big event in their lives."

"Yes," said Jayson. "It is, but so is the birth of the first child. I know you are thinking that we place to much emphasis on our rituals, but these rituals come to us from a time in human history before man even thought of space travel. Even before he had completely explored his own world of origin. There was a time when a Great Leader was to marry, other Leaders would travel great distances to be witnesses to the union. These Leaders would bring gifts and offerings to the couple. Why in ancient times there would be a celebration that would last for months. Now they knew how to party!" Jayson was unaware that they had a shadow as they walked down the long corridor.

"Just what kind of gifts do they give at a wedding? asked Roeman.

"Now that depends on just who the couple getting married are." said Nika as she came up beside them. They stopped and Nika took Roeman's arm. "If you really want to know about such things you are talking to the wrong person. Jayson has always left such things to me. He is more interested in watching the fun unfold at such things." She turned to her brother. "Jayson, you remember Perry's wedding. They held it at the river park, near that foot bridge. It was spring time and the flowering trees were in full bloom." she smiled at the memory.

"Yes, I also recall a shoving match that led to a dozen people being pulled out of the river too. A word of advice my boy, leave the party early." Jayson leaned towards Roman as he said that.

'Now Jayson!" chided Nika. "You're frightening the boy. Don't pay him any mind Roeman." she said as they started to walk again. "By the way, what have you two been up to?"

Jayson looked at his sister. "There is a slight problem on Terra Two." He explained what was going on. "We told Henson we would get back to him when we came up with a solution."

"You said that they are demanding transport?" she asked. "Well there you have it."

"What do we have?" asked Roeman. Jayson didn't say a word. He knew how much Nika loved dropping the proverbial other shoe. He also loved the way her mind worked.

"Let's just see how much they demand when they find out that they have to pay for their passage. Sinsee did say that she was going to allow travel between the worlds again. Surly they don't think that she is going to do this for free.?"

"She is right Roeman. Well that should take care of most of them, but there are still those who can pay the price." said Jayson, hoping to catch his sister off guard.

"While you boys have been off playing, I have been looking into the number of available accommodations. There are empty quarters on all but the third sphere that does not include the center sphere. Some are large enough to accommodate groups up to twenty people." said Nika, looking at her brother.

"Wait a minute, what do you mean, accommodate?"

Roeman could not understand why she would need those empty quarters. All the staff she had brought with her had already been given living quarters.

"The guests have to stay somewhere while they are here." she told him.

"Guests!" exclaimed Roeman.

"It is just like I was saying," said Jayson as he joined in at this point, seeing that Nika's little game was making Roeman nervous. "When a great Leader marries, People come from all over. Mostly only the high ranking members of other countries. In this case, other worlds."

"I have sent a number of invitations out via ship relay. I started this even before we left Terra Two. Haven't you noticed that half your ships are out?" asked Nika

"I thought they were out running missions for Sinsee." Roeman answered her. He was becoming aware of just how much personal power this woman held over others. Ship Captain's were taking her orders without clearing it with Home Station. How does she do it? How does she get anyone to do just what she wants.

"They are, in a way." said Jayson.

"Only the closest Colony Worlds will be able to get here in time for the wedding." said Nika.

"And you did all this from Terra Two. Does Sinsee know about this?" He was told that she did not.

"So just what are we looking at here?" He asked Nika.

"It is really rather simple. Only twenty guests from each world will attend the wedding. The reception itself will go on for a long time. Those who don't make the wedding can still have the opportunity to attend the reception. I for one am looking forward to seeing what they bring to the table." Nika held onto Roeman's arm as they made their way to Sinsee's office.

"Some how I get the feeling this is all over my head."

Roeman shook his head. "What do you mean by bring to the table?"

"Why gifts my boy!" said Jayson. "You can expect some very interesting things."

"So what are we expected to give in return?" he asked them. Nika looked at her brother and shook her head. She had her work cut out for her bringing Roeman up to speed. She sighed.

"They are coming to a wedding, not an open market." said Jayson. "This is how it is done."

"I don't know brother," said Nika. "There may be some who would want to take this opportunity to beg favors of the Millally. We should use this to our advantage." They reached the office and Roeman opened the door, Nika entered first. Sinsee was there to greet them.

With everything that was going on Sinsee and Roeman had spent very little time together. Nika suggested that they take some time and try to relax, even if only for a few hours.

Alone in their quarters for the first time in a long time, Sinsee and Roeman enjoyed each others company. Laying back on their bed, Sinsee snuggled up against Roeman, his left arm wrapped around her, his fingers playing with a strand of her long hair. It had amused him that other women on the station had begun to let their hair grow long.

"I have missed this." sighed Sinsee as she stretched, then she looked into Roeman's eyes. "How about a bath instead of a shower?" she asked him. He nodded, and she got up to go and draw the bath. He watched her as she walked away from the bed. Her body did not yet show her condition, and he enjoyed the view.

"Has Jewbee found a way to keep the Lionesses from going out and seeking dens when their times come?" he asked her as he stretched the muscles in his neck.

"Halley and Dr. Parry have been working on simulating

the dens they use on Terry Two. Halley got one of the older Lionesses to describe a den to him." Roeman heard the water running and missed what she said next so he got out of bed and joined her in the other room.

"Sorry, I didn't catch that last part." Roeman came up behind her, he encircled her waist in his arms and kissed the back of her neck.

"I said that some of the boys over in fabrication are proving to have a real artistic talent. Halley managed to install medical monitors in the flooring of the dens with out interfering with the readings. Jewbee can keep an eye on the progress with out adding any undue stress on the Lionesses. If a problem comes up, she can intervene. Otherwise the Lioness does it on their own." Sinsee turned in his arms to face him, they kissed each other passionately. Sinsee reached out with her hand to find the bath controls, she shut the water flow off. Their bath would have to wait, Roeman picked her up in his arms and carried her back to the bed.

Some time later Sinsee joined Jewbee in the Lion Nursery and found the women there hand feeding some of the cubs. Jewbee explained that one of the Lionesses could not produce enough milk for her eight cubs. Jewbee had noticed that they were not putting on any weight, which they should have been.

Sinsee asked if she could help and was handed a bottle of heated milk. Jewbee showed her to a seat and laid a thick pad on her lap. "You will need this, the cubs have a tendency to claw at your legs when they are feeding." She was given one of the cubs by an aid and the cub went for the bottle, sucking, purring, and clawing at the pad. Sinsee looked around at the other nurses in the room. The older one was familiar. Sinsee remembered her from the training sphere, she was the one who spoke up and had asked Sinsee to find her babies. Now that the children were staying with there parents there was no reason for the old nurse to stay in the training center. Sinsee was glad that she had found something else to take the place of the children she had lost.

The older nurse was busy feeding the cub in her lap, she took the bottle away and started to half rub and half pat the back of the not so small cub, it gave a loud burp and she gave the bottle back to the cub. "It is nice to be looking after babies again, even though they are covered in fur. All they need is a comfortable bed and loving hands to see them fed. Isn't that right my little love." She rubbed behind the cub's ear. "Chandler, you should burp your cub now."

Sinsee did just what the old nurse had done and she was rewarded with a rather loud burp. Sinsee became acutely aware that she didn't know anything about new born babies. It might be a good idea to have someone like this old nurse around. She seemed to know what she was doing.

"It wont be long and I will have to do this for my own child." said Sinsee, hoping to open a dialog with the old nurse.

"But surely Chandler, you will want a fulltime nurse for the child. Babies take up so much of ones time and you have your duties as well. One of the young aids should do well in this capacity." the old nurse suggested.

"I thought that I would raise my own child." Sinsee's mother had raised her and her brother without any outside help. But then again, her mother didn't have to deal with a huge space station and a fleet of ships. Maybe she should rethink this.

"Even so, it may be that you can do this, but you will need help. Someone who's job it will be to look after the child when you can not be there." said the old nurse.

Jewbee came back into the room at this point with two more cubs in her hands. She switched them with the two Sinsee and the old nurse had. "Personally, I don't know what I would do without Kreeote to look after his sister Reekee." The young aid came behind her with fresh bottles of milk. Sinsee handed her the empty one in exchange for a full one. She was on her third cub when Halley and Patrick showed up.

"So this is where you have been hiding out. Here, let me try that." said Patrick as he took the cub from Sinsee. "You have to lift the bottle like this." He tilted the bottle almost on end. "This way you wont be spending all your time burping the cub and he can spend less time getting food into his gut. The air stays in the back of the bottle. See what I mean."

The women exchanged looks and smiled at Patrick but it was the old nurse who spoke up. "Young man, you would make a wonderful mother. Just where did you learn how to do that?"

"Besides being a Doctor, I spent a few years traveling with a troop of Lions back home. We never had this many cubs though. There isn't much that I don't know about them." said Patrick.

"Well why didn't you say something before now!" complained Jewbee. "I could have used your help around here."

"I wasn't aware that there was a problem." replied Patrick. Jewbee threw her hands up in the air in disgust. "Well I am here now so why don't you tell me what you think is wrong."

Jewbee sat down across from Patrick. "Nothing and everything. OK. Give me a minute." She tried to get her thoughts together. "To start with, the Med units don't work on the Lions or the Catsman. Your Father has been teaching me old style medicine to handle them." Patrick was with her so far. "The reason Halley keeps doing what he does is because he knows that our med units can regenerate his fingers. It is the same with everyone else on the station. Our people take risks that they shouldn't because of that knowledge. But when a Catsman gets a finger cut off, that's it. We can't grow it back. Now do you understand?"

"The Catsman see our taking risks as some kind of

bravery. So they take risks that they normally would not." said Halley.

"That is it." said Jewbee. "And now this thing with the Lions. I've gone over the blue prints of the Med units and there is nothing I can see that will convert the process over to Catsman DNA or the Lions for that matter."

"Well, maybe the Tec's on ZENTEX could come up with a med unit that will work on both the Catsman's and the Lions." said Patrick.

"What are you talking about?" asked Jewbee.

"The Tec's are the ones who invented the rejuvenation tanks. They never let them out of their control, so when someone needed the use of one, they would have to go to ZENTEX for treatment. Wait, are you saying that you didn't know that?" asked Patrick. Jewbee said that she did not know that. She only knew about her people converting the cryo chambers over to the medical units they used today. She was unsure just who it was who came up with the first one.

Sinsee spoke up then, "I think that Allison must have had something that the Tec's needed real bad, badly enough that they parted with one of their tanks, giving it to Her.."

"Sure!" said Halley. "Then all we would have had to do is back engineer it, just like we are doing with the Catsman ship."

"Yes, but you can't back engineer something you don't have." said Jewbee.

"If we only had a ZENTEX Tec, we might be able to refit a med unit so it could work on the Catsman's." said Halley.

"And the Lions!" The old nurse piped up.

"I believe I can help you in that respect." said Nika, she stood in the entrance way to the nursery. "I see you have found a pleasant past time." she was speaking to Sinsee. "As to the ZENTEX, they are on their way here. It would seem that they have been very busy. Your Grandfather and I would like to talk to you and Roeman, now."

✸

Nika and Sinsee found the others still in the communication room. Roeman was deep in conversation with the shift manager and did not see them come in. Sinsee walked up to Jayson and asked what was going on. Jayson tried to explain. "It would appear that the ZENTEX Tec's put a lot of faith in their tools. For some time now, they won't say how long, they have been monitoring every communication signal that has been sent. They wish to make a deal with the Millally and Terry Two, for certain privileges. They do not say rights, they do make that distinction. They would install a communications system that is vastly superior to anything known. They claimed that this system would not need any relay satellites."

"And what are they arguing about?" Sinsee indicated Roeman and the shift manager, who were starting to raise their voices.

"She doesn't want any outsider messing with her stuff." said Jayson.

The conversation was really starting to heat up. Their bantering words back and forth were starting to get on Sinsee's nerves.

"Enough! The both of You! I'm starting to get sick with all this noise!" To everyone's surprise, including her own, Sinsee did get sick, all over the floor. Nika was at her side instantly, she held Sinsee's head as she once again lost more of her last meal.

Kit's roar could be heard right outside the door to the communication room. The door opened and in came Jewbee with Kit right behind her. When she was asked how she had gotten there so fast, she told them that Kit had told her that something was wrong with Sinsee.

"But Doctor, you are not a telepath.!" said Jayson.

"I am now." she replied. "At first I thought my scalp was going to come off, then I heard Kit and the cubs, who were yammering to be fed again. Kit told them to shut up and they

101

did, then he told me that Sinsee was not right. That she was in pain." Jewbee took over for Nika.

"Fascinating!" said Jayson. "I'm starting to see a pattern here."

"Brother, Are you thinking that the Lion cubs are responsible for her latent talent?" Everyone knew that Jewbee had been spending more time with the Lionesses and the cubs because of their need of her medical services. It could be a matter of long exposure to the young cubs who did not know about their ability as yet.

"How about it Jewbee? Have any of your staff started to hear voices in their heads?" asked Jayson. The Doctor was to busy right then to answer his question. Kit gave another roar.

"Yes, I know." Jewbee said to him as she grabbed a small waste basket and placed it in front of Sinsee who lost even more of her last meal. "I think that is the last of it Sinsee. Can you make it back to your quarters?" Kit stepped up. "Good idea. Come on Sinsee." Jewbee and Roeman helped Sinsee to climb onto Kits back, she leaned forward and laid her head into his massive main. "now take it easy Kit." The others followed them out of the communication room and back to the center sphere and Sinsee's quarters.

"Fascinating." said Jayson one more time.

"So it is True." said Jayson as he talked to Jewbee. "The Lions are the catalyst to releasing latent talents."

"Yes, both the nursery aids and the old nurse are picking up signals from the cubs. Most of it is only feelings of hunger or the need to be touched. You have to remember that the cubs are still babies after all." She reminded him.

"And YOU on the other hand have been dealing with the adults." remarked Jayson, as he gave this more thought.

"Maybe." said Jewbee. "But if that were the case, then why did it take so long for it to happen? No. I Think it was because

Kit felt Sinsee getting sick and he focused in on me, knowing that I could help her. It was a deliberate act."

"I see." Jayson had hoped that long term exposure to the Lions would activate the telepathic talent in humans. But if it was a matter of choice on the part of the Lions, he knew that he couldn't force them to do it. At least now he knew it could be done, if the Lion was willing. "I must stop by the nursery one of these times and see how the cubs are doing."

Jewbee gave him a look and thought, You sly Old Dog. Aloud she said, "You would be welcome anytime. Mostly around feeding time." she would love to see him trying to feed one of her cubs. She heard Kit give a deep mental rumble, and she broke out laughing. Jayson did not bother to ask her what was so funny.

✳

Jayson's attempt to influence one of the Lions into activating his latent talents did not materialize. When he voiced his disappointment to the others it got Sinsee to thinking.

"If it takes a Terry Two Lion to activate the telepathic talents, how do you explain Allison Millally's telepathic ability?"

"I don't know." said Jayson but I intend to find out." He and Sinsee went to communications. "You know my dear, You should really have a direct link to communication in your office and your quarters. I for one am getting tired of these long walks. An old man like myself has just so much energy.

"You are not that much out of shape Jayson. But perhaps you are right. I'll talk to Roeman and see if we can get something put in our quarters and the office." She saw the raise of one eyebrow and the start of a smile on Jayson's face before he could conceal his intent. "I saw that!" she challenged him.

"I am only thinking about you and the child my dear. Have you ever been around a woman in her last stage of pregnancy?" asked Jayson. Sinsee had to admit that she had not. "Well take it from me, you are not going to want to be

103

walking these corridors. Long walks will be the last thing you will want to have to do."

"I don't know if that is true where I am concerned. I am not like other women, I never have been. But if it will make you feel better, I will have the link from communications set up." She saw the relief on his face. "That doesn't mean that I am going to set on my ass until the baby comes."

Jayson chuckled under his breath.

In communications, it took some time to get a link with Terra Two, and then there was an even longer wait while someone went to get Allison Millally.

"It would seem that the relay satellites are not the only things out of place. I told them that Allison was not to leave the Foundation." Jayson began to pace.

"Maybe you should have put a link in my old apartment. After all it is a long walk to your office from there." said Sinsee in a teasing way. Jayson looked at her as if he had never seen her before.

"Sir," interrupted the shift manager. "The Chandler is waiting for you." She stepped aside and let Jayson and Sinsee take her place at the screen. There was still no visual and the time lag seemed to be getting worse. Jayson explained about the Lions being the catalyst for the telepathic abilities. "Now what I want to know is how were those latent talents activated in you."

[Over]

Jayson waited for the answer and the silence in the room was nerve racking. He looked at the shift manager who was timing the laps in time, which didn't help him at the moment.

"I know what you are asking and I know why you are asking it. I am sorry that I have to disappoint you on this one Jayson. You see it was part of my job to see to live cargo in the hold of our ship. I remember that we transported some of your Lions to one of the other colony worlds. Some rich man had his own personal zoo. Come to think of it I thought that the Lions had given me fleas. I scratched myself until I drew blood. Then the itching just stopped." said Allison.

[Over]

"You wouldn't happen to remember which of the colony worlds the Lions went to and how many were transported.?" asked Jayson.

[Over]

"There were four males and four females. But as to which world they went to, I couldn't say. As I told you, my job was in the hold, not on the bridge. I am sorry Jayson. That is all I can tell you." said Allison.

[Over]

"That is alright Allison. It was just that I was hoping that there was another catalyst other then the Terra Two Lions. Thanks anyway."

[Over and Out]

Jayson turned to Sinsee and saw the glint in her eye. He smiled and tilted his head. "You can't blame an old man for trying."

"Oh I don't. But this means that Terra Two has a commodity that can not be found anywhere else in the universe." smiled Sinsee.

"Yes, I guess it does. Now what I want to know is what do the Terry Two Lions and the Catsman's have in common that allows them to be born with the talent?" said Jayson.

"I am not all that sure that The Catsman young are born with the talent, or if they learn it the same way our young learn to speak." said Sinsee as she and Jayson made their way out of communications.

"Maybe I should have a talk with Doctor Jewbee and see if her daughter has shown any signs of telepathic communication yet." Jayson turned and headed towards the hospital, knowing that he would find the good Doctor in the Lion nursery at this time of day.

"YOU be nice to her when you talk to her about Reekee. She can be more protective of that little bundle then a Terra Two Lioness. Believe me, I know first hand about that." Sinsee laughed as Jayson waved good by to her over his shoulder.

"Yes, yes. I heard all about that. They say she really went after the Captain with blood in her eyes. Don't worry about me, I will be the concerned grandfather all the way. He walked on down the corridor, Sinsee wondered if she should give Jewbee a heads up that he was coming her way.

{["She already knows."]} came Kits touch. {["Roeman is looking for you."]}

{["Thank you Kit."]} she answered him. {["Where is he now?"]}

{["He is in your rooms."]}

Sinsee turned and headed for her quarters. {["Don't let him leave."]}

One week later there was an incoming transmission from Captain Dee. Roeman greeted his old Friend.

"We are about a week out from Homestation. Now before you blow a seal hear me out." said Dee.

"This better be good." said Roeman.

"Oh it is. The ZENTEX Tec's met us more then half way. You should see the shuttle they have got! I wouldn't mind having a few of those in my holds. I have already asked them what they want for one but they wont deal with me. Anyway, they have already up graded my communication systems. Nice!"

"I was wondering why we don't have a lag time. So it works just like they said it would." Roeman looked at the shift manager as if to say, I told you so. She just snorted at him and turned away. "I hope these Tec's are as good as they think they are." said Roeman.

"Something up?" asked Dee.

"Not on the com, Dee." ears seem to be everywhere.

"I get your point." said Dee. "There is something else you should know about these Tec's, They come in pairs and speak in tandem. If you don't try to watch which one is speaking you wont get dizzy. I've got their shuttle locked up in my hold and I have restricted their movements on my ship. They seem to be handling it pretty well."

"I will give you points for this one, Dee. Get here soonest."

"See you in a week. Over and Out."

At an improvised meeting Roeman called of key personal, he explained about the ZENTEX and their shuttle. "From what I understand, these shuttles can match speeds with our ships." said Roeman. "Other wise they would not have been able to meet Dee at more then the half way point."

"Well we know that they have been listening in on our transmissions. They would have known that we had dispatched a ship to ZENTEX. They would also know about the invitations to the wedding. Seems to me that they want to be first in more ways then one." said Captain Lane. Nika looked at her with agreement. She liked Captain Lane, the women was not bothered by what others may or may not think of her. When it came to getting the job done, Lane could get more out of people then they thought they had.

"Does anyone have any ideas as to what kind of privileges they might be expecting?" asked Halley from his side of the room. A buzz of speculation went up around the room.

"All I know is that the Tec's have something that we need. Themselves." said Jewbee.

"That is for sure." said Halley. "If there shuttle is any example of the advances they have been making, I could sure use their help on New Home."

"That's It!" said Sinsee with excitement. "They know about New Home and they want a close look at Her." Everyone looked at Sinsee. "The Tec's are scientists, inventors of the highest quality. No offence Halley." She looked his way to see if she had hurt the boy's feelings and he just smiled at her. "What we need to do is keep them off balance. Lets make them work for what they want. For now, no matter how much they offer, New Home is off limits to them."

"That is cruel Sinsee. That ship out there is the size of a small moon. They take one look at her and the only thing they are going to be able to do is salivate." chuckled Nika.

"Good ." said Roeman. "We keep them baited, then we can see just how much they are willing to bring to the table." Roeman looked over at Nika for her reaction. He remembered their conversation in the corridor.

"You are learning." she said to him. "Now we prepare to meet our guests. Sinsee, Roeman. You two are going to do a little role playing." She held up her hand to prevent any questions until she was done speaking. "You two are going to play the part of King and Queen while our guests are here, and that goes for the Wedding Guests as well. All of Us, from now on will call Sinsee, High Chandler." Sinsee bulked at the word High being used. "Yes Dear. I know how you feel about that, but we must make your rank perfectly clear from the very start." Nika turned to Roeman. "You will have to forgive me Captain, but the Leader of the Millally can not marry a lowly captain. There for You are now given two ranks. Lord Roeman and Fleet Admiral Roeman."

"Wow! That's one Hell of a promotion!" said Captain Lane.

"Is all this really necessary?" asked Sinsee.

"Yes it is. Now all ships that come in must be made aware of our plot. That means that the crews will have to stay onboard while the guests disembark. Then a runner can go onboard and tell the crew what we are up to. It has to be this way because we can't send them a transmission, not with the ZENTEX Tec's listening in on every communication." Nika looked around the room and saw that everyone was in agreement with her.

"OK people, you heard the Countess. Lets get this ball rolling." said Roeman. His look dared Nika to protest her new title, and she did.

"If you don't mind, I would rather be a Duchess then a Countess. From the way you say the word countess you make it sound like some kind of blood sucker." She wrinkled her nose at Roeman. Something Sinsee had never seen her do before. Sinsee also thought that Nika was enjoying this far to much or maybe she, Sinsee, was not enjoying it enough.

"Speaking of getting things started, just what are we going to do first?" asked Captain Lane, as she looked from one to the other.

Nika had an answer for that one too. "We start by outfitting our King and Queen. Then we move on to the Great Hall. Redo the whole thing. The Black Guard already had a regal look to them, so we don't have to change a thing there." Nika was in her element here. She had always wanted to play at Royal Court, and now she had her opportunity. "Lord Roeman, I think it is time for your Fleet to have a code of uniform. Level and rank should be reflected in the uniforms. Also expertise." She turned to Sinsee. "Do you remember the military insignias from your military studies?"

"Military Studies!" said Roeman, as he looked with shock at the woman he loved.

Sinsee looked back at Roeman and blushed. "It was only studies, Roeman. I never actually did any military training." She gave Nika a scathing look. Nika ignored the look and continued what she was saying.

"There are two sides to our house, one is the military side and the other of course is the civilian. I am sure that I don't have to tell you which one is which. I think that a nice dark blue will be just the ticket for the Fleet. Lower ranks should be trimmed in silver while the higher ranks should be trimmed with gold." Nika looked around the room, then called out loud. "Abby! Where are you!"

Abby came trotting into the room. "Yes Mam, I'm right here." It was obvious to everyone that Abby had been listening in on the whole conversation.

"I want you to find me enough cloth to outfit at least three ships crews to start with, and don't forget the trim. Sinsee will provide you with the diagrams for the insignia. I want those to be made with colored silk threads. Do we have silk thread?" she asked her.

"Yes Mam." said Abby with excitement. "We also have a lovely Rich Red Velvet that would look good in the Great Hall. I am going to need to gather the best seamstresses we have. Shall I set up a meeting, so you can tell them just what is expected of them?"

"Yes. Can you have them meet in the Great Hall in about three hours from now." Abby said that she could. "Good. Now Sinsee, I need you to start on those Diagrams. The rest of you can get started on spreading the word around the station. Don't miss a single person. I don't want any slip ups."

They all took off for different parts of the station to spread the word. The Catsman's didn't understand what all the fuss was about. To them Sinsee had always been the High Chandler because she was the strongest telepath among them, but they were more then willing to play along with the humans. This new concept of a Royal Court intrigued them.

Chapter Four

NIKA OVERSAW THE REDECORATING of The Great Hall. There was enough of the red velvet to create an overhead canopy with a back drop and flowing side curtains. Two ornate chairs were placed on raised flooring with three steps leading up to it. Someone found two ornate free standing candles holders to go on each side of the raised floor. There was a little trouble finding candles though. The storage crew had to go through so many crates before they found one that must have been in storage for at least a hundred years. In side it were the candles that went with the stands. Royal was what Nika wanted and Royal was what she got.

One of the seamstresses came up with a design for a flag to represent the Millally. It was simple yet elegant. A black field with bands of gold quartering the field on an angle, in the upper left half was a depiction of a male Terra Two Lion that looked very much like Kit. In the lower right half was an opened eye that seemed to follow the on looker around the Hall. Nika approved the design and ordered a number of smaller banners in the same design. She suggested that the banners be trimmed with a mix of silver and gold tassels.

While The Great Hall was undergoing its transformation,

Sinsee and Roeman were also underwent there own transformation. Roeman was being fitted with a uniform that reflected his new rank. Abby was directing the work that was being done by another seamstress on the deep blue jacket and vest. Sinsee was in the other room being fitted into yet another gown. When she came out to show him this outfit, Roeman gave a whistle. "I might have to fight off the Tec's if you wear that one." he said. "Ouch!" He jumped. "Watch those pins!" he said to the seamstress. "Your going to have me full of holes if you're not careful."

"Sorry Lord Roeman. If you would only stand still, perhaps the pins would not stick you so often." she said to him as she tried not to giggle.

"How much longer is this going to take? I have got other work to do you know." He looked down at the women who held up another pin in her hand. Roeman rolled his eyes up and tried to stand perfectly still. Sinsee started to laugh and had to leave the room. As she went into the other room she heard Roeman again. "Ouch! You did that on purpose."

Fabrication came up with the idea of making full battle gear for the Lions, complete with silver studs for the saddles that were as comfortable to sit on as they were to look at. The male Lions had to have special face guards made while the females were fitted with neck guards which were as flexible as the free motion of their own necks. The breast plates were the same for both. As if the Lions weren't impressive enough on their own, the battle armor gave them such a fierce look that even Patrick was taken back by them.

Patrick made an observation that he had not noticed before now. "Has anyone noticed that the majority of female Lions have chosen human males as their mind mates and male Lions as a whole have paired with human females? Granted there are some same sex pairings, but only a few."

"Seems pretty natural to me." said Sinsee. "Human males are more aggressive and mach well with the hunting Lionesses.

Male Lions are more like female humans, they keep the peace in the pride."

"I guess that is one way of looking at it, but that does not explain the same sex pairings." said Patrick, believing he had found the flaw in her explanation.

"Not all men are aggressive Patrick. Just like not all women are submissive. You of all people should understand this."

"Good point. Ouch!" Patrick flinched at the punch Sinsee gave to his arm. "What was that for?"

"Just a little reminder to you. Just because I am paired with Kit does not make me a pussycat. The same goes for any rider. So don't go selling them short."

"I never have. As much as I have worked with the Lions, believe me, the last thing I want to do is sell them short. Male or female." He rubbed on his sore arm.

They were all having so much fun getting ready that the week went by before they knew it. Sinsee was still trying to decide which gown to wear when word came that Captain Dee was requesting Docking instructions.

"Oh Gees!" exclaimed Sinsee. "I'm not ready yet!"

"Take it easy, you have got plenty of time." Jewbee helped her into the gown. "Now breath out so I can get this fastened, there. Is it to tight?" she asked, then checked the seams. "You are starting to put on weight already. Just how much have you been eating?" Before Sinsee could stop him, Kit started to tell the Doctor everything that Sinsee had consumed for breakfast. "By the void! No wonder you put on all this weight. Sinsee, how can you eat that much food?" asked Jewbee with astonishment.

"I don't know! I have always got this feeling that I am hungry, even when I'm stuffed! I can't control myself!" she started to cry.

"Oh NO!" said Jewbee. "Sinsee, listen to me. There is nothing wrong with you. Don't you get it! It's the cubs. They must be projecting their hunger and with your higher level of telepathy you are picking up on them. With the number of cubs that are now in the nursery it is no wonder."

"The cubs?" sniffed Sinsee. "Really? Then there is nothing wrong with me?" She started to giggle and then to laugh. One of the clasps on the back of the gown gave way.

✱

Docking control managed to let Captain Dee know something was up before he docked. Silent word went through the crew to stay put. Dee escorted the ZENTEX Tec's off the ship and turned them over to their new escorts, The Black Guard. Before Dee reentered his ship he saw a young man whom he knew very well.

Halley came walking up the ramp dressed in a black suit with a silver sash. He carried a large package under his arm. "Dispatch sends his regards Captain." Halley winked in the direction of the retreating ZENTEX Tec's. Dee motioned for Halley to follow him into the ship, the hatch clanged shut behind them.

"I hope this fits." said Halley as he handed over the package to the Captain.

"What is all this?" asked Dee.

"It's your new uniform, Sector Marshal Dee." Halley grinned at the Captain's reaction. "Get me of cup of hot coffee and I'll fill you in on what has been going on around here sense your last transmission."

Dee was pounding on his knees and roaring with laughter. The others who had gathered around their Captain and Halley, to find out what was going on, were also laughing and slapping each other on the back. It was good humor all the way around. A few had gone to spread the word to the rest of the crew.

"You better get dressed. The Lord Roeman and the High Chandler are expecting you to attend the fun." said Halley.

"Even if this thing fits, we will be late getting there." said Dee as he picked up the package with his new uniform in it.

"No we wont. The Tec's are walking to the center sphere. We on the other hand are taking The Rail." "The What?" asked Dee. "You will see." said Halley. "Just a little thing I have been working on for Lord Roeman."

"Does he expect me to call him, Lord Roeman?" asked Dee.

"Only in public. It is for show only, Sector Marshal Dee." Halley bowed to the Captain.

"I could get to like this." said Dee as he looked at Halley. "Give me a minute and I'll meet you at the hatch."

Halley was there waiting when Sector Marshal Dee came strutting down the passageway. He looked so regal in his dark blue uniform that Halley bowed to him again. The boy could not wait to get Dee into one of his personnel rail pods. At the end of the trip, Dee wanted to do it again.

"Later! Right now Roeman and Sinsee want to see you before the Tec's get to the Great Hall." said Halley. Dee gave one last look over his shoulder to see one of the pods heading back out to the outer sphere, then he followed Halley out into the main corridor where he got another surprise. He wondered just how long he had been gone.

✱

The stage was set and everyone was in their places.. As the ZENTEX Tec's came into the Hall they were announced as Ambassadors from The planet of ZENTEX. A young boy came up to their group and bowed to them. "This way Ambassadors, if you please." He led them up to the bottom step of the raised floor, He then bowed to Roeman and Sinsee. "Lord Roeman, High Chandler. These are the Ambassadors from ZENTEX." The boy bowed again and stepped back out of the way.

Sinsee looked at the two women who had placed themselves at the front of their group. She then looked at those who stood behind them. She once again looked at the two women in the lead.

"Your early arrival has caused a bit of a situation." Sinsee paused so that her next words would carry the full impact of their meaning. "I thought I had made it perfectly clear, that even though I am once again allowing travel between the Colony Worlds, It is We, The Millally, who rule space! Why have you built a ship, no matter its size, that trespasses against Us?!"

Oh very good Sinsee, thought Nika. Kick their power right out from under them. Take away any control they might think they have.

Roeman stood to his feet, towering over the entire room. He held in his hand the printout of the scans from Dee's ship. "Your little ship is flawed. If you thought to use it to sneak around our backs, forget it! That thing leaves an energy trail that even one of our toddlers could follow." He tossed the printout at their feet, Turning to retake his seat, he winked at Sinsee.

"We meant no harm." said the first of the Tec's. "It is a gift for you." said the second one. "Yes, a gift." said the first one again.

In a more gentle voice Sinsee said, "A wedding gift, you say. Then you should not have taken it into space. You should have waited for Captain Dee." She motioned for Captain Dee to step forward from where he stood. Dee came forward and bowed to her. "Captain," said Sinsee. "You have spent some time with these ZENTEX. What is your impression of them?"

"They are good at what they do, High Chandler. I believe them when they say that they meant no harm. Surly the High Chandler can over look this breach in etiquette this one time. He bowed to Roeman and Sinsee and stepped back.

Sinsee looked at the two Tec's again. "It would seem you have an advocate in My Sector Marshal. Do not give him reason to regret his choice." She stood, and then Roeman stood and kissed Sinsee's hand. She smiled at him and turned to step down the stairs, two guards came to help her, each one offering her their hand on either side. Once she was down she was surrounded by a flock of women. They made their way to the back exit.

Roeman stepped down to stand on the first step. "So," he said as he looked into their eyes, getting their full attention. "Just what is it you want from US?"

✳

Later, after the ZENTEX Tec's had been shown to their quarters, Roeman confirmed what Sinsee had suspected. The Tec's had asked if they could look at the Catsman Ship.

"They didn't push it when I said no. They also need large shipments of ore from some of the mining worlds. I wonder what their need for all that ore is. They also asked if we could procure some gold and refined copper for them. They must need that for the microscopic chips that they use in the new communication systems. We've got the gold and the copper, it's the ore we don't have." said Roeman as he pored himself a drink. He lifted the juice bottle to see if Sinsee wanted any, she shook her head, so he put it back.

"With our new friend at the mining colony, I don't foresee any problems getting the ore. The Tec's say they don't want smelted ore, but the amounts that they want. They want more then ten ships could possibly move. I just don't see how we could transport that much ore."

"Maybe it doesn't have to be in the cargo holds. What if you attach it to the out side of the ship in cargo pods." suggested Sinsee.

"That is a lot of cargo pods. Think of all the work it would take to get the pods up to the ship. Not to mention the effect all those pods would have on the handling of the ship. You could end up shaking the ship apart before you even get it out of the system into open space." said Halley. "I don't think it can be done."

"Well if the Tec's want that ore so badly, why don't you ask them to solve this little problem." said Jewbee. "After all, solving problems is what they are reputed to be good at. But not before I get my new Med Units."

Sinsee knew how important it was to get those units. "Halley, why don't you take our guests on a tour of the station tomorrow. Make sure you show them just a glimpse of New Home from observation, then take them to the Hospital. When you get there, something will come up and you can leave them in the care of our good Doctor here. How about it Jewbee, you think you are up to putting on a little show of your own?" Jewbee nodded.

The next day, Halley took the Tec's on the tour of the station. He made it a point of showing them the observation rim, just above the docking ring. From the point that they entered you could just see one third of Ship New Home. More then once Halley had to say, "This way Ambassadors.", as he tried to move them along.

Finally they reached the Hospital. Halley was explaining the running lights that surrounded a sealed hatch. "Inside this chamber we have our Med Units. The lights indicate that the chamber is now at zero gravity." The Tec's nodded their understanding. "Now if you will follow me this way, we can visit our nursery." They followed him to a set of double doors. Inside they found a number of curtained apertures. Jewbee entered the room carrying a cub in her arms.

"Hello Halley, I'll be right with you just as soon as I return this little girl to her mother." Jewbee drew back on of the curtains to reveal a full grown Lioness and a number of cubs.

"Still hand feeding the cubs Doctor?" asked Halley.

"Yes, this lioness is not producing enough milk for all of her cubs. Some of the older ones are starting to drink from pans on the floor. They will need bigger portions soon." Just then a Lioness came in through the double doors. Jewbee took her scanner off the shelf, she ran it over the Lionesses extended belly. "You are right Lena, your time is close. I have three empty dens . Would you like to choose one?" she asked the

Lioness. Jewbee opened the curtain to the first empty den and the Lioness looked inside, she shook her head. Jewbee went to the next curtain, the Lioness must have like this one because she jumped inside.

Jewbee turned on its monitoring screen and coded it to her pager on her belt. The Tec's moved closer to have a better look. Jewbee explained that this kind of monitoring was better for the expectant mothers. If they went into stress, the sensors would instantly notify her that there was a problem.

Jewbee made a point of looking over to the doorway. The Tec's turned to see what she was looking at. There was Halley talking to someone, he nodded his head and made his way back to the group. " I have been called away. Doctor do you think that you can see to it that our guests make it back to their quarters for me, I really have to go."

"Yes of course I will." she said. Halley took his leave of the Tec's saying that He hoped to see them again.

Jewbee's young aid came in at the moment carrying a tray with bandages on it along with some creams. "Excuse me, I will just be a minute." Jewbee pulled out a small shelf from the wall next to one of the curtains, the aid put the tray down on this. Jewbee opened the curtain to reveal a Lioness who's stomach was bandaged. Very carefully Jewbee removed the old bandage to reveal the long incision that had been sewn shut. The Tec's watched as the Lioness twitched in pain as the new bandages went on. "I am so sorry dear." said Jewbee. She took out a hypo injection and injected the Lioness, who instantly relaxed.

The Tec's were visibly shaken by this. Jewbee realized that they had never seen another being in pain before. Even if that being was not human, it still disturbed them. "I am sorry," said Jewbee. "I was not thinking. Your people do not suffer the pain of injuries very long do they?" She escorted them out into the corridor. "The Lions would not suffer if I had only been able to convert some of my Med Units over to their physiology." At that moment a Catsman came hobbling down the corridor on a pair of crutches, his right leg was in a cast. He disappeared into another room and the door shut behind him.

"With this, We, Can, Help you. If we, May see, Your medical, Records, On the, Lions, And the, Catsman's, We can, Have, A working, Med Unit, For you, By tomorrow, Evening."

Jewbee had to blink, a conversation in this type of stereo was enough to make a person dizzy. "I would be so very grateful if you could help in this matter." said Jewbee. "But what could I possibly give you for your service?"

"No," said the Tec's. "This, We, Do, To, End, The, Pain."

It was all Jewbee could so to keep from jumping for joy. While four Tec's remained at the Hospital to begin work on the Med Units, Jewbee took the rest of them back to their quarters. From there she headed towards the center sphere.

"I'm telling you Roeman, They really want to help. They didn't ask for anything. What surprised me was the fact that they can not stand the sight of anything, human or otherwise in pain. It really effects them." Jewbee was trying to convince Roeman that the Tec's were sincere.

"I still think that they are trying to weasel their way onto New Home." Roeman was passing the floor.

"Excuse me Roeman, But isn't that where we want them?" asked Halley.

"Yes, but only on our terms, not theirs. Give it some more time. I want to see just how far they are willing to go." Roeman thought for a moment. "Halley, I want you to get about six bars of gold along with a hundred pounds of pure copper and take it to their quarters. Ask them if the quality is good enough for what they want. Try to find out what they intend to do with it. Maybe we can get some leverage on them."

"Roeman," said Sinsee. "Do we have that much gold?"

Roeman and Halley both laughed at the same time. Jewbee

leaned over and whispered into Sinsee's ear, at which point her mouth dropped.

Roeman smiled, "That is why I did not object when you gave that gold mine to Jeffery. Which reminds me. Jeffery is part Millally."

"Does He know?" asked Sinsee.

"No. I thought that the next time we visit, you can explain it to him, his father and mother. The Doctor on the Claw told the Canes that they might have picked up a bug from Kit and He just wanted to check their blood to make sure they had nothing to worry about. He gave them the all clear and sent me the results of the tests." Roeman finally stopped passing.

"You know something," said Halley. "We should have put surveillance in those quarters the ZENTEX Tec's are in. I would love to have a record of their reaction tomorrow."

"Good for you Halley. At least someone else is on the ball." Nika entered the office and sat down in the chair next to Halley. "I already had all the guest quarters set up with surveillance." From the look on Halley's face Nika could tell that he was impressed. "And if you are a good boy, I will let you see them." She reached over and ruffled his hair. "Now how about going and making a drink for this tired old woman."

"Yes Mam." said Halley with a spring in his step as he went to the beverage counter.

"Nika, you are a gem!" Roeman had the biggest smile on his face. "But when did you do all this, and why was I not informed about what is happening on my Station?"

"When I was having the quarters made ready for our guests. And that is just the point. You want to know what all these people think. They certainty are not going to tell you to your face. What you need to know is what They don't want you to know. Just don't move on what you hear right away. Let the wind die down, then make your move." Nika took a sip of the drink Halley handed her.

"You have done this before, haven't you, Miss Nika?"

accused Halley. Nika just took another sip of her drink then she smiled up at the boy.

"Done what?" asked Jayson, as he came into the office.

"Nika bugged all of the guest's quarters." said Halley with a big grin on his face.

"She did? Come to think of it, I seem to remember a certain vent grating." said Jayson as he looked at his sister.

"You knew about that!" accused Nika, as she sat foreword in her chair.

"Not at first. You made the mistake of leaving it open one to many times." he smiled at her.

"And you continued to let me listen in on your meetings all this time. Why Jayson?"

"Because my dear sister, I am not a fool. You have a unique mind that can think on many different levels at the same time. When I had a problem that I could not seem to get around, you would always come up with a way to help me find the answer. Have I or have I not always listened to your advice. Sometimes I think that if it were not for all your help, I would not have kept my position as Planetary President." Nika could except that.

Sinsee was thinking about someone else who would enjoy all this, her brother, Seenan. All the plotting they had done as children. The hours they had spent together in his room studying and the times they would run in the woods out behind their parent's home. She wished with all her heart that they would have come with Jayson and Nika to Home Station. She remembered her mother's hugs and kisses that last night she spent with them. A tear rolled down her cheek and she quickly wiped it away.

Kit relayed Sinsee's thoughts to Jewbee, who signaled to Nika to join her. She told the others that they needed to check on something and that they would be right back. Shortly after Nika and Jewbee left there was a knock at the door and Roeman went to answer it.

"Sinsee," he said. "There is someone here to see you." She looked up and there stood her brother Seenan, behind him was her Father and Mother. They had been in hiding, their presence was to be a surprise at the wedding. It was certainly a surprise for Sinsee to see them standing there. After all the crying and hugging was over, Dr. Brion joined them.

"You know Sinsee, I am really hurt. I would have thought that you would have missed me all this time." Now that he mentioned it, she could not remember seeing him around for quite some time.

"Dr. Brion has been very good to us." said Fone, Sinsee's mother. "He has shown us around the station and we watched you in the Great Hall, when you met with the ZENTEX." Her mother dropped her gaze to the floor. For a moment Sinsee was ashamed of her behavior, but only a moment, for when she saw the look on her father's face. She saw great pride in his eyes.

"You were in the Hall? I didn't see you." she looked at the others to confirm this.

"No. We weren't in the Hall. We were watching you on a remote screen. Nika thought that our presence in the Hall would be a distraction for you. You needed to keep your mind focused on the ZENTEX Tec's." Her Father said. "You were wonderful."

"You frightened me Sinsee." said her Mother, Fone. "You have so much power." Fone looked over at Jayson. "You have done so much for my daughter and yet. I have to wonder. Will this be the way of it now on Terra Two? Will we women be given the opportunity to better ourselves as Sinsee has?"

"Fone!" said her husband. "Mind who you are talking to."

Fone looked at her husband and for the first time she did not back down when he used that tone of voice on her. Instead she told him to shove it.

Jayson chuckled, it was just enough to distract Mr. Tang away from Fone. "Come now Lee, you really don't expect the

Mother of The High Chandler to back down now do you. I think Fone is beginning to understand her unique roll in all this."

"Yes," said Nika. "You are right Jayson. Her life will never be the same, will it." Nika looked directly at Fone, who's eyes began to grow larger with anticipation.

Sinsee watched as her mother was breaking free of her father's dominance. Years of male dominance had made Fone timid and obedient to any male. Now she was standing up for herself, a true sign of what was to come. Maybe not for all the women on Terra Two, but there would be enough to start a movement that sooner or later would sweep the planet.

"Try to remember Lee, your wife is of the Millally blood line, as are You." said Jayson.

"I see." said Lee as he looked at his daughter then his wife. "This will take me some getting used to. Just how much power do you have, Sinsee, and how much of it will I have to expect from Fone?"

"I am afraid that you will have to learn that on your own Father. Who am I to know what lies ahead for you and Mother. I can tell you that it is better to have an equal by your side who will tell you the truth rather then to tell you what you want to hear." Sinsee smiled at her Father, knowing that he would have to get to know his wife all over again. Only this time it would be on equal terms. Sinsee intended for both her parents to be in the Great Hall for the next reception. She and Nika would have to school her mother in manners and carriage if she was to look the new part. Sinsee was sure that her mother would enjoy every minute of it. In fact the whole family would enjoy this.

Even with all the activity that was going on around him, Patrick managed to continue His work on the embryo gestation tanks. As luck would have it, he was transferring one of the tanks from New home to the station Hospital wing when he ran into the Tec's in the corridor. Their curiosity got the better of them and they followed Patrick to his finale destination. When they saw the line of gestation tanks, their speech patterns went into over drive and Patrick could not understand a word they were saying. They also seemed to be using their hands in some form of communication as well. Try as he might, Patrick could not understand anything that was going on between the Tec's. Then all of a sudden they stopped.

Two of the Tec's came up to Patrick and asked if they could help him in his work. Patrick sure could use the help, but he was unsure if he should let them at this stage. He told them that he would have to ask permission of the High Chandler.

Later in Roeman's office, Patrick was pacing the floor and running his fingers through his hair. "I wish you could have seen it! I have never seen anything like it before. No one! No one can talk that fast. You should have seen It!"

"I have." said Roeman, who had been enjoying Patrick's reaction to the Tec's. "Come here and have a look at this and tell me if it is what you saw in the Hospital." Roeman turned on the screen that was on his desk and inserted a disk into the playback.

There was Halley, with a small hand pull hover cart. On the hover cart were two crates, one large and one small. Halley was surrounded by the Tec's, trying to get a look at what he had brought them. He opened the large crate first, within it were sheets of refined copper. These were passed around to the Tec's, who examined them with great care. But it was their reaction to what was in the smaller crate that Roeman wanted Patrick to see.

Halley opened the second crate and lifted out a bar of pure gold. The scene became a repeat of what happened in the Hospital, including the hand movements.

"Now watch this. I slow it down and up the volume. Here is where it gets interesting."

"This, Is, Pure, Gold . I have, Not seen, Any, Like this, In our, Life time. Yes. More, Twins, Will be, Born. The, Capsules, Can be, Made Fresh. We will, Survive!"

Roeman turned it off. "It goes on like that for some time. We still don't know what all that hand signal stuff is about. One thing is for sure, the twin Tec's are not born. They seem to be created in some kind of tank, and that tank needs gold to function properly."

"No wonder they went nuts when they saw the gestation tanks in my lab. Come to think of it, one of the panels on the inside is made of gold. I thought it was platted at first, you know, with a thin layer of gold, but it is not. The whole panel is gold." said Patrick. "Could it be that we have more in common with the Tec's then we know of."

"I think it is time that the Tec's are given another audience with The High Chandler and The Lord Roeman." Roeman grinned at Patrick. "It is time for you to play a roll in all this. Do you think you can keep a straight face? This won't be anything like the last roll you played, this time you will have to speak." Patrick nodded his head. "Good. I'll call everyone and have them stop by for dinner. We can work out the details then."

At dinner, Nika once again reminded Roeman not to move on what he knew to soon. "Take your time Roeman. The Tec's are not going any where for some time. Let them feel that they can trust you."

"Just don't let them think that they can walk all over you." said Jayson.

"Right. This is about our tanks, not theirs." said Sinsee. "What we want is for them to tell us to our face what we already know. Trust must come with time." She looked at the others in the room. "This might be a good time to bring up the matter of the raw ore. They may even tell you why they need so much of it."

"If key personnel start supporting them in the Hall before

you, We could start to give them a free hand. Build the trust that we want." said Jewbee.

"On the station, maybe, but not on New Home. We need to hang onto that as bait." Roeman looked at the disappointment on Halley's face. "Sorry Halley, but until they open up to us, I don't want them on that ship. You, Tiny and his crew, will just have to do your best for now."

"I thought that was what we were doing." Halley looked across the table. "May I have some of that boiled grain?" Nika passed him the dish, and told him that it was called rice, not grain. She was amazed at how much food this young man was putting away. In fact she found that everyone seemed to be eating a lot more lately. She made a mental note to ask Jewbee if this was normal behavior for humans in space. Perhaps it had something to do with the artificial gravity.

The next day the ZENTEX Tec's were summoned to the Great Hall. They had no idea why they had been summoned and when they entered they saw Patrick on one knee before the High Chandler. She was speaking to him in a soft voice.

Patrick regained his feet and turned to them, he was smiling and motioning them to come closer. Sinsee pointed to the two Leaders of the group. They came even closer then the others.

"You have seen what you should not have seen." She held up her hand to prevent any reply. "Hear me out. Your willingness to help our Doctor is greatly appreciated. Our Catsman are so few. They have suffered such great lose of life. It causes us pain to remember the deaths we could not prevent. In time you will learn of this." She looked deeply into their eyes. "If we let you help, you must never speak of what you see or may learn. I will not have the other colony worlds learn of this thing we are trying to do for our beloved Catsman. Too, I will not allow you to use this to your advantage, thinking to use this information against us at some other time. I will give you no favors, for you do this on your own. You will swear before me that you will tell no one. Not even the Leaders of your home world. I must worn you. I know when someone speaks the truth or not. So do not tempt me."

They agreed to her terms and took an oath of silence. At the end of their oath the Hall erupted in a roar of clapping hands which surprised the Tec's. Sinsee smiled at them. "Now I believe that Lord Roeman would like to have a word with you." She motioned a young boy to come forward. "If you would please follow this young page, he will take you to Lord Roeman."

As soon as the Tec's had left the Hall Sinsee began to tug at the top of her gown. " Someone help me undo this stupid thing. I can barely breath in it." Someone came running to her aid and unhooked the gown from the back which allowed Sinsee to take a deep breath and she sighed with relief. "That does it, the next gown, I am going to design it myself. There is no reason for me to be uncomfortable." Someone reminded her that the gown she was wearing was designed by Miss Nika. "Nika is not the one who has to wear this stupid thing." Sinsee remembered the white and gold gown she wore when the ship arrived. Now if she got rid of all the under gowns and took in that gown just a little, it would be just right for her. Better yet, she would copy the style of that gown for her wedding dress, with a few alterations it would be quite stunning.

The young page showed the Tec's to a work room where a number of people were going over blueprints, most of which were half hearted attempts at cargo pods, designed for the oar that the Tec's had requested.

Two of the Tec's were looking at one of the prints on a large table. They picked it up to have a better look and show it to the others, underneath it was a schematic of a portion of New Home. Before they could have a good look at this, someone snatched it off the table.

Roeman entered the room from the back at this point.

"Ambassadors," he indicated the work tables. "As you can see, I have a problem. Transporting base metals is easier then transporting raw oar. The volume alone makes it impossible. If we were to do it in small shipments, the cost alone would be staggering. I am sorry, it just is not possible."

"If we, May work, With your, Designers, We may, Find a, Way to, Make, Large, Shipments, Possible." they said. Roeman was starting to wish that they would talk like everyone else. Trying to follow who was speaking and when was enough to make him crazy.

"If you can make this work, can you also make it work for cargo that needs an atmosphere?" asked Roeman.

"That, Would be, More, Difficult, But it, Could be, Done, If, We have, The right, Equipment."

"If you make this work, I will give you twice the copper and gold that was sent to you the other day. You have my word on this." said Roeman.

When he told them that, they huddled together and this time they only used their hand signals. When they were done, two of the Tec's went to work at one of the tables. The young page escorted the rest of them back to their quarters. Roeman nodded to his men in the room then he left them there to keep an eye on the Tec's. What Roeman did not expect was that when the Tec's had been returned to their quarters, they immediately dispersed in pairs of two, all over the station. They were determined to help in any way they could and set out to do just that.

✸

While Sinsee was getting out of her gown in the other room, Roeman was telling the others just what the Tec's had said they would try and do with the transport pods.

"If they can do it, we can increase our shipments." said Halley. "It will have an effect on the price of products. Drive the price down."

"Yes, but we make up the difference in volume. It will take

the pressure off some of the colony worlds. Make life a whole lot easier for most of them." said Jayson "And the more easier we make it for them, the more likely they are to come around to our way of thinking."

"Just what is our way of thinking?" Halley looked around at the others for an answer to his question. Sinsee walked into the room at this point, she had heard the conversation from the other room. She walked over to Halley and ruffled his hair. Halley was getting used to that.

"Our way of thinking is to unite all the colony worlds under one banner. The colonies have horded their talents and secrets far to long. For hundreds of years they have held onto this mind set. Point in fact, the Tec's themselves have horded major leaps in science. They once lived off the income generated by the fact that a person had to travel to ZENTEX in order to have a severed limb regenerated. When the Millally stopped all space travel between the worlds, their income became almost nothing. Yet they still continued to horde their technology. True, the Millally have been able, over the years, to acquire some of that new technology. But what about the rest of it? If the Tec's were to open this vast vault of knowledge to the rest of the colony worlds, the day to day struggles of the average person would be reduced greatly. Do you see what I am getting at?"

"I think so." said Halley. "It is not just the Millally that you want to benefit. You are thinking of the human race as a whole."

"Not just the human race, all the races. Think about the fact that just in the past few years we have been introduced to not just one new race, but two. How many more races are out there do you think? It took the Catsman generations to reach that point where we found them. Does that mean that it will take us many more generations to find other life forms. I don't know. But wouldn't it be fun to try?" Sinsee had a far away look on her face for a moment. "We will need the cooperation of all the colony worlds to attempt a feat such as that. We will never see it in our lifetime, but our descendants should have that opportunity."

"OK." said Halley. "I can understand that, But right now it seems to me that everyone is getting help but me." He turned to Roeman. "Just when do I get a chance at the Tec's. Frankly, Tiny and I have hit a brick wall on New Home. We need those Tec's."

Roeman nodded his head. "Why don't you and Patrick go visiting our guests tomorrow morning. It might be time to start bring them up to speed anyway. Start with the Chandlers story but don't tell them about the Foundation. Stay with the original story, the one that drew us in to rescue her in the first place. Get their attention. I want to see their reaction to her telepathic link with the boy Kreeote. If it is what I hope, I will send you a signal through your wrist com. Then and only then can you tell them about Sinsee's confession to Chandler Allison. I am sure that from their monitoring our communication that they have a good Idea about the truth."

"I don't know Roeman, don't you think that will lessen us in some way?" asked Nika.

"It might, then it might give us an even higher standing in their eyes. They will see a commonality between our two people." said Roeman.

"I don't believe that everyone on ZENTEX is grown in one of those tanks. Only the Tec's, because of something I heard the day Halley delivered the copper and gold. It led me to believe that the Tec's are completely different humans from those who originally colonized ZENTEX. It might also be that the Tec's don't trust their Leaders."

"Then we are dealing with a double factor on ZENTEX?" asked Jayson.

"I believe so. I need to know if we need to send another ship to ZENTEX, to pick up a real Government representative. The Tec's may be hiding things from their own Government."

said Roeman. "If they are, can we actually trust them not to do the same to us. Can we take that chance?"

"Some one has to make the first move." said Sinsee. "I can, and I will. The first thing we have to find out is the Tec's relationship with their own Government." She turned to Halley. "Do what Roeman told you to do. I will also be watching to see their reaction."

The next morning, Roeman, Jayson, and Sinsee were watching the screen as Halley and Patrick made their visit to the Tec's. Roeman could almost swear that he saw a reaction from the Tec's as Halley started to tell Sinsee's story, but it was when Patrick started to add his voice to the story that they got reactions. Patrick was more animated in telling his view of what happened, he used his hands and then his whole body to reenact this or that part of the story. He was good at it too. Sinsee looked at Roeman. "I didn't do that, did I?" He nodded his head and Sinsee made a puckered face. Roeman decided to send the signal to Halley and he punched in the code on his own wrist com.

That day the Tec's learned everything about Sinsee. At one point they went into their hand language and left Patrick and Halley standing there not knowing what to do.

"We will, Do, What ever, the, High Chandler, Needs us, To do for, Her. She is, The one, We have, Been waiting, For." they told Patrick. "Purity of, Spirit and, Mind. The, High, Chandler, Is, The, One." The last three words were spoken in unison.

"Then your government will support the High Chandler?" asked Halley.

"No. We alone will, Support, The, One." Halley looked at Patrick who looked at the Tec's.

"Does your government know that you are here?" he asked them out right.

"No." they all said at the same time.

Patrick looked at Halley. "We've got a problem!" He turned back to the Tec's. "You will have to stay here in your quarters until I can reach the High Chandler. She will know how to help you." He turned to face Halley. "There has to be a way to protect the Tec's." Halley nodded his agreement and the two of them set out to join the others in Roeman's office.

The others were already trying to think of a way to prevent the ZENTEX government from finding out that the Tec's were on the Station.

"Well it is to late to get a representative here for the wedding, but we can still send a ship to bring them here anyway. Each colony has to have an ambassador to represent them. Otherwise this isn't going to work. The Tec's still have some time here on the station before that ship can return from ZENTEX. I suggest that we give them a free hand while they are here. Captain Dee can return them to ZENTEX in that shuttle of theirs. It must have gone undetected by their scanners for them to have lifted off without their government knowing about it. We will use the same thing to get them home again. We can't deprive ZENTEX of all their Tec's, but we can, using that shuttle, remove those who want to leave ZENTEX." said Jayson. "For those who want to remain we will have to find a way to stay in contact with them without the ZENTEX government knowing about it."

"If we had more of those shuttles the Tec's could have more freedom to come and go as they wished." Roeman liked the idea of having more of those shuttles. "If we could get some of the Tec's onto a Mining Colony, they could set up a manufacturing plant for the shuttles. We are already in production for the space station rings. How much more trouble would it be to set up for the shuttles?"

"It shouldn't be that difficult. Will the Mining Colony allow the Tec's on their world is the more important question." said Jayson. There was a nock on the door, Patrick and Halley entered the office and Sinsee brought them up to speed.

"We still don't know what they want with all that ore." said Roeman. He looked at Halley and Patrick. "Guess it is my turn to have a go with them again."

A short while later Roeman was surprised to learn that the two leading Tec's were requesting a meeting with him. The resulting conversation with them turned out to be most informative.

They told him how they created sets of twins in their own tanks, similar to those now in Doctor Patrick's lab. The creativity of these twins, Tec's, was what kept ZENTEX products in such high demand over the years. Recently though, those tanks had produced more failures in the twins then ever before. The reason was two fold. First, the gold plates that filtered the fluids were wearing out. Second, the nutrients needed to build strong bones came from a coral in their oceans. These same oceans were now becoming depleted of certain trace elements, the result was that the coral was dying. The Tec's hoped that they could find enough of these trace elements in the ore to replenish their oceans. That was the reason they needed such large shipments of raw ore.

"I wish you had told us about this before." said Roeman. "It would be much simpler to remove the elements that you need from the ore on the mining colony itself. That way you would not have to dispose of what you don't need and it can go directly to the smelting plant." He sat at his desk, his chin resting on his hand, his eyes closed in thought. "Perhaps the High Chandler can get her friend on one of the mining colonies to convince the government to allow a group of your people to search for what you need. The mining colony doesn't really have anything that they need to hide. Most anyone can dig a hole in the ground. Some of the aspects of their smelting process might be restricted. Though I can't imagine why."

Knowing the Tec's as he now did, he had no doubt that they would, if given to opportunity, find a way to improve the smelting operations on the mining colony.

"We would still like those cargo pods, if you can make them work. The Chandler would like to increase cargo shipments to the colony worlds. With those pods, we could reduce the cost of products, making life a lot easier for a lot of people." He decided to give them one more thing. "Our relationship has now changed. It would seem that you are suited to our way of life. I will ask the High Chandler to grant the ZENTEX Tec's the same privileges that Terra Two now holds."

This pleased the Tec's to no end and they started to talk so fast Roeman didn't think that even the recorders could handle it. As the Tec's left his office they turned around and bowed low to him, he could have sworn that their eyes sparkled.

"Two worlds and climbing." said Sinsee as she entered his office.

"Have you got my office bugged?" he looked at her with an accusing expression on his face. She smiled at him as she took her seat.

"I would never do that to you Roeman. No, I passed the Tec's just now out in the corridor. They seem to be very happy."

Roeman told her about his offer to The Tec's. "Considering the fact that their government doesn't know they are here, I thought it wise to give them our protection. We may have trouble with the ZENTEX government, but I figure the benefits we can get out of the Tec's out weigh any trouble we may have with them."

"Anything the Tec's want, we should do our best to see that they get it." Sinsee touched Jewbee's mind and asked her to join them. She also asked her to bring Patrick with her. A short while later they arrived and went over what they now knew about the Tec's.

"We should have them check out the fluids in our gestation tanks. I don't want anything going wrong with them when we turn them on." said Patrick. "I don't know if the fluids are the same or if there is a difference in the makeup. Catsman are different from us." He turned to Jewbee. "Do you have a working Med Unit for the Catsman yet?"

"Yes, and the Terra Two Lions. I don't want the back engineering to start on them until the end of this birthing cycle. The next cycle wont begin for another one hundred and fifty to one hundred and eighty days." she said.

"Why so soon?" asked Roeman.

"Some of the Lionesses come from different climate zones on Terra Two. When it is winter in one place it is summer in the other. I think we should be grateful that they only breed once every few years. Otherwise we would be overrun with Lions in a very short time. As it is now, we have more then our fair share of cubs. I still have not figured out why they are having such large litters." she said with a frown.

"Yes," said Sinsee. "Kit assures me that the most they have ever given birth to is only one to two cubs, and two at the same time is very rare."

"How many cubs do we now have on the station?" Roeman looked at Jewbee.

"You never read my reports, do you?" she sighed. "At this point, twenty five Lionesses have given birth, with an average of six to eight cubs. I have already had to expand the nursery to accommodate one hundred and sixty four cubs." She waited for the numbers to sink in and was not disappointed in Roeman's reaction.

"How many Lionesses are going to go into heat this next time?" asked Sinsee. Roeman didn't know if he wanted that question answered or not. As it was, Jewbee did not have that answer so she left to find out just how many there were of breeding age.

"I sure hope she can find out what is causing so many births. I know that we need the Lions once we get the space station rings operational, but right now don't you think that we have enough Lions?" Roeman was scratching his chin. "What if we send the Females back to Terra Two. That might slow down the birth rate."

Sinsee didn't think so. "What ever caused it, the Lionesses have already been exposed to it. It could have something to do with the artificial gravity."

"If that were the case then the Millally would out number the populations on all the colony worlds by now." Roeman chuckled to himself and shook his head.

"I guess you are right about that." Just then Sinsee's stomach growled. "Wow, I guess this time I am hungry."

"What do you mean, this time?" asked Roeman.

"Jewbee told me that the reason I was eating so much was because I was picking up on the cubs hunger. For a while there I could not tell if it was the cubs or myself who was hungry. I guess I still can't." she said.

"Well in that case, lets go get some food. I am rather hungry myself right now." He stood up to go and noticed that Sinsee was not moving. "Is something wrong?"

"Trouble at the Hospital!" she said. "One of the Tec's is down! Jewbee says to hurry."

"Come on! We'll take Halley's Rail." Roeman took her by the hand and they were out the door in a flash.

✱

The Halley's Rail got Sinsee and Roeman to the Hospital in record time, though Sinsee wondered if her stomach would ever catch up to her. As they came in through the hatch they could see the crowd that was gathering around one of the exam room doors.

Roeman started to push his way through the crowd when all of a sudden he heard Sinsee's voice inside his head. {["**Move It!**"]} Instantly there was a clear passage before them.

"Damn it, women, let me know the next time you are going to do something like that. I almost jumped out of my skin!"

"Sorry." said Sinsee as she moved past him and entered the

exam room. The Tec's was laying on the exam table, Jewbee was hooking him up to the monitors. Dr. Parry was checking his eyes with a light pen. "What happened to him?"

"No one seems to know." said Jewbee. "One minute he was fine and the next he was laying on his back with a cub licking his face."

Sinsee heard a tiny voice inside her head saying, {[mine, mine, pretty boy mine.]} Sinsee looked around and found the cub under the exam table, she picked it up. "What did you do?" she asked the cub. All it would say was, {[mine, mine, mine.]} Everyone in the room was watching Sinsee's attempt to talk to the cub.

Jewbee looked from the cub to the Tec's on her exam table. "Damn!" was all she said.

It was some time before the Tec's regained his senses. He tried to explain what had happened to him. While they had been working and he was taking notes, this cub kept bumping against his leg. Every time he moved away from the cub it followed him. Finally he reached down and picked her up, the cub had touched her nose to his own and the next thing he knew he was looking at himself, only it wasn't him, it was what the cub was seeing.

Jewbee pulled Sinsee away from the Tec's. "High Chandler, this Tec's is not speaking like a Tec's any more." It was true, the man was forming full sentences all on his own. The other Tec's seemed to be in shock. Sinsee could tell that he was this ones twin.

"Can he walk?" she indicated the Tec's on the table and was told that it looked like he could. "I want all the ZENTEX Tec's in the Great Hall in one hour." She Told them, "Come on Lord Roeman, we have a lot of work to do." She turned to Jewbee. "I need you to bring Kreeote, your son, to the Hall, I'll explain later." She and Roeman made their way out passed the onlookers, leaving a perplexed Jewbee behind.

"What is all this about Sinsee?" asked Roeman as they headed back to the Halley's Rail.

"The Tec's are what you would call telampathic not telepathic, but a form of it. Just like Kreeote with his pictures in my head. It is no wonder they work best as twins!" she told him.

Sinsee was having trouble making the Tec's understand what she was trying to tell them. Jewbee finally showed up with Kreeote and Sinsee called the boy to her. Telepathically she told the boy to look into the minds of the Tec's and show them the inside of the ship New Home. She had him stand in front of her and she put her hands on his shoulders, this way she could piggyback on his brain waves.

Telampathically and Telepathically they reached into the minds of the Tec's. As the pictures formed in their minds, Sinsee was able to tell them what they were looking at and how this was possible. Kreeote even showed them his little sister who was half Human and half Catsman.

"Thank you Kreeote." said Sinsee as she sent him back to his mother. The boy had grown in the past few years, he was almost as tall as Sinsee herself.

"This we, Must tell, Other, Tec's. We must, Go home, Now! Much wrong, Has been, Done. Those we, Thought, Flawed, Are, Not, Flawed. We, Thought, They were, Mad. Out, Of, Their, Minds. We, Locked them, Away. We must, Go, Home, Now!"

"Yes," said Sinsee. "I will have a ship made ready for you. There is one other thing." She looked at the Tec's who had made contact with the cub. "You must stay here with us. The cub has chosen you for some reason. If you leave now, it will break her spirit. I can not allow that. If you truly want to return home, you must take the cub with you." Sinsee stepped up to stand in front of the Tec's. "I would rather that you would chose to stay with us. At least until the cub can take care of herself." She waited for his reply.

He looked over to his twin for support, his twin took his hand and as everyone watched, the other twins' eyes rolled back into his head and he spoke in a strange voice. "You, And, Your, Friends, Destiny, Will, Set, Us, All, Free."

Jayson leaned over to whisper into Nika's ear. "I think we can add precognitive to their list of talents."

Sinsee continued. "I would like to send a team of researchers with you to ZENTEX My Brothers." she said to them. "If there are things that you do not want them to see, they will respect your wishes." The fact that Sinsee called them her Brothers gave them much to think about. As One they bowed low to her and left the Hall.

Roeman contacted Captain Dee and told him to get his ship ready to depart. He also told him to reload the Tec's shuttle and why he was getting the shuttle. Dee asked if someone else could make this run. "I thought you liked the Tec's?" asked Roeman.

"I do, but I also don't want to miss your wedding. I have a right to be there. She is still a woman of my house." he said.

"Not for long." laughed Roeman. "Alright, I'll get someone else to make this run." That was easier said then done. Most of the Captains who were at Home Station didn't want to take the job. They wanted to stay and watch the fun. Sinsee had to step in and order a captain to take the Tec's back to ZENTEX and then bring the ZENTEX Ambassador to Home Station. The Captains may bulk at Roeman's request, but they would not dare to challenge their Chandler.

"The problem is that they all think of me as a Captain, just like them." said Roeman after the incident. "I guess I forgot that I was playing at being Lord Admiral Roeman."

"Yes," said Jayson. "I think it is time that you stopped playing at it and really became Lord Roeman."

"What do you mean?" asked Roeman.

"I intend to perform the ceremony at your wedding. At

that time I will also confirm your title as Lord Admiral. You wont have any more trouble after that." said Jayson.

"Can you do that?" asked Roeman.

"My boy, I can do anything I want too." he said.

"And he usually does." said Nika as she came into the room. "We have another incoming message from Terra Two."

Chapter Five

WITH THE TEC'S NOW gone from Home Station, Sinsee and
Roeman found that they had some time on their hands before
the Wedding. Nika suggested that they spend some time with
Sinsee's family that is if they could get her brother, Seenan, off
of the Halley's Rail.

In their quarters, Seenan was telling them that each Rail
around the station was different. "There's even one up in the
north section that has a spiral that runs through three levels
and then takes you into a clear tunnel over to the quarter's
section of the third sphere." Seenan was so enthusiastic about
the Halley's Rail, that when he returned to Terra Two, he
wanted to build his own form of the Halley's Rail.

"Why would you want to give up a perfectly good career
at the University?" His mother, wanted to know.

"Oh, I'll stay on at the University. If Sinsee can handle so
many things here going on at the same time, so can I." Seenan
puffed out his chest and squared his shoulder, readying himself
for his mother's lecture that he knew was coming.

"Seenan, if you had bothered to look around, you would
see that your sister has a large number of people who help her

run this station. She does not do it by herself." Fone looked to her husband for help in convincing the boy.

"I know that Mother. All I am going to do is build one small Halley's Rail to start. I can get some of the other younger professors at the University to help me. They might even want to invest some of their own credits into the project." he told her in a reassuring way. "The Rail will be in the open of course. More of a thrill ride that way. I'll have to make the whole casing out of clear plexy, the same type that runs between the spheres."

Lee Tang liked the idea, and wanted to help his son. "I have been on the Rail a number of times myself. I don't think you should use it as a transport though. Build it all in one area. That way the people have to come to you." He paused for a moment. "You know, when I was a kid I would have given anything for a thrill like that."

The two of them started to brain storm on different designs for their Rails. Little did they know that in the years to come they would transform parts of Terra Two into the Hottest Vacation Spots in the Universe. Visitors would vie for a chance to spend even one week on Terra Two.

*

While the Tang family enjoyed their rest, Nika, Jayson, Halley, Patrick, and Sector Marshal Dee kept things running as smoothly as could be, considering they were expecting an invasion of wedding guests.

With the new communication system installed on the station they could reach any ship, any where, instantly. Even more, the visuals worked at the longer ranges now. Some times the visual was fuzzy because the ships didn't all have the new systems yet, but they still worked.

The R.S.V.P.'s were coming in at a fast rate and Dee was working out a departure schedule from each planet within the planned time frame for the wedding to arrive within a few days of the event. Give a few days one way or the other. Those who would be on the station the longest would have to find some form of entertainment. Which they did, much to the dismay of the Rail Handlers who spent their time cursing Halley.

Henson's ship arrived with more supplies and guests from Terra Two, along with a news crew. Fortunately for Henson, the man who's jaw he busted was not among them.

The cargo dispatcher was besieged with requests for urgently needed shipments to be rushed to this, that, and the other place. Each time he was contacted he told them that as soon as it came out of the hold he would send it their way.

"You would think that by now they would understand that cargo goes in one way and comes out one way. It's not our fault if what they want is all the way in the back under a ton of crates. They'll get it when they get it!"

"Hay!" said the cargo assistant. "Here's that frozen milk the Doctor has been screaming for. What's this! She gets meat too?"

"It must be for all those cubs she has." said the cargo dispatcher.

"You mean those things are carnivorous!" The assistant looked across the Docking Bay at a pair of extremely large Lions and their riders. "I thought they were vegetarians like the Catsman."

"Nope, they do eat grains and only some vegetables when they can't get meat. You better move that crate along before they get a chance to smell that meat." said the dispatcher. The assistant moved the crate over to the Rail that went to the sphere were the Hospital was located, all the while he kept one eye on the Lions, hoping that they would not smell what was in the crate.

At the Hospital, Patrick and the ZENTEX Tec's, who's name was Sebastian, were monitoring the gestation tanks. The growth rate was accelerating. "Are you sure those readings are right?" asked Patrick.

"Yes, there is no mistake." said Sebastian. "These tanks are not the same as our tanks. Maybe they were designed to do this once the embryos reached a certain level of development. It does make sense, if their intention was to populate a new planet. This would explain the acceleration growth that is now taking place."

Patrick had to agree with him, but right now they weren't trying to populate a planet. Only thirty tanks had been brought on line. There were five hundred tanks in all found in the chamber. There were also thirty thousand cartridges of fluid for those tanks.

"At this rate we should have fully developed infants in four months or less if the process continues to accelerate. You better tell fabrication to put a rush on that new nursery." said Sebastian. "I am going to have a look at one of the other tanks on New Home and see if I can find the component that is causing the acceleration. If we can slow it down I think we should."

"Why?" asked Patrick. "So long as it works, I see no reason to slow it down. We have control over how many will be born at any given time. Besides, there are a number of Catsman females waiting for a chance to take one of these little guys."

"You don't understand, the acceleration might create problems in the development of the infants. To rapid a growth could cause a under developed heart or lungs. We need to slow the acceleration down to a normal rate of development." Sebastian explained.

"Are you sure you are not a Doctor?" Patrick was impressed with Sebastian's explanation and also a bit put off for not thinking of it himself. "I'll have a talk with the boys in fabrication just in case we can't slow down the acceleration. The hospital is getting rather crowded these days, what with all the cubs running around and getting under foot."

"Why not transfer them to New Home. There is more then enough room in some of the big chambers that even the adults could get up enough steam for a good run without having a bulkhead getting in their way." suggested Sebastian.

"That's a great idea! It might even solve the problem of some people thinking that they are hungry when they are not." Patrick's stomach chose that moment to growl. "Or maybe not." he said with a grin. Sebastian laughed at his new friend and then his own stomach growled.

Dr. Parry and Dr. Brion came in at that moment and wanted to know what was so funny so Patrick told them.

"Then it is a good thing we are here to relieve the two of you but first, how are things going with our little friends here?" said his father. Sebastian explained about the acceleration and his concern that it may cause problems.

"I don't think so." said Brion. "When I helped Jewbee, her pregnancy accelerated in the beginning and slowed down near the end. I was also concerned about the health of the child but as it turns out this is a normal development for the Catsman race."

"Why didn't you tell us sooner?" asked Patrick.

"Because OBGYN is not your field. Plus it slipped my mind." his uncle said. "Now you two boys go find some food and get some rest." Patrick and Sebastian were more then willing to do just that.

The next day Patrick and Sebastian went to see Jewbee. "You want me to move part of the hospital onto New Home!"

"Not everything, just what is needed for the cubs." said Patrick. "We can build them all kinds of thing that they can climb on and cause no damage to. The mothers will have plenty of room to get some exercise."

"Maybe," said Jewbee. "But I am not letting a single cub over there until I have checked out every inch of the place. You have no idea the places that a cub can get into. And getting them out again is a nightmare. Come with me, I want to show you something."

They followed her into another room where work crews were busy replacing a wall section. Cut sections of the old wall were stacked over to one side of the room. Jewbee picked up a section that had a grate that measured six by ten. She held it up so that they could get a good look at it.

"You see this, one of the cubs got inside the bulkhead through this little opening. Now, as you can see, we had to take the wall apart to get him out."

"I see." said Sebastian. "I will personally check every chamber that will be used for the cubs."

"Thank you." said Jewbee. "And I hope you won't mind if I check them when you are done."

"Not at all Doctor. Two pairs of eyes are always better then one." replied Sebastian. Well at least he has a sense of humor thought Jewbee.

✳

Roeman had just left his office when he tripped over a cub in the corridor. "How did you get here?" he asked the cub. "You there." he called to a guard. "Take this cub back to the hospital." He handed the cub to the guard, at which point the cub started to have a fit, so Roeman took the cub back and it stopped fighting.

"Sir," said the guard. "I think she likes you. How do you think she got here all the way from the hospital?"

"I don't know." he said. "But I am going to find out." Instead of taking the cub back to the hospital, Roeman took it to his and Sinsee's quarters.

While Sinsee contacted Jewbee, Roeman watched the cub as she pounced on Kit's tail. Kit flicked his tail and the cub stood up on her hind legs and fell over backwards. Roeman chuckled and gave Kit a big grin, he seemed to be enjoying the cub as much as Roeman was.

{["I was wondering if we had lost another cub in a wall somewhere."]} thought Jewbee to Sinsee. {["I'll send someone to pick her up."]}

{["Don't bother,"]} thought Sinsee. {["I think we will keep this one. She is old enough to be eating on her own and I think Roeman likes her. I know Kit does."]} Sinsee was smiling at the antics of the cub as she tried again to get Kit's tail.

Jewbee could feel Sinsee's laughter. {["What is happening there?"]}

{["The cub is trying to catch Kit's tail. Ooops, there she goes again."]}

{["Are you sure about this Sinsee? A cub at this stage can be a real handful."]}

{["I'm sure Jewbee."]}

That was how Roeman got his very own Lion. He named her Celeste. For the rest of the evening they occupied themselves with cub proofing their quarters.

As the ships began to arrive and the guests shown to their quarters a number of them were requesting a private meeting with the High Chandler. They were informed that she was preparing for her wedding to the Lord Admiral Roeman. Perhaps they would like to speak to the Sector Marshal, if he was free at this time. Some excepted the offer but most declined, much to the relief of Sector Marshal Dee.

The Delegates from the mining colony were on their way to the station but they would not make it in time for the wedding, so the Captain put through a transmission call to Lord Roeman for them. In this way they were the only ones given a private meeting with Lord Roeman. What they wanted was for the High Chandler to arrange for a ZENTEX Tec's to come to their world and see if there was a way to increase production of their smelting plants that were having trouble keeping up with the needs of fabrication. Roeman was pleased to learn that they wanted the Millally to be the ones to make arrangements for them. He told the delegates that he would speak to the High Chandler.

"Don't worry about this." said Roeman. "At the moment,

the mining colony has top priority as far as the High Chandler is concerned. I do not know at this time what the price of the ZENTEX Tec's services will be, but the Millally will cover half of that cost. Is there anything else I can do for you at this time?" There was not, so the connection was ended.

✳

The real test of the new communication system was made when the news crew made a pre-emptive broadcast and sent it out to all the ships, and the colony worlds which had ships in orbit relaying the transmission to the planets surface. It announce that the Wedding Ceremony of the High Chandler of the Millally to the Lord Roeman would be broadcasted live as it happened.

A view of the Great Hall was shown. The reporter was showing just where the High Chandler was expected to enter the Hall. Workers were bringing in floral arrangements from Terra Two that would decorate the hall. Just then an extremely large Lion and his rider came into view. His rider in formal dress, looked to be in full control of her mount. The reporter was saying that the Honor Guard seemed to be as excited as everyone else on the Millally Home Station about the up coming wedding.

The Lion roared at that very moment, his head going back and the onlookers got a real good look into his opened mouth, teeth and all.

"And that seems to make it unanimous." the reporter was saying as he moved further away from the Lion. "So don't forget folks, in twenty four hours from now, we will bring you the broadcast of a life time. So Don't miss it!" The reporter looked at his camera crew and they gave him the signal that the transmission had stopped. "How was it? Did you get a shot of that lion? Oh Good! That was a real once in a life time shot, it was great the way he roared like that. I'll bet that will never happen again."

The Lions rider was smiling to herself. {["Thanks Tiger."]}

she said as she patted her friend on his shoulder. {["You're welcome."]} he said as he touched his riders mind.

✳

Sinsee had more butterflies in her stomach then she knew what to do with. Right in the middle of dressing she had to run to the bathroom, where she immediately threw up. There were more then enough helping hands to assist her and she was soon back in the other room finishing her preparations. Someone helped her into the dress she had designed for this very day. Now if only her stomach would cooperate.

In another part of the central sphere, Roeman was having his own problems. His head pounded like nothing he had ever experienced before.

"Here, drink this." Dr. Brion handed him a glass filled with a yellow liquid. "It will stop that head of yours from falling off. I can't do anything for your butterflies though. Sorry."

Roeman gulped down the contents of the glass and the pounding in his head began to ease up some. "Do all the men on your world go through this?"

"I wouldn't know, I've never been married." said Brion. Patrick came in and said that they were seating the guests now.

"You better go take your seat now Uncle. I'll take care of things here. Say, where is Sector Marshal Dee?" Patrick heard a noise coming from the other room.

"I'm right here." said Dee, as he came out of the bathroom. He looked no better then Roeman had. "What the hell was that stuff we were drinking last night.?"

Patrick pored him a glass of his Uncle's fix all. "Here, this stuff will fix most of it."

"Thanks." Dee downed the drink, then he looked at Patrick. "How come you aren't sick like the rest of us?"

"Are you kidding! Do you two know how much you drank last night. I have never seen anyone drink that much and live."

Patrick shook his head. "It is a good thing Sinsee didn't see you, or the wedding would be off."

"We weren't that far out of line were we?" asked Roeman.

"Just be grateful that no one recorded that party. Sinsee would probable hold it over your head for the rest of your life." He took a peek out the door at one of the young pages who was keeping an eye on things for him. The boy nodded excitedly. "Almost time Roeman."

"Oooo!" moaned Roeman as he made a dash for the bathroom. A few moments later he was standing in the doorway with a bottle of mouth wash in his hand. He handed it to Dee, who took a big swig then spat it out into an empty glass.

"Well old friend, let's do this thing." said Dee, as Patrick opened the door for them.

Sinsee was shaking so much that she had to hold onto her fathers arm for support. The bride's maids had already entered the Hall, now it was her turn. She could hear the music that was being played inside the Hall. Jewbee was making last minute adjustments to the long train of her gown.

Sinsee was glad that she had insisted on the gold thread design that mirrored her ceremonial gown. She had to over rule a number of objections, including one from her mother, but when the women saw her in her wedding dress, they had to admit she was right.

"You amaze me Sinsee." said her father. "You go charging off into space, knowing that you could die at any moment. You save an unknown race, become the Leader of the most powerful people in the universe, and now look at you. You cling to me like a little girl, shaking like you did that day they came to test you. I wanted to fight for you then. Did you know that? Now look at all these people, it seems that I don't have to fight for you any more. It seems to me that no one has to do your fighting any more. I love you daughter." He smiled down at her and she smiled back at him. He always knew just what to say.

Sinsee took a deep breath, squared her shoulders, and they began their walk into the Great Hall. It seemed to take forever to walk the distance from the entrance to the base of the steps to the raised flooring, the music was slow, and they moved as if they floated down the aisle, each step taking her closer to Him.

They stopped before Roeman. Lee stepped in front of his daughter, he gently lifted her vale and kissed her on the cheek. Taking her hand in his, he placed it in Roeman's. Turning, he went to take his seat next to her mother, who was crying silently.

Together they ascended the stairs to stand before Jayson, who cleared his throat. The music stopped.

"We have come this day to stand as witness to the joining of these two great Houses. Lord Roeman, we bestow upon you this day, our greatest treasure. This child of Terra Two, to be your life mate. Never did I think to see this day, and yet it has come to pass. It shall forever more be known that by decree of law, all that you have and all that you will have shall in its time be passed to any child made of this union. All shall recognize such children as your rightful heirs. I ask you Lord Roeman, do you accept this Law?"

"I accept this Law with open heart and open hand." replied Roeman.

"High Chandler of all Millally, beloved and most loved Grand Daughter, I ask you, do you accept this Law?"

"Grandfather, I accept this Law with open heart and open hand." Sinsee smiled at him.

"Then I bid that the two of you step forward and place your prints upon the contract."

As Roeman and Sinsee stepped up to the table behind Jayson and placed their hand first on the ink pads and then on the contract.

"Let all the worlds of man stand as witness to the pledge you make one to the other. Bound to each other for all to see. None may stand between you for now two are one. As you have pledged your lives to each other, so too have your people pledged themselves in this union. Let it be know that from this day forward, the Millally and Terra Two are now one people. Terra Two now stands as Home World to all Millally. We embrace our brothers of the Millally Spacing Guild." said Jayson as he placed a white silk sash around Roeman's and Sinsee's joined hands. He then knelt down on one knee. "I pledge my service to the High Chandler and Lord Roeman."

Roeman and Sinsee were both surprised by this last part, Jayson had not told them of his intentions to pledge himself to them and their reaction was plain for all to see.

Sebastian came forward and knelt before them. "I have been given authority by the Tec's of ZENTEX to speak on their behalf. The Tec's of ZENTEX pledge their services and ask to be aloud to join the United worlds of Millally and Terra Two. To stand by your side, to aid you in what ever way that the Tec's may serve." Sebastian then took hold of one of the ends of the silk sash and pressed it to his lips.

All the Lions that ringed the Great Hall rose to stand their full height, their silver armor clanking as they moved. In unison they lifted their heads and roared, the vibrations of that roar could be felt as well as heard by everyone in the central and second spheres.

Roeman smiled at Sinsee, she had told him what she had intended to do with the Lions.

Only a few of the guests fainted. Hand in hand they left the Hall.

Jayson addressed the guests. "For those of you who wish to remain while we prepare this Hall for the reception, you will find that we have provided beverages for you at the far side of the Hall. Those of you with companions who are in need of assistance, please stay were you are. Help is on the way."

Jewbee entered the Hall with a staff of medical personal. They dispersed among the guests to see to those who had fainted.

On the other colony worlds there was a buzz of speculation. On some worlds the general population demanded to know why their governments had not sent representatives to the wedding of such high ranking individuals. On one such world the government was over thrown within one week of the wedding being aired. Yet there were still some colonies which held the Millally in contempt. The airing of the wedding only served to fuel that contempt.

Nika made sure that the food and beverages continued to be refreshed. A tower of Glasses was set up and the guests watched as the top glass was filled to overflowing and in turn, each glass under that filled to overflowing and so on until the very bottom glasses that formed the base filled to the rims.

The ornate chairs had been returned to the raised flooring, a small table had been placed before the chairs and covered with a hand embroidered white and gold table cloth. When Roeman and Sinsee returned to the Hall for the reception they took their seats and Kit stretched out on the main floor just to their right. Celeste was content to stay by Roeman's feet, she tried to play with the ends of the table cloth until Sinsee told her to behave.

Each group of guests made their way, at one time or the other during the celebration, up the steps to pay their respects to the newlyweds. Roeman was surprised at how many merely wanted to wish them well. The few who asked for favors at this time, well, Roeman felt that they needed watching. "This is neither the time nor the place for such things. This is a time of celebration." he would say to those who approached him for favors.

As the party continued, Roeman and Sinsee found that they were beginning to enjoy themselves. Nika had managed to drag Roeman out onto the dance floor for a rather fast pace dance, next he found himself dancing with Sinsee's Mother. To Jewbee's dismay, Roeman pulled her out onto the dance floor next.

Sinsee was not about to be out done by the other women, so she got out onto the dance floor with Sector Marshal Dee, then her Father had a slow dance with her. To everyone's surprise Kit wanted to dance with Sinsee as well. The floor was cleared as the large Lion made his way out onto the dance floor. At first the two just seemed to be circling each other until someone recognized their movement as part of a very old dance style. Soon they were striding side by side, Sinsee was hanging onto Kit's long mane and with the swing of his massive head, he flung her up and onto his back. It was as if the onlookers were watching a story unfold in the dance.

"What are they doing?" asked Jewbee.

"I think I know." said Patrick. "It is the story of how they met."

"Do tell it." said Jewbee.

Others gathered around him as he told the story of how Sinsee and Kit met. He brought the story up rapidly to the point where the two dancers were now at in the dance. "Now they have found the pack of the beast, but he is not there among them. Look now, It comes for her. Oh brave and faithful Kit, see how he saves her life. Look now, the triumphant hunters come home." Patrick moved out onto the dance floor and Sinsee came running up to him, he lifted her in the air, a joyful meeting of old friends. Kit came up to the two of them and Patrick pretended to be afraid of him. Sinsee danced a reassurance to Patrick and the three of them walked off the dance floor.

The uproar from the onlookers and the Lions was enough to have deafened everyone's hearing for a few minutes. Sinsee and Kit came back out onto the dance floor and took a bow. Roeman went out and took her in his arms and just starred into her eyes as she breathed deeply trying to catch her breath. They looked around at their guests and saw the joy in their eyes.

"Now This," said Roeman as he indicated the room at large. "This is a party!"

Unbeknown to everyone, Nika had set up small surveillance cameras around the Great Hall. A record of Sinsee's and Kit's dance was made, and in the years to come, symphony directors would compose operas based on those recordings.

Roeman and Sinsee left the next day for a quite honeymoon on Terra Two. They took Kit and Celeste with them.

Mr. and Mrs. Kenny were more then happy to have the couple stay with them at the farm.

As the sun was going down, Roeman and Sinsee sat on the front porch swing. Little Celeste was curled up on Roeman's lap and Kit lay out in the yard on the cool grass. Celeste uncurled herself and put her front paws on Roeman's chest, she touched her nose to his. Roeman's vision blurred for a moment and then he was seeing himself through the eyes of Celeste.

Sinsee giggled. "Isn't it nice to know that we are not alone."

Roeman smiled at her. "You knew this would happen."

She looked at him. {["Yes."]} Her thought was a gentle touch in his mind. She giggled again.

Chapter Six

FOR THE PAST FIVE years Sebastian had been trying to solve the enigma of what appeared to be a second engine on New Home. At first they thought it might be part of the ships shields because a spider web of conduits wrapped themselves around the ship and then back again to this engine. As Sebastian studied the back engineering and also helped in the restoration of the ship, he hypothesized that it was an engine, but that he had no clue as to how it worked. Even after five years, he would not give up.

Right now Sebastian had his head inside one of the control panels on the bridge. "Well, this matches up." he said to his Lioness, Destiny. She made a rumbling sound deep in her throat. "Just a minute and I will be out of here." He could feel her concern for him. She had felt that he had been working on this thing far to long. "I am working on it because I want to turn it on, silly." She projected an image of what he looked like with his head stuck in that box. He had to chuckle. "You win, I am the one who is silly." She rumbled in her throat again. Sebastian came out from under the controls and replaced the cover panel back to its rightful place. He stood there next to the control console and looked at the view screen in front of him. He leaned against the control panel, his right hand resting on a spot that was worn from countless generations of Catsman who had done the very same thing.

The view screen showed a full view of Home Station before him. He could see the many new shuttles, that his fellow Tec's had made for the Millally, zipping around the station like bees around the hive. Destiny came to sit next to him, she wanted her ear scratched. Sebastian reached out with his left hand and started to scratch her in just the right spot.

"Maybe I have been here to long." said Sebastian to her. "I need to go home." Destiny projected a view of their quarters. "No, not that home. My home on ZENTEX." He concentrated on what his world looked like and projected it to Destiny. The panel under his right hand began to shimmer and glow, then the whole bridge began to shimmer and glow a soft blue. Suddenly there was a flash of white light and when Sebastian looked up at the view screen he did not see the station. Destiny nudged him because he had been ignoring her attempts at getting his attention. She wanted to know what that was.

"That Destiny, is My Home. We are at ZENTEX!"

Roeman checked in to see if Cayla needed anything before he headed to his office. The young nanny was just finishing up giving Bethany her bath. Roeman thought that Bethany was looking more and more like her mother. "Do you need anything before I leave?" She said no, she had everything she needed for now. "Where are Sinsee and Danny?"

"They are over in the second sphere, in the zero gravity chamber." said Cayla as she was trying to get Bethany into her new jumper.

"Again?" Roeman knew that Danny loved the zero gravity chamber as much as his mother did. The boy had a real talent and could do everything that Sinsee could do in zero gravity, even though he was only five years old.

Roeman wished that he could join them but there was that

new Delegation from Windgall. They were requesting entry into the Union of Worlds. Their world produced some of the finest cloth. From what he understood, they got the fiber from a small worm that thrived in their marsh lands. Sinsee had received some rather provocative outfits as a gift. Roeman had forbidden her to wear them in public, but he had no problem with her wearing them around him.

Roeman checked the time, he had just enough time to stop by his office and pick up a few things before the meeting with the Union Senators to discuss Windgall. It was all pure formality, show boating really. Sinsee had made it clear that she wanted Windgall in the Union. Roeman remembered the first time Sinsee had denied a world entry into the Union. They were no more than a planet full of thugs and bullies. Sinsee had raged for hours after dealing with their representative. In fact it had taken all of his own willpower to not have the man thrown out the nearest airlock. For a time Sinsee had stopped all transports to Chronis Three, thinking that that would curb their attitude. It didn't, but Sinsee just could not bring herself to punish the innocent along with the guilty. Instead she placed restriction on their off world travels. The moment they stepped out of line she would hit them with all kinds of fines, or worse.

Chronis Three was not the only planet that had been denied entry into the Union, though it was the worst of the lot so for. There were four other worlds who's Leaders were the type of men you wouldn't want to meet on a lonely road no matter what time of day it was.

Roeman actually had to pull out the aid workers Sinsee had sent to help the people of the planet Norvox. Just as the last shuttle lifted off the building in which they had been housed exploded in a massive fire ball.

There were those in the Union who wanted to retaliate against Norvox. Sinsee would not let them take action against Norvox. No one had been killed or injured and the only loss was to a building that did not belong to them in the first place. "You have to wonder about a government that shoots it's self in the foot."

Tolly, Kearney, and Muddy Gulch were also added to the list of undesirable, but Roeman still had hope that Kearney could turn itself around and one day join the Union, but for now he had to agree With Sinsee. Kearney was steeped in a government of religious rule that distrusted everyone and everything, including themselves.

"Sir, can I take Bethany to the play chamber today?" asked Cayla.

"Sure, just keep her within arms reach. You know how she loves to try and get away from you." He bent down and kissed Bethany on her forehead.

Roeman left their quarters and headed for his office when one of his aids came running up to him.. "Lord Roeman! Ship New Home is gone!"

"What?!" Roeman turned and headed for the nearest Halley's Rail.

{[**"Roeman!"**]} Came Sinsee's mind touch.

{[**"I know, I know!"**]} Roeman thought back at her. {[" I am on my way to our shuttle right now."]}

{["I will drop Danny off and head for Observation."]} she told him.

{["Cayla has taken Bethany to the play chamber, so drop him off there."]} came Roeman's reply.

{["Alright. I'll let the docking bay crew know that you are coming. They can have the shuttle ready for you when you get there. Roeman, be careful out there."]}

Telepathy was faster then reaching for a com unit. Sinsee touched one of the minds of the Catsman working in the docking bay and he relayed her orders to the rest of the crew. By the time Roeman reached the bay his shuttle engines were up and running, the shuttle had been positioned for a fast take off .

Roeman took the shuttle out through the baffling shields even before docking control had a chance to dampen them down. These new shuttles were really an advancement in technology. Roeman was checking his scanners for any sign of debris, just in case.

Collision alarms went off and Roeman looked up just in time to see that he was headed right for the hull of New Home. He pulled the controls hard over, the shuttle groaned under the strain of the maneuver, the port side of the shuttle made contact with New Home as the sound of metal on metal reached Roeman's ears.

The com speaker came alive with everyone trying talk at once. Roeman felt Sinsee's mind touch and braced himself for what he knew was to come.

["Get off those coms, clear the air NOW!]

There was no stopping his wife when she wanted to be heard and that was a fact that everyone was learning the hard way. None telepaths would end up with a pounding in their heads every time she let loose like this.

Roeman tuned his com to New Home's frequency. "New Home. Can you hear Me?' he asked in a controlled voice.

"Yes Lord Roeman, I can hear you." came Sebastian's reply. "I am really sorry about that. Did we hurt anyone when we Folded back?' he asked.

"Just my pride." said Roeman. "Stay where you are. I am coming onboard!"

"Yes, Lord Roeman." Sebastian cut the com signal. He opened the link to the docking bay in New Home. "Shuttle arriving in the foreword docking bay. Prepare for the arrival of Lord Roeman."

Destiny growled low in her throat. "No, I don't think that we are in any kind of trouble." She growled again, but this time she was shaking. "We will see about that." Sebastian opened the com to the shuttle again. "Lord Roman, could you do me a favor?"

"What is it boy?" said Roeman in a rather pleased tone of voice.

"The other Lions are giving my Destiny a bad time right now. Could you ask the High Chandler to tell them to back off." There was an edge to his voice that told Roeman his Lion was in some form of distress from the other Lions. A moment later Sebastian thanked Roeman and said he would be on the main bridge of New Home awaiting his arrival.

Roeman sat in the captain's chair and Sebastian sat in the chair at the consol. "It is so simple, that I missed it all these years. I kept looking for some complicated reason behind the second engine. I knew that it had to be controlled from this panel but there are no controls what so ever. This ship was designed to fold space. What we assumed were the main engines are actually in system engines. The fold engines have not been used in generations, that is why none of the Catsman knew how they worked or that they were even there in the first place. Most likely because telampathic births stopped for some reason or other. By the time Kreeote was born the knowledge of the fold engine had been lost for countless generations. That was also why they thought the boy was damaged."

"So what you are saying is that it takes a telampathic to use the fold engine." said Roeman as he rubbed his chin.

"Yes Sir. Contact with this panel here is the linking point. I only need to place my hand here and concentrate on the place in space that I want the ship to go and then we go there." said Sebastian.

"Show me." said Roeman. "Take us to ZENTEX."

Sebastian put his hand on the heavily worn plate. As before, the bridge began to shimmer, turn a soft blue and then the flash of white light.

Roeman slowly stood to his feet. He looked at the main viewing screen. There before him was the planet ZENTEX. He and Sebastian just stood there for a while admiring the view. Then Roeman said they should contact the surface.

✳

The second time New Home disappeared, Sinsee ordered all shuttle craft grounded. She sat there in Observation with a number of other people around her. She kept her eyes on the spot where New Home had last been.

"It has been six hours." someone to her left said.

"Wait for it." was all Sinsee would say. She cursed herself for not thinking to have New Home fitted with one of the new communication systems. Then again, no one thought that New Home was going anywhere.

The time dragged on and then, "There!" The space where New Home had been stationed off of Home Station began to shimmer with a blue haze like fog, then there was that flash of white light, the same white light that had marked the disappearance of New Home in the first place. Now that New Home was back, safe and sound, Sinsee relaxed the tension that had been building up inside of her.

{["Roeman, are you alright?"]} she asked him.

{["Yes, I'm fine."]} he replied.

{["Well you wont be when I get my hands on you."]}

The reason it had taken so long was because Roeman had shuttled up a number of Tec's from the planets surface, they were now going over the fold engine with a fine tooth comb.

✳

Later in their quarters. "What I can't understand," said Sinsee, "is if a telampath has to envision the place he is sending the ship to, how can he send it to a some place he has never seen before?"

Roeman shrugged his shoulders. "I know what you mean. It doesn't work for an exploration ship looking for new planets."

"I think you mean colony ship, don't you?" she corrected

him. "I wish the Catsman had kept better records about their past. All they know about their home world is that it is dead. This generation does not even know where it is."

"Sinsee, How does a planet die? I mean, if their planet had been destroyed, they would have told each following generation that it was destroyed, but the Catsman insist that their home world is dead. So just how does a planet die?" Roeman shifted his weight on the couch and he heard the crinkling sound of paper underneath him. He reached under his right thigh and pulled out a sealed folder. "I forgot all about this. It is from the researchers you sent to ZENTEX over five years ago. They asked me to give it to you."

She started to read the report, about half way through it she put it down. Roeman asked her if something was wrong. "I think it is time to bring the researchers home. It says here that there have been a number of fights among them. Mostly from short tempers stemming from having to deal with the Tec's themselves."

Roeman remembered what it had been like with just ten pairs of Tec's on the station. He didn't even want to think of how it must be for the researchers having to deal with countless numbers of twins, all talking in that round de round speak of theirs. It was no wonder that they had short tempers.

"What they need is a place where they can scream their heads off and no one will think any different about them, you know, like they are nuts or something." said Roeman. "Say, what about that park your Dad and Seenan have on Terra Two. I hear that people are screaming all the time there. A few weeks of rest there and they should be good as new. I better stop those Tec's before they take the fold drive apart. We will need New Home to fetch our boys from ZENTEX, then take them to Terra Two. They can stay in the shuttles while they are there. Just another home away from home. I'll go set things up with your brother now." Roeman left to make the arrangements. Sinsee got herself a cup of coffee and sat down to finish reading the report.

By the time Roeman returned she has finished to report. "Well?" he asked her.

"It is not what I was hoping for, but then I am not really sure what it was I was hoping for in the first place." she sighed.

"So put it away for now. Are you up for a little trip with the Kids?" he smiled at her.

"Sure, just what do you have in mind.?" she asked him.

"I thought we would pop over to ZENTEX, pick up our boys and then pop over to Terra Two for a Holliday. I can't remember when the last time was that we took some time off, can you?" he asked her.

"Are you sure we should be using New Home this way?" She looked at him with a strange look on her face.

"Why not, now that we have got the damn thing working, lets use it." he said. "Go pack some things for us and the kids, and tell Cayla she is coming too."

Word went through the station like a fire storm that the High Chandler and her family were going on vacation and taking Ship New Home with them. Shuttles made bee lines between Home Station and New Home, transporting goods and personnel back and forth. A number of the Senators wanted to tag along, some of them had heard about Seenan's Rail Park and wanted to see it for themselves.

When Danny learned where they were going he would not stop jumping up and down. Cayla had a hell of a time strapping him into his seat in the shuttle for the short trip to New Home.

Sebastian had never been to Terra Two so Roeman took his seat at the control panel, just in case, Sebastian stayed by his side. Roeman put his hand on the plate and thought with all his might just how Terra Two looked from space. He really did not have to think as hard as he was. He had spent long hours looking at Terra Two from the bridge of the Antiack, that was, before he met Sinsee.

✷

Seenan was amazed at the number of shuttles that were landing in the valley field next to his Rail Rider Park. As a group of people made their way towards him, he saw a small figure break away from the others and start to run towards him ahead of the rest.

"Uncle!, Uncle!" Seenan caught the boy up in his arms and swung him around in the air.

"My goodness, Danny, but you have grown. Did you bring the whole station with you?" He tickled the boy on his stomach, which caused Danny to squeal with delight. Roeman and Sinsee walked up to them.

Seenan put out his hand and shook Roeman's. "Nice to see you again, Roeman." He turned to his sister, who was holding Bethany. "And who do we have here." He took Bethany from her mother and looked closely at the girl. This was the first time he had seen his niece, she looked just like Sinsee when she was her age. Seenan leaned over and kissed his sister on the cheek. "Terry told me to make sure that I brought you home for dinner, but I don't think she made enough food." He indicated the shuttles and the crowd of people that were coming out of them.

Roeman laughed. "Sorry about all this. We just couldn't get away with out all the hoopla." He turned to have a look at the height of the tallest Rail Rider, his head tilting back as he followed the path of a line of connected pods making its way to the top of the highest Rail. That was when Roeman noticed that the pods were open to the air. His mouth dropped open as he heard the screams of the passengers within the pods. "Holly Shit!" He lost color to his face. "I think I am going to pass on this one. You got anything smaller?"

"Not me." said Sinsee. "I came here for a thrill and that is just what I want."

"That thing is in the open." said Roeman as he followed the path of the pods as they dropped down the casing. "It is not like the rails on Home Station that are inside sealed tunnels and tubs." The more he watched, the more he did not like this type of rail.

"How about it Danny," said his mother. "You want to go on the big one with me?" The boy looked from his father to his mother. When Sinsee smiled and nodded her head at him, the boy began to jump up and dawn again.

As they made their way to the Park, Seenan turned to look back at the shuttles. Someone had raised a flagpole and was now raising the flag of the Millally Royal Court. After all his sister had accomplished, he felt that she deserved this. No one was more proud of her then he was, except maybe their Father.

Roeman had been right about the Tec's improving the smelting posses on the mining world. They had done such a good job, that they had even come up with a new type of metal which had to be smelted on a new space platform refinery that now orbited the planet. Roeman had been assured that the refinery could produce any length or width of metal that was required of it. To augment the new refinery, another space platform was built where the new fold engines were being produced, but on a smaller scale then the one on New Home. Before long the space above the mining world was filling up with platforms that formed the new ship yards for the construction of the new line of ships that would fold space.

It wasn't long before the first ship came off the production line. Sebastian was given the honor of piloting this first ship, a fact that did not go unnoticed by other Tec's.

Sector Marshal Dee became swamped with requests from a number of Tec's who had been found to be telampathic and who wanted to become a part of the new fleet that was being built.

Roeman was grateful for those volunteers, because he really did not want to have to order any of the Tec's into Fleet Service.

While the new ships were being constructed, Sebastian took the new recruits out, in the newly commissioned Miss Destiny, for training on fold jumps. Visuals of each world were shown to the new pilots in training and they were given the chance to fold to the planet of their choice.

One such fold some how went wrong and the ship popped into space just beyond the gravity pull of a water world that was not on any of their files of known worlds.

A buzz of excitement raced through the crew, as Sebastian confirmed that this world was in fact a new planet. It had been the cloud cover that had been the cause of the mistaken fold. Sebastian played back the recording of their first sight of the planet, sure enough, the clouds had taken the shape of the land mass on the planet that the young twins at the controls had intended the ship to go to.

Captain Lane decided to take advantage of this situation and she ordered the launch of a number of probes, to be sent into the atmosphere to take readings. Water meant air, weather or not it was breathable, they were about to find out.

Sebastian made visual recording from every bit of data the probes transmitted back to the ship. There was one hell of a storm going on down there at the moment and they lost contact with one of the probes. The humidity readings were off the scales, temperatures varied from the poles to the equator. That was to be expected. All to soon the gravity took over and the probes were pulled down into the vast ocean of this water world.

"That's it." said Captain Lane. "Lets get this information back to Home Station. Sebastian, would you please take the controls. We don't want to get lost again." She looked at the twins and smiled at them to reassure them that she meant no disrespect. She also wanted them to know that it wasn't their fault that this happened.

✹

Dee had studied the files four times now. He looked up from his screen to see Lane smiling at him. "Who did you say made this fold?"

"Antella. They are the youngest twins we have. That's probably why the jump went arrantly wrong, that and the fact that the cloud cover took the shape of the land mass at the instant of fold." She just kept smiling at him. "If it hadn't been for that, we would never have found it."

"Antella, you say. Well that sounds like a good name to me. We'll give this one to the twins. Planet Antella, it even sounds better each time I say it. A world with their name on it should make up for how badly they must be feeling about flubbing their first fold." He looked at the clear photo of the planet from space. "I dub you the Planet Antella." He looked at Lane again. "You will let the twins know."

"Of course. I would love to see the look on Roeman's face when you show him that photo but I should be getting back to my ship." She rose from her seat.

"Tell your crew that they have Lord Roeman's gratitude and mine. I am sure that Roeman will send them and you his complements." he said.

"Have him send it to the twins, if having a whole planet named after them doesn't lift their spirits, his personnel thanks will." She closed the door behind her as she left his office.

Roeman did indeed send his complements to the twins, Antella, along with orders to return to the water world with a team of researcher. He wanted more data on the Planet Antella. He also suggested that the Antella twins try the fold again.

"That was sweet of you Roeman." said Sinsee as she sat in his lap. "I'll bet you that the Antella twins become our best pilots."

"So you think I'm not the best anymore, do you?" He pulled her closer to him and started to nibble on her neck.

"Oh, you are still the best!" she giggled. She pulled away from him. "Did I forget to tell you, the Tec's want to fit one of the shuttles with a fold engine."

"I don't think that is such a good idea. I don't want shuttles popping out to who knows where. Some fool might pop right into a sun or even into the core of a planet. Best to leave that alone."

"If you say so." She leaned into his embrace and thoughts of planets, ships, and shuttles were soon forgotten.

With all the help from the researchers and the tons of equipment they brought along with them, it didn't take long before they found what the probes had missed. The storms had died down and there it was, a small island in the equatorial region of the planet. It was only a few miles wide and fifteen to eighteen miles long, and completely covered in a lush green vegetation. The research team prepared to go down in one of the shuttles and check it out. The Antella twins were aloud to make the first trip down because the planet had been named after them and it was only right that they should be the first to set foot on this new world.

After circling the island to have a good look at what they had to work with, the shuttle landed on the shore line of a natural cove. A jetty of rocks extended out into the water to form a natural breaker, and waters of the cove were as clear as glass.

The team members walked out onto the jetty to what should have been the deepest section. They could see the different types of aquatic life forms from this advantage point. There seemed to be vast numbers of sea life in the cove. More then likely they stayed here because the jetty protected them from the many storms that ravaged the planet.

They wasted time that first day just pointing out the

different life forms in the cove. The team members were surprised at the variety of colors and shapes. Every now and then someone would point out a really exotic looking life form. The others would rush over the rocks to get a look at the life form.

"OK People!" said the team leader. "We have got work to do, so lets get started." He led the way back along the jetty to the shuttle on the beach. He turned to his group.

"Finder," he called the young man up from the back. "I want you to try and find a route into the interior that wont be a hazard to the others. You know how some of them can be, so find the easiest route you can." He turned to look at the rest. "Any of you who go into that jungle, I want you to be wearing your anti-grave harnesses at all time. Is that understood!"

"Sure Philip." said Jewl. "No telling what is in their. This place might be small, but some of the most deadliest things come in the smallest packages.

"We can setup the base camp on this beach." said Philip. "Everyone, except Finder, start unloading the shuttle."

It took them the rest of the day to setup the base camp. The lab domes were setup close to the shuttle so they could be powered by the power hook cables that ran from the small ship to the domes. The men had the option of sleeping in the shuttle itself or setting up smaller domes on the beach.

Jewl said that there was no way he was going to sleep on that beach. "What if one of those things out there in the cave can walk on land? No sir, not me." Jewl was one of the best lab workers that Philip ever had, but he also thought that Jewl was a bit of a sissy.

Finder returned just before dark with an arm load of fresh fruits. "I thought I would bring these in on my way back. There is a lot more out there where these came from. If they test out to be safe to eat, at least we have a fresh supply of food while we are here." He placed them on the work bench along with a vile of clear water. "There is a small spring about two miles in. I did not smell any sulfur and there is no sign of salt in the water and no salt around the ground either."

"Good work Finder." said Philip. "Did you see any signs of life forms?"

"I thought you would never ask." smiled Finder. "There is no sign of life on the ground larger then my little finger. But." He opened his coat and took out a blue handkerchief, very carefully he unfolded the edges. In side it was what looked like a small Butterfly Bird. The others gathered around to have a look and jumped back when the bird stood up on its feet and buzzed like a bee. "She flew right up to me and acted like she was glad to see me. When I touched her, she seemed to vibrate with excitement." He held out his finger and the Butterfly Bird zipped over to perch on the tip, tilting her head this way and that.

"She is beautiful." said Jewl. "Will she let me hold her." Jewl held out his finger. "Come here girl and let me have a good look at you." She zipped over to him, landing on his finger, she presented her open wings for him to look at them. "Did you see that! I think she is intelligent."

"Now hold on Jewl. Don't go jumping to conclusions on this." said Philip. "You know as well as I do, that thing is only a bird."

"You think so. Well lets just see about that." He looked at the Butterfly Bird. "You hear what he said Girl. He thinks you're just a simple little bird." Jewl set up a number of small objects on the table. He pointed to each object and out load he spoke its name. "Now, put the paper clip into the cup." To every ones amazement she zipped down and picked up the paper clip and dropped it into the cup. Jewl looked at Philip who now took more interest in the little bird.

"I wonder just how intelligent she is." Philip tried to pick her up and she zipped away from him, buzzing violently. She landed on Jewl's shoulder and moved closer to his neck.

"I don't think she likes you Philip." said Finder. "Maybe

you should apologize to her." Philip gave Finder a look that said, you have got to be kidding.

"I don't think this will do any good, but what the heck." He turned to face Jewl and looked at the bird on his shoulder. "OK Girl. I was wrong, you are a very smart little thing, and I am sorry if I hurt your feelings." She zipped over to his shoulder then and snuggled up to him. "Well I'll be damned."

"Told you so." Jewl boasted. Everyone agreed that the little Butterfly Bird was intelligent and they made a huge fuss over her. There was so much of a fuss that she zipped away, back into the jungle. "Now look what you have done!" groaned Jewl.

"Don't worry about her, Jewl." said Finder. "This is her home and she knows what she doing."

" I know, but I wanted her to stay." Jewl seemed very sad about the little bird flying off that way.

"We will be here for some time, maybe she will come back." said Philip. "In the mean time we have work to do. Jewl, check the fruit for toxins. Terry, have a go at the water, see if it is safe to drink. We still have about an hour of sun light left, so lets at least get some work done."

Checking the fruit and water was about all they were able to do for the next few days because one of the planets storms came up from the south and the team was stuck in the base camp. The rain came down so hard that it actually stung the flesh. Movement around the camp was limited to only what was absolutely necessary. The water turned out to be drinkable and only two of the fruit samples were toxic.

Once the storm cleared the survey team set out to chart the small island. The work was slow going because of the vegetation. The anti-grave harnesses helped some, but even the overhead growth was covered in vines that cress crossed back and forth so many times, it was like trying to make their way through a test maze. Slowly but surly they began to make their grid map of the island.

Two weeks into the job they made an astonishing discovery.

Covered in a mass of vine growth was an intact space ship. The survey team sent word back to base camp and base camp sent word to the ship. It wasn't long after that that the ship the White Dove was in orbit around the water world Antella.

Three more shuttles touched down at the cove. Captain Duvale would have sent more, but the little beach could not accommodate any more.

It was hard work digging the ship out from all that vegetation, even using the laser hand cutters on the vines proved to be slow going. When two thirds of the ship had been uncovered there was no mistaking it, it was an old style Earth Ship. Giving the age of the ship and the fact that it had survived the harsh environment of Antella was no small miracle. The hatch was rusted shut and the team set about to gain entry into the ship with out causing to much damage to the hatch.

Captain Duvale wanted to be there when they breached the ship, so one of the shuttles had to return to the ship while yet another shuttle descended to the island. The shuttle pilot who had to return to New Home was disappointed because she wanted to get a chance to see inside the old ship. Now she wasn't due for pilot rotation for at least ten shifts.

Work on the hatch was interrupted by another heavy down pore of rain. The workers ran for what ever from of cover they could find. The stinging rain was not dangerous as such, but it was not something that one wanted to be out in with out cover. The large trees in the area provided some relief from the rain. Their over sized leaves formed umbrella like shelter for the workers.

When work resumed on the hatch everyone was drenched to the bone, but they ignored this fact and put all their effort into opening the hatch. Excitement permeated the air as the hatch finally gave way to their efforts. Still they had to wait for that first glimpse inside. Portable fans were set up in the hatchway to circulate fresh air into the ship. Even with the fans working at top speeds, those who went into the ship had to wear breather masks. In the high humidity wearing the masks was one of the most uncomfortable experiences you could imagine.

The ship was an archeological find. Inside the ship was a complete laboratory, along with hand written ledgers and notes on medical experiments by a Doctor named Lawrence Lightenglow. They even found the mummified body of Doctor Lightenglow laying in a bunk just beyond the laboratory.

That night Captain Duvale made his report to Home Station. The moment Sinsee heard the name Lightenglow she ordered that everything on that ship be carefully crated up and sealed, to be returned to Home Station. She contacted all three Doctor Nathan's and put a call in to Jayson at the Foundation.

When Roeman wanted to know what all the fuss was about, Sinsee explained to him that Doctor Lightenglow was the original geneticist who had created the codes that were the foundation of the development of the first Millally. "Don't you see, He is in effect the Father of the Millally."

"You mean the father of slaves." said Roeman.

"No Roeman. Lightenglow didn't create slaves. That was done later by greedy government men who didn't know any better. Lightenglow was a good man of science. When the government took his work away from him, he disappeared." she smiled at him as her words sunk in.

"How do you know all this?" He asked her.

"Because the first Doctor Nathin on Terra Two was a geneticist who studied the work of Doctor Lightenglow for years. Not even Jayson knows that the original design was meant to be a free willed individual. I came across one of his old journals that had an inscription code embedded in it. I cracked the code but I never told anyone about it." She lowered her head. "Maybe I should have."

"Even if you had, I don't see what good that would have

done at that time." Roeman reassured her. "What we can do now is to bring Lightenglow home. We can tell the truth now about his work and who knows, one day he may even be claimed as a hero."

"That may not be the wisest thing to do right now." she said.

"Why? Don't you trust our people to do the right thing?" he asked.

"Of coarse I trust our people. I also want to protect them, the last thing we need right now is another controversy about the former slaves of space just when we are establishing ourselves. We should have the Foundation's people go over everything that comes off that ship. It can be put under high security at the Foundation." That had been one of the reasons she had contacted Jayson, that, and to give him the access codes to Doctor Nate Nathan's private journals. Jayson had been a little put out that she had not confided in him before now, but he also understood her caution.

Roeman contacted Captain Duvale again and told him that no one was to speak of this discovery to anyone and learned that it was already to late for that. News of the discovery had already reached half the fleet and every Senator on New Home was trying to contact his or her own planet with the news.

"That does it," said Roeman. "From now on, anything we find out there is restricted knowledge until it is cleared through Sinsee or Me.

We can't control what happens on individual planets, but we sure as hell are not going to lose control of what goes on out here in space." Sinsee agreed with him and put out an order to that effect.

Shuttles landed at Terra Two's space port and began to unload crate after crate into Foundation ground transports. Port cargo workers were not allowed to touch the crates, so they stood off to one side and watched as crews of workers from the ships and the Foundation worked to move the crates. This was all right with them because they got paid their credits weather they bent their backs or not. Standing there watching someone else do the work was a treat for them. Once someone almost dropped a crate and a port worker called out, "Ant so easy is it fellow, now you know what we go through every time a shipment comes through." There was a lot of cat calling then from the dock workers, but that soon stopped when armed guards started heading their way.

At the Foundation, seven teams of investigators were painstakingly going through each crate as they came in from the port. Some of the items were resealed and sent on to be housed in one of the Foundations storage rooms. Years later these items would be put on display in the Capitals Historical Preservation Exhibits Building.

Hours on end were spent going over Doctor Lightenglow's notes and medical files. One of the crates held his personal journals, unfortunately they were so well encrypted that not even Sinsee could break the code, so she had them sent to Sebastian.

With in weeks Sinsee had a transcribed copy of Lightenglow's journals in her hands. Most of what she read, she already knew, right up to the point where Lightenglow had disappeared.

Lightenglow had liquidated all of his own assets in order to build his own space ship. He had taken his work out beyond the control of the Earth government, where he would continue his work the way he had meant it to be. In another entry he stated that he had taken his work to the colony world of ZENTEX. He hoped that it was far enough away that he would not raise the interest of the Earth Government. He chose a small city far away from their space port. Things went well for him there and then it was time to move on. He wanted to find a new world that the Earth Government knew nothing about.

That was all there was. Sinsee had the Foundation check to

see if they had missed anything in the crates. She was told that the medical files had been sent to ZENTEX for decoding.

"Well," said Roeman. "It looks like he found his world and that is as far as he got. I wish he could have continued his work the way he wanted to"

"Who is to say he didn't." said Sinsee.

"What do you mean?" asked Roeman.

"His journal said that he went to ZENTEX to continue his work, there is nothing in them that says he didn't, only that things went well and then he had to move on. Why move on?" Sinsee rubbed her eyes. "I don't know, maybe I'm just grasping at straws."

"Well, it is all over now." said Roeman.

"Is it?" she said. " What about what happened at Burning One. They paid a horrible price for their experiments in genetics."

"Are you thinking that something like that could happen again?" The memory of what had happened that day made Roeman very angry and it showed on his face.

"Not if we and our children and their children can prevent it." She reached out and gently placed her hand on his arm. "I know how you feel about being called a slave, I feel the same way. Our descendants must never forget where they come from. We will write a true history of the Millally that will be for the Millally only. Maybe one day our descendants can make it public, but for now, we must wait and watch." Roeman wrapped his arms around her and held her close to him.

"When that day comes, we will show all the worlds what was done to us in the name of profit for only the few." He kissed her gently on the forehead.

Weeks later, a package arrived from ZENTEX. Within it were more of Doctor Lightenglow's notes. They proved that the Tec's were actually another genetic outcome of Lightenglow's work. Roeman wanted to add this information to the Millally

History then thought better of it. Perhaps the Tec's didn't want to be part of this history.

"You want to leave it out of history. Maybe that is the way all history was recorded. Just enough truth to give us a glimpse into the past without telling the whole story. That way somewhere down the line someone else can make the same mistakes." said Sinsee in a disgusted tone of voice.

"Ouch!" said Roeman. "You win. I'll contact the Tec's and ask them if they want to be included after Dr. Parry has a chance to fill in some of their own history for them."

"Thank you Roeman, I knew you would do the right thing." said Sinsee. "I wonder how the Tec's came under the control of the ZENTEX government in the first place?"

"Probably the same way the Earth government took over Lightenglow's work. They did something that got the governments attention. It saw them as a tool, just like us." Roeman shrugged his shoulders.

"Speaking of tools. Lightenglow mentions something about using a remote probe in his notes. The probe, when launched, would travel at light plus. That is how he knew where he was going. The probe would go into a system and check for habitable worlds." Sinsee was looking over Lightenglow's new notes.

"With the new fold engines, we don't need any probes." said Roeman.

"Yes, but we still need to know where we are going in order to fold to that place." she replied.

"If we used some of our shuttles as advanced scouts for the main ships, I'll bet we could find even more worlds out there just like Terra Two. The only limitations on the shuttles are the human factor and how much food supplies they can carry. Other then that, I have been told that the shuttles range is unlimited." Roeman was rubbing his chin in deep thought.

"Sounds like you want to go into the exploration business. We can work our way out from Antella and see what we come up with. Has anyone been able to figure out just where in the galaxy Antella is located?" She put down the notes she was reading and poured another cup of coffee for herself and Roeman.

"The Tec's are working on a homing device that will allow us to pin point the exact location." He took a sip of his coffee then added some sweetener to it.

"That island on Antella, it has not been given a name yet. I think we should call it Lightenglow's Island." said Sinsee, deep in thought.

"I think that the Doctor would have liked that." Roeman smiled at her. "The research team there says that they have a surprise for us. They are sending us another gift from that island. They wouldn't say what it was though."

"When will it arrive?" He had perked her interest.

"The ship from Antella is due to fold sometime this afternoon." Roeman yawned and stretched. "I have a meeting with the Senators this morning. I'll probably be tied up all morning. You will have to meet the ship without me when she comes in." He got to his feet, leaned down and kissed her. "If it turns out to be important, give me a shout and I'll join you." He scooped up the case that held his file disks and headed out the door.

Abby came in to clear the remains of their breakfast from the table. For once, she didn't have anything to say and Sinsee watched the women as she did her job and left the room. Sinsee scratched her head. [{" Kit. Is there something bothering Abby?"}]

[{She and Tessa have been arguing for days now. They will work it out.}] came Kits reply.

Sinsee certainly hoped so. There had been a lot of arguments on the station lately and Sinsee spent a lot of her time settling disputes. It was getting out of hand because most of the disputes were over trivial matters.

Chapter Seven

WORD CAME TO SINSEE through Kit that a number of the new Catsman young have been fighting. Station personal had been injured when they attempted to pull the combatants apart. Sinsee made contact with Jewbee and asked her what was going on.

[{"Sorry Sinsee, I would have called you before now, but I have had my hands full at the moment."}] She could tell Jewbee was very busy with something. She told Jewbee that she was coming to help. [{"That might not be such a good idea right now. We just had to pull two young bucks off of each other, right here in treatment. I took a gash to my shoulder. The Med Units are full right now. Patrick is here and he is attempting to suture the gash closed. Ouch!"}]

Sinsee flinched at the pain she felt from her friend. [{"Does anyone know why all the fighting is breaking out?"}]

[{"Preegar says this is some kind of right of passage. A kind of pecking order if you will. Right now it is just the males that are doing the damage. The females are just shoving each other around, they are not using their talons, unlike the males who have no problem with that."}] Sinsee could feel Jewbee thanking someone. [{"I have put the word out, anyone who tries to breakup these fights has to be in body armor. These kids are just plain out of control."}]

[{"Maybe we should just let them fight and get it out of their systems."}] Sinsee thought to Jewbee.

[{"That won't work. I have two kids in Med Units who were injured so badly they almost died. These kids are serious about this thing."}] replied Jewbee.

[{"If we can stop them now, maybe we can control the fights."}] said Sinsee.

[{"How! I damn near got my arm cut off trying to stop a fight."}] This situation was really starting to get to Jewbee. Even the patterns of her thoughts showed that she was frustrated.

[{"Jewbee, I am going to setup a fight competition for the Catsman youth. They want a pecking order, I'll give them a pecking order, My way.

Hang onto something Jewbee, I am about to open up." Sinsee warned Roeman and her kids that she was about to cut loose. They didn't have long to wait.

[{"**Catsman Youth. This is your Chandler. Hear My Words. You want to fight, So Be It. You will Fight before Me, in the Great Hall. I will be the judge, and I will say who among You will be know as the First Ones. See your Elders for your time of Judgment.**"}]

[{"Sinsee! You did it! They stopped fighting, for now."}] thought Jewbee. [{"But how are you going to keep them from killing each other in the Great Hall?"}]

[{"Simple, we tape and pad their hands. The worst that can happen is they give each other black eyes."}] Sinsee told her.

[{"Yes, well don't forget their feet too."}] Jewbee was right. They had talons on their feet as well. [{"You want to know something Sinsee, I'm glad Kreeote is the only one in his age group and that goes for Reekee too."}]

[{"I don't think Reekee would be affected and Kreeote is a telampath. He is already in a much higher standing then the others."}] she told her friend.

[{"Thank You Sinsee. I should get back to work now. If I get some time I'll stop in later to see you."}] Jewbee had not considered her son as being above this pecking order thing and she was truly grateful that Sinsee saw her son as special. She also hoped that the human half of her daughter would prevent her form wanting to fight.

✳

"The problem is that every one wants to see this competition. I don't get it. You would think that everyone had enough fighting in the revolution." said Roeman.

"That is human nature again. I told you that already." Sinsee was going over the names of the young Catsman. She was trying to rank them by size and weight. "You know, we should have some skill competition as well. The Catsman don't like being immersed in water. Maybe we could have a tank of water with a plank over it just wide enough to put one foot in front of the other. Give the kids padded poles and see who gets knocked off first."

"You're enjoying this!" Roeman accused her.

"No I am not. I am trying to come up with ways that they wont kill each other. I could really use some help with this. Instead of complaining about it, you could at least try to help me keep them from ripping themselves to shreds." She gave him a look that said it was the only way.

"Alright," he gave in. "You can't make it easy for them. Grease the plank. With those toe talons of theirs they could get a good grip on the plank. Grease it up, and it becomes more difficult." He took a deep breath. "Let me see that raster, I've seen some of these kids. I think I know what they are capable of doing." Sinsee was glad that he was coming around to seeing it her way. This competition was not just about the standing of the Catsman youth, it was about keeping them safe during this phase of their development. Sinsee just realized that they would have to go through this three times a year. Roeman picked up on her thought. "That's all we need!"

✳

Requests came in from Terra Two and from ZENTEX for transmission of the competitions. "That's not such a bad idea." said Roeman. "We can transmit to all the worlds. Let those kids know that the Union of Worlds would be watching them and maybe they will look at the skills program a little differently. Take it more to heart."

"That would do it." said Patrick. "Sinsee, do you remember the show we put on that day in the gym long ago. You think we could do it again?"

"I have not worked out like that in a long time. I don't know if I can do it now." she told him.

"I have seen you working out in the heavy gravity room. It's not that much different from what we used to do." Patrick wanted to convince her that it was a good idea. "We could show these kids what real skill truly is."

"What is he talking about?" Roeman asked her. Sinsee looked at Patrick for help in trying to explain it to Roeman.

Patrick explained how he and Sinsee would work out in the gym on a daily basses. He explained about the equipment that they used and how they used it. The whole time Patrick explained this, Roeman's mouth was wide open and he would look from his wife to Patrick in disbelief. "You're not kidding!" He turned his gaze on Sinsee, she just smiled at him. It seemed that he still did not know everything about his wife.

"Can you still do those things?" asked Jewbee.

"There is only one way to find out." said Patrick. "I'll have our old equipment sent from Terra Two. Quicker to send for it then it would be to manufacture it." He saw the look of doubt on Sinsee's face. "We can practice in private for a while. See if we still have it." He turned to the others. "Only after I am sure of our skills will I let you see for yourselves."

"Sounds reasonable." said Jewbee when she saw the look on Roeman's face. She could have sworn that Roeman was getting jealous of Patrick.

✴

Sinsee was amazed that her body remembered the moves so well. It felt great to be back on the bars again. Even holding the cross on the rings seemed as if it had only been days instead of years from the last time she had done this. Her muscles rippled with strength she did not remember.

It was Patrick who could not keep up with her. Sweat rolled off his face and he missed his dismount. "I give up! There is no way I can be ready by the day of the competition. You are going to have to do this one on your own."

"Maybe that is for the best Patrick. Watching their Chandler do this alone might be better for the kids." she told him. "Hay Patrick! Catch Me!" She did not give him much time to get ready for her and he almost missed her. They tumbled to the mat, Sinsee laughing all the way down.

"OK. You fly and I catch." he laughed. "How do you want to work this run out?" He got to his feet and helped her up off the mat. She worked out a pattern of flight from one peace of equipment to the next. "You sure you can keep up that kind of pace?" She assured him that she could. "OK. Lets try it."

Sinsee made it through the whole flight with only one mistake. They worked on it until she had it right ten times in a row.

"You sure are stronger now Sinsee. Maybe I should work out in the heavy gravity chamber more often." She told him that his body would not take that kind of abuse. "I think you might be right." he had to admit.

Roeman was made speechless by his wife's skill on the strange equipment. "And to think, I once thought of you as a helpless little girl."

Danny and Bethany both wanted to learn to do this new exercise. Even Kreeote and Reekee showed an interest in trying to use the parallel bars. When Roeman said that he wouldn't mind learning right along with the kids, Patrick's jaw dropped. "If it is alright with Patrick, I would rather teach you myself,

Roeman." said Sinsee. Knowing the difference between a normal human and a Millally human, Patrick was relieved that Sinsee would be teaching Roeman.

✳

The day of the competition arrived and Bethany was helping her mother dress in a leopard print skin tight body suit. Bethany asked her mom if she would look like that one day. Sinsee had to laugh.

"I believe you will be surprised at the difference only a few years will make. You are growing like a weed as it is now." Sinsee took Bethany to stand in front of the mirror, she stood behind her daughter. "See how much bigger you are now then you were just six months ago. You are out growing the clothes on your back. I thought Abby fit you with new clothes a few weeks ago. Why are you still wearing these?"

"The new clothes feel funny. Besides, I like these." said Bethany.

"Yes, but they don't fit you right anymore. I'll tell Abby to make you an outfit just like this one, only bigger, if this is what you really want." she told her.

"Can I have a suit like the one you have on?" Bethany turned to look up at her mother with those big dark eyes of hers. She had a sweet look on her face. The kind that an adult could not resist. Sinsee had to laugh again.

"Now you don't actually think that is going to work on me, do you. I'm the one who invented that look." Sinsee spun her daughter around to look in the mirror again. Bethany now had a very sad look on her face and Sinsee could not stand it anymore. She had been keeping something from Bethany. "Well if you want it so badly I guess you better go get changed then. You will find your very own leopard suit and over gown in your room. Abby is waiting for you there, to help you get into it." Bethany was out of her mother room in a shot and heading to her own room. She ran past her father in the hall almost bumping into him.

"Slow down there!" said Roeman as he side stepped his daughter. She ran past him saying that she couldn't stop now, she had to get dressed. "You look dressed to me." he called after her. He shook his head and turned to enter their bedroom when he got a look at Sinsee. He made a long drawn out whistle. "You look like you are part Catsman in that outfit. You do realize that all the Union Worlds will be watching this competition don't you? Everyone is going to be looking at you in that thing."

"Jealous? Because if you are, you should know that I had one of these made for all of us. Yours is in that box over there." she pointed to the box on the chair in the corner of the room. "They are for wearing when we work out on the gymnastic equipment."

"You mean I have to wear one of those things?" He had a shocked look on his face.

"Don't worry, yours is more masculine then the one I am wearing. Would you help me with this over gown? It turned out to be heavier then I expected." Roeman picked up the gown from off the bed, it was made of a thick brocade with Sinsee's favorite golden thread pattern running through it. The gown was more like a huge over coat then a dress. It had only one fastener in the front at the waist in the design of a Lions head.

"Wow! This thing weighs a ton. It's a good thing you wont be wearing it for too long. Even an AECS doesn't weigh this much." He helped her put the over gown on and she actually seemed to be alright with its weight. "I guess you have been spending a lot of time in the heavy gravity Chamber haven't you. I better start making time in my schedule for some work out in there myself so I can get back into shape. I've been so busy with the Union of Worlds Senators that I just haven't had any time for much else."

"You once told me that I didn't have to do it all by myself. You should take your own advice and let your aids handle most of the Senators." She put her hand on his cheek and kissed him lightly on the lips. "Stop trying to be the only one in control. Dee lets his boys do most of the work for him and his department runs along just fine."

"Dee is dealing with the ships and their crews. It's not the same thing as dealing with the Senators." said Roeman as he put his arms around her waist. "For now, I'll just make some time for us." He began to nuzzle her neck.

"Roeman, we have the competition this afternoon and you are not dressed yet." she lightly pushed him away from her as if she were reluctant to leave his embrace. "The people are expecting to see Lord Roeman in his uniform."

Roeman sighed. "Remind me to have someone change the design of my uniform. The neck line is so uncomfortable." Sinsee giggled at him. "What is so funny?" She told him to go have a look at his uniform. He went into their walk in closet. "Hey! When did you have this done?" He came out with his new uniform still on the hanger. It was still the same shade of blue but now it sported a new look. Instead of the stiff collar around the neck there was now a thin collar and a double row of gold buttons that connected a removable front panel trimmed in gold, epaulets adorned the shoulders and there was a sash that matched. A small emblem of the royal court was hand sewn over a breast pocket on the left. The cuffs were also trimmed in a fine gold thread pattern, and the same pattern ran down the outer seams of his trousers. Roeman kissed his wife and then started to get dressed.

When they were finished dressing they joined the others in the antechamber to the Great Hall. Bethany was dressed like her mother and Danny looked just like Roeman only now he was catching up to his father in height. Roeman took a good look at his children. He wondered how they had gotten so big. Danny was almost fifteen now, and Bethany was what, twelve, no, she was thirteen or close enough that it didn't matter.

Sinsee nodded and the doors to the Great Hall opened,

She and Roeman entered first with their children walking behind them. They made their way to the raised flooring and their seats. The young Catsman boys and girls lined the walls that encircled the hall. When everyone had settled down Sinsee rose to her feet and stepped foreword to the edge of the steps. She used her mind to reach out to the Catsman youths at the same time she spoke aloud.

"You see this field of battle." she drew her hand around the hall bringing everyone's attention to the equipment that was now bolted to the floor or hanging from the domed ceiling. "This I say to each of you. Know your own body and you shall truly know yourself." This was Patrick's signal to lower the rings from the ceiling, which he did. Then he went to stand at the foot of the stares.

Roeman came up to his wife and removed her gown coat and stepped back. Sinsee crouched down and then sprang up into the air, Patrick was there waiting for her and he caught her as she came out of a mid air somersault and flipped her body to end up standing with her back to him. At this point they both crouched and with Patrick's hands on her waist as they sprang upward he was able to give her just the right amount of lift that her hands grabbed the rings high above their heads.

Her movements were flawless, she swung her body up and into a perfect hand stand. The ropes the rings were attached to barely moved. She lowered her body until her shoulders were even with the rings, then she flipped around four times and pulled herself up into a perfect cross, still there was no movement of the rings as she held them out at the full length of her arms. She slowly lowered herself to hang by the rings, then up, over and into another spin this time with her legs split so that the ropes would wrap around her legs and she came up being supported by the ropes, her hands now free of the rings she started to spin twinning the ropes from the ceiling all the way down to where she was and then reversed the spin. The ropes stopped spinning at that every moment the twinning parted.

Patrick prepared himself for her dismount. She did one more body spin and dismounted in a backward flip. Patrick seemed to grab her out of the air as she came down to lightly touch the mat on the floor. The onlookers cheered and stomped the floor.

Not waiting for the cheering to die down, Sinsee took a flying run at the horse, she hit the jump spring and went into a triple foreword tuck and landed right at the foot of the bars. She was up and over before anyone had a chance the breath.

She spun her body back and forth between the bars. She held her hand stand for a good half minute then swung into her dismount. The balance beam came next. She cart wheeled across it never touching the beam with her hands. She dismounted with a flying wing and this time Patrick was ready for her.

Roeman was there at the end of her run and he draped her coat gown over her shoulders. Sinsee looked at the young boys and girls. "This is what it means to have skill, your body is your skill. Respect it!"

The cheers, clapping, and stomping followed Sinsee and Roeman back to their seats. Roeman leaned over to talk to Sinsee while her equipment was being replaced with the equipment that had been designed for the Catsman youth.

"I still find it hard to believe that you were doing this kind of thing when you were just a kid." he said in a soft voice..

"I was younger then Bethany when I first started to train with Patrick. To tell the truth, it was a lot more fun back then. Now it is just a lot of hard work." She was still breathing heavily from her run and Roeman signaled for someone to bring her a drink of high energy mix. She took a sip, it was cold and tasted of mixed fruits. She thanked him and downed the rest of the drink, then turned her attention to the main floor. The new equipment was now in place.

First came the larger males, who would fight in the boxing ring that was now in place. They had to put their hands and Feet into a machine that would coat them with an expandable fabric that the ZENTEX Tec's had come up with for just this purpose. It would prevent them from using their talons and cutting themselves to shreds. Their hands and Feet had to be shaved of all their fur. The only way to remove the coating was to peel it off and any fur that was coated would be painfully pulled away with the coating.

The males approached Sinsee and Roeman, bowing low, they then took their places by the boxing ring. They would go into the ring by twos. The one who walked out under his own power would advance to the next round.

The first two entered the ring and began to circle each other in an attempt to find the first advantage. Then in an instant they were joined. They bunched, they kicked, they even body slammed each other into the guard ropes. Within three minutes they both sported bloody snouts. They would not give up and the fight went on. It took longer then expected for one of them to finally go down, now the one left standing had to make it outside of the ropes before the other one could regain his feet. The apparent victor staggered to the ropes, almost falling as he did so. He grabbed the top rope and managed to climb through the ropes. As soon as he was on the other side the Hall was filled with the sound of stomping feet from the adult Catsman. It was there equivalent of cheering and clapping. There was a lot of that as well. And so it went for five sets of large males and in the end there were five winners.

The next weight class came foreword, first stepping up to the Tec's machine to receive their fabric coating. Sinsee was very grateful to the Tec's for coming up with the fabric coating. It was flexible and yet so strong you could not cut it, so it literally had to be sprayed on in a controlled environment, hence the machine that the youths now put their hands and feet into. The Tec's had even found a way to recycle the fabric.

Roman leaned over to whisper into Sinsee's ear. "Preegar told me that the alpha male and the alpha female will mate once they get past this stage of their development." Sinsee did not know that. It seem that the Catsman went from childhood to adulthood in a matter of weeks. She looked at the two who were now entering the ring. It was true, their growth had accelerated from the last time she had seen them when she and Roeman had made out the weight class roster just three weeks ago.

She watched this round with more interest. This pair seemed to be more evenly matched in their fighting skills. Then all of a sudden one of them took a flying leap at his opponent and planted his feet right in the middle of his chest sending him over the ropes and out of the ring. Medics came running up to help the boy, he was out cold.

Sinsee got to her feet and stepped foreword, she started to stomp her feet even before the standing boy made it to the outside of the ring. Roeman joined her and added his stomping feet to hers. The young male turned to face them and bowed deeply, he then left the ring. At the end of this weight class they had another five winners. Now it was the girls turn.

In the center ring stood an adult Catsman female, she would judge this round. The girls had only one objective, and that was to shove, push, or fling their opponent out of the marked circle, they would receive one point every time their opponent went out. The winner would need ten points to win. The first two girls faced off and the match was on. By now everyone in the hall was shouting for their favorite combatant. Even Sinsee's own heart raced as she watch these two females go at it. One would think that shoving and pushing was not as rough as what the males had just gone through but as it turned out, this was a long drawn out struggle that lasted a very long time. When a winner was finally declared, the two females were exhausted to the point of collapse. By the end of this round there were five more winners. Next would come the elimination rounds, but before that there would be a break to give the combatants time to rest and take nourishment, while preparations were being made for this round.

Meanwhile, on the many Union Worlds, bets were being wagered on who would make it through this next round. In bars, offices, restaurants, and homes, people had been jumping and shouting in an attempt to encourage one combatant or the other. It did not matter to them weather or not the combatant on Home Station could hear them. They raised their voices anyway.

In this next round there would be only two females that would make it to the finale round. For the males, two from the heavy weight class would go on, and the same from the next weight class. The workers had set up for the elimination round. A large cargo net now hung from the ceiling, at the top of the net there were two gold flags. This was not going to be easy, for the combatants had to climb the net, retrieve the flag and make it all the way back down the cargo net to the floor before being declared the winner. Two adult Catsman males stood at the corners of the cargo net and shook it violently while two more males came foreword with long poles that had been padded on the ends. It was their job to try and knock the combatants off the cargo net before they got out of reach. The floor under the net was piled high with mats to cushion their fall.

The first five winners stepped up to the net, it was Sinsee who set the mark and they were off. One male was gaining ahead of the others and a ramming pole knocked him down even with the others. A violent shake caused two of them to loose their footings, but they made a quick recovery. Another shake of the net and one of them had his leg slip through the net and he lost his grip, now he was dangling upside down, struggling to right himself. He pulled himself upright and continued to climb.

One male had now reached beyond the ramming poles and was almost at the top of the net and his goal, the gold flag. He made it, he got the flag, now all he had to do was make it down the net without loosing his flag to one of the other males.

Another male made it to the top and was now on his way down. The ramming poles were removed and the net was drawn tight. Now it was a battle for the two flag holders to get past the other three males and make it to the floor.

One of the males made a grab for the flag and lost his grip on the net, he fell to the mats on the floor. Now it was a one on one match as the two flag holders squared off against their opponents, each one trying to avoid that one set on taking the flag from them. One of them managed to get past his opponent and when he got close enough to the floor he jumped off the net. This left the other flag holder to deal with two opponents now.

The onlookers began to cheer him on even louder. Danny and Bethany added their voices to the fray. Roeman and Sinsee watched as the flag holder began to climb again, in an attempt to get away from the others. He worked his way to the edge of the net and swung himself around to the back side. As one of his opponents came even to him, he kicked through the net and sent the other falling to the floor. Now he had only one opponent to deal with.

His opponent stopped and assessed the situation, he decided to come at him on the back side of the net and to the side. As he came within reach of the flag holder, he shoved his leg through the net and grabbed the flag holder by the leg, he then pulled him off the net and they hung there upside down. He then lifted the flag holder until he could reach for the flag that was now draped through his opponent's belt. Once he got the flag he dropped his opponent to the mats below. Pulling himself to an upright position, he then waved the flag and started to make his way down the net. The stomping and cheering reverberated through the Hall. Sinsee leaned over to say something to Roeman and he nodded his head.

The next set of winners stepped up to the net, and it began all over again, only these boys seemed to be more agile on the net and managed to avoid the ramming poles. It did not take long and they had two more winners.

The ramming poles were removed and the net was once again drawn tight. The five females stepped up to the net, at Sinsee's signal they began to climb. The females started to pull, push, and even kick each other off the net even before anyone had reached the flags. It was a cat fight all the way to the top and then down again. Roeman lost count as to how many times the flags changed owners. During the whole climb up and down not one female was knocked off the net, but it wasn't for a lack of trying.

By the end of this round only four males and two females remained. Of the females, one would be the omega and the other would be the alpha of this generation of Catsman. With the males only one of the larger males would become the alpha male. From the next weight class would come the omega male. Now came the real test.

The water tank was rolled into place, from either side a short ladder led up to the plank that crossed the center of the tank. Once the combatants were at the top of the ladder they were handed padded rods with which to knock their opponent off the plank and into the water. Catsman do not like water. This point must be made clear.

With their foot covering now removed the two potential alpha males made their way out onto the plank. Their toe talons helping them to keep their balance on the greased plank.

To everyone who was watching, this was a very comical competition, but to the Catsman, who could not stand to be in water, It was a very frightening experience. Even for the adults who looked on, it was enough to have them shaking where they stood. Some of the viewers began to understand just what this meant to the Catsman and they thought it was a very cruel thing to do to them.

It didn't take long for one opponent to knock the other off the plank and into the water. Human hands quickly helped the loser out of the tank and rushed him away wrapped in blankets.

Next came the males who were competing for the omega position. They seemed more sure of themselves on the plank then the larger males had been. This bout proved to be more exciting then the first, because it took longer, but in the end there was only one winner.

The females were next. They climbed up the ladders and took the rods that were handed up to them. They started to inch their way out over the water, one of the girls looked down and started to back up. She was shaking her head. Only those humans with telepathic abilities knew what she was screaming. None of them ever revealed what had gone through her mind that day. She climbed down the ladder, waving her hands in front of her face. She had given the win to the other female, who then walked the full length of the plank to the other side.

The four winners were presented to Sinsee and Roeman. Standing beside their parents, Danny and Bethany held red velvet pillows. Resting on these pillows were gauntlets, two of which were made of silver and the other two were made of gold.

The alpha male and female came forward to receive the golden gauntlets from Sinsee. She picked up the gauntlets from the pillow that Bethany held for her mother, then raised them over the heads of the recipients. "You are the First, and will be taught to lead others of your age group. So say I." Sinsee thought and spoke the words at the same time. She then placed the gauntlets on the winners. Stomping feet reverberated through the Hall, and the alpha male and female stepped aside so that the omegas could come forward.

Roeman took the silver gauntlets from Danny's pillow and did the same for the omegas as Sinsee had done for the alphas. Again there was a round of stomping feet in the Hall as the four winners stepped back and turned to face the rest of the Hall, lifting their gauntleted right hands high in the air. Before leaving the Hall they once again faced Sinsee and Roeman, bowing as deeply as they could and grinning as only the Catsman could.

The stomping of feet and the roaring of Lions could be heard all over the station. For the first time in The Catsman memory, the right of passage into adulthood had not claimed a single life.

A celebration was held on the station that night. The new alpha and omega pairs sat at the head of the table with their High Chandler and her family. It seemed that everyone on the station had come up to them to congratulate them and admirer their gauntlets. Pats on their backs were like hand shakes for the Catsman, and they received so many that Sinsee feared they would have black and blue marks on their backs come the morning.

After a well earned dinner there was music and dancing. There was even some good natured arm wrestling going on for those who wanted to prove themselves, but when Tiny sat down to get in on the fun, there were no takers. Even Roeman shook his head when Tiny asked him to have a go.

"You're just going to have to face the fact that you are in a class all by your self my old friend." Roeman slapped Tiny on the back. "But I will have a drink with you, even though I know that you can out drink me as well." laughed Roeman, as he and Tiny headed for the bar.

All in all, it had been a very exciting day.

✳

Somewhere out in the cold depths of space, Captain Lane was leap forging her ship every three weeks, just behind her scout shuttle. She nodded to Sebastian and he folded the ship to the last transmitted view they had received from the scout. The ship popped in just beyond a massive asteroid belt.

"Give me a close up of that belt." she ordered. The screen zoomed in for a closer look, something glinted back at them from one of the larger asteroids. "Zoom in closer on that big one." She leaned foreword in her chair.

"Captain, is that what I think it is?" asked Sebastian from his seat at the fold control panel.

"Now don't get your hopes up, Sebastian. Lets get a sample onboard for analysis before we go jumping to conclusions." admonished his captain, but her heart was racing just like everyone else on the bridge.

Lane sent out the next shuttle crew in AECS's to retrieve a chunk of that asteroid and bring it back to the ship. The time it took for the shuttle to reach the asteroid and get back to the ship was the longest time Lane or anyone on the ship had ever spent. It was as if time had slowed down.

As Sebastian analyzed the mineral content of the rather large chunk of clear crystal, Lane hovered over him like a worried mother hen. Other crewmembers gathered around the open hatch to his lab. He put down his tools and picked up the fist size stone and tossed it to Lane. "It is just what I thought it was." He looked up at Lane as she turned the large stone over in her hand. "What you are holding there is the largest diamond anyone has ever seen, and there were other gems inside that chunk the crew brought back." He smiled up at Lane. "Care to do a little space mining Captain?"

"Hell yes!" She turned to one of the men standing in the hatchway. "Ben! Get all the AECS's out of storage and get all the shuttles prepared for shift work. I want as much of that asteroid in our holds as we can get in there. We're going into the mining business!" Ben gave her a sharp salute and headed down the passageway. "I think I'll make a call to Home Station and get as many ships out here as we can. You want to say hello to the folks at home Sebastian?" she asked him as she tossed the diamond into the air and caught it in her other hand.

"I wouldn't miss this for anything." He smiled and looked

over to where Destiny lay in the corner of his lab. "What about it girl. You think they will be pleased with this find?" Destiny roared her approval of contacting Home Station and sent Sebastian an image of Roeman and Sinsee jumping up and down. "You might not be to far off on that one." he said to Destiny.

Lane had become accustom to the private conversations between Sebastian and Destiny, what she still had a problem with was when Destiny roared within the confines of the ship. Her ears were still ringing as they made there way to the bridge.

Roeman was trying to wipe the sleep from his eyes as he took the call from Captain Lane. "This better be good Lane. We have had a long day here and a long night to go with it."

She held up the stone to the screen. "Would you care to guess what this is?" she asked him. He knew she would not be asking him that question unless she already knew the answer. His eyes focused on the stone. "And we have got bigger ones then this that are being extracted as we speak."

"Extracted from where?" he asked her. Lane switched the screen to an outside view and Roeman got his first look at the asteroid belt. The screen zoomed in on a work crew who were working on what looked like a vain of pure gold the width of five men.

"Sinsee! Wake up! Wake up! You have got to see this!"

As tired as everyone was, the docking bays were in a state of pandemonium. Ships were being loaded with supplies, equipment, and extra shuttles to be sent out to meet Miss Destiny, Captained by Captain Lane. Ships were sent out as soon as they could be loaded.

Personal from the mining consortium were inspecting each piece of equipment before it was loaded onto the ships.

They couldn't wait to get to the belt, even though they knew that they would not be allowed to leave the ships, it was just to dangerous for them. They had settled for coordinating the work from the safety of the ships.

By the next afternoon Miss Destiny had returned to Home Station with the first of many ships with there holds full the mined asteroids precious metals and gems.

Lane requested some well earned R&R for herself and her crew. Roeman said that they could do anything they wanted to do, he was not surprised when he learned that they had taken the Miss Destiny to Terra Two and had spent their entire leave at Seenan's Rail Rider Park.

Chapter Eight

THERE HAD BEEN MORE then just one ship playing the leap frog game. Captain Tankfull and his new ship, The Upper Class, had been mapping the stars from a different vector out from the planet Antella.

"Alright, Antella." he looked at his twin telampathices. "Take your time and your views from the shuttle, when you are ready, fold to his location." The twins nodded and focused their attention on the small screen before them, the bridge began to shimmer.

The Upper Class reappeared outside of a system that had thirteen planets. Three giants, two ringed, four frozen, one red, and three blue marbles. "It looks like we hit the jackpot." said Tankfull. "Bring the shuttle in Antella and have the pilot report to me in the mess." Tank left the bridge and headed down to the mess with a spring in his step. The twins smiled at each other and then got back to work.

The shuttle pilot walked into the mess room and spotted his captain at one of the table in the back. Tank waved him over to the table. Talbit dropped his hat down on one of the chair and sat down across from his captain. Tank poured him a cup of coffee from the decanter on the table and handed him the cup. Talbit took a sip and then leaned back in his chair.

"Well, what did it feel like coming up on that system?" Tank leaned forward in his chair and placed his arms on the table, waiting for an answer.

"Tank, have you ever had the shakes?" Talbit held out his hand so that his captain could see that he was still shaking from the experience. He took another sip from the coffee cup. Tank had added some of his own personal stock to the coffee. "At first I thought I was seeing things, so I kept checking the scanners the closer I got to the system." He reached for the decanter and refilled his cup then filled tank's cup. "Gees Tank. Three of them! Can you believe the luck?"

"You want to talk about luck, wait until you hear what the Miss Destiny has been up to." Tank filled Talbit in on what had been going on in the other direction. "I thought about pulling you in and heading off to join the fun but then I thought about all that hard work. Now I'm glad I didn't pull you in. We'll take the ship in for a closer look at those worlds. See if there is any signs of life. Hopefully we just might have our own colony world that we can lay claim to."

"Luck seems to be on our side ever sense the High Chandler came to us, so there is no reason to think it will fail us now." said Talbit.

Tank topped off their cups one more time. "To the luck of our High Chandler, may she rule forever!" They raised their cups and then drank them down. "Well, lets go have a look at these worlds you found."

Only one of the blue planets proved to have some form of higher life form. There were artificial landing that extended out into the waterways, and cultivated fields and orchards could also be seen from the fly by probes. There were no sings of any buildings or even primitive huts for that matter. What life forms they did see could not have possibly been responsible for the cultivated fields and orchards.

Tank contacted Roeman and gave him his report on what they had found. Roeman made the decision that this world should be left alone. He told Tank to concentrate on the other two worlds and let him know if they could be colonized, Tank said, will do, and cut the connection.

Good news was good news, and Roeman sure needed that right now. The Union of Worlds was climbing down his neck about the asteroid belt. Each one felt that they had a right to a share in the wealth that was coming out of the belt.

Roeman had completely lost it with one of the Senators who was being very belligerent. Roeman had ordered that the man be taken and put into an AECS and shoved out an airlock. It took Sinsee six hours to convince Roeman to bring the man back inside the station.

Roeman faced the man as he was brought back inside the station. "That is the environment that my people are working in! Now, tell me one more time what gives you the right to that wealth and I'll put you out there without the benefit of an AECS."

The subdued Senator had taken the first ship he could get on that would take him to his home world and he never came back. His replacement was a gentle, soft spoken woman, who seemed to understand the pressures Roeman was under from the other Senators. A few well timed words from her and things quieted down and no more was said about who the wealth of the asteroid belt belonged to. Sinsee liked this new Senator.

Tank confirmed that the other two worlds could be colonized. Roeman sent word to the other worlds in the Union that two new worlds were going to be opened for colonization. Volunteers would be needed to establish new settlements on these worlds. A screening program would be set up on each Union World for those who wanted to colonize the new worlds. Only ten thousand applicants would be excepted at first. These first must have construction skills, hydro energy skills, infrastructure knowledge, and support skills such as medical, maintenance, cooks and the like. Families of the applicants could accompany them to the new worlds.

Roeman told Sinsee that the screening process was to weed out the riff raff. There was no need to tell those who were turned down the reason for their rejection.

✳

Captain Duvale came across a system that had four worlds. When he contacted Roeman to tell him what he had found the look on his face told Roeman that something was wrong. "I'm not really sure how to put this." said Duvale as he rubbed his chin. "Lord Roeman, I think we found the Catsman home world." he lowered his gaze. "It is a dead world alright. Along with the entire population. I think someone should come out here and look at this."

"I will come out myself and I think I should bring Preegar with me. Send me a visual to fold to." Roeman set his screen to record, and Duvale sent the visual. Roeman contacted Captain Lane. "Captain, I have a favor to ask of you. I need you to take me somewhere."

"Sure Lord Roeman, any where you want to go, but don't you usually use New Home?" she asked him.

"Not this time." He explained about where he was going and what Duvale had said.

"I see what you mean. Most of the Catsman have taken to living on New Home. OK, I'll be there shortly."

"Thank you Lane." After talking to Lane, Roeman contacted Jewbee and told her the news. "Would you and Preegar please join me on Miss Destiny, she will be in Bay Eighty." Jewbee said that they would be there.

Roeman touched Sinsee's mind, he told her what he was going to do and asked if she wanted to join them. [{"I don't think I should Roeman. Not in my condition, I was going to tell you tonight but.]} She left her words unfinished.

[{I might be gone for a few days. I'll check in with you

as often as I can. I love you my wife.}] He felt her leave his mind and suddenly he felt very much alone. He took out the recording and put it in his breast pocket and headed for Bay Eighty where Miss Destiny was docked.

Jewbee and Preegar were waiting for Roeman, the three of them entered the ship in silence and walked to the bridge where they found Captain Lane and Sebastian. "Take us out." said Roeman. Once the ship was out of the docking bay and in clear space Roeman handed Sebastian the recording disk. "Take us there lad."

Sebastian played the recording and a shiver went through his body, he looked at Roeman who only nodded once. Sebastian engaged the fold engine that would take them to a planet that would have otherwise taken countless generations to reach. They now had a good idea how far away the planet Antella was from Home Station. Very far indeed.

Roeman and the others joined Captain Duvale on his ship, The White Dove. Captain Duvale met them in his docking bay and said that he wished that they were meeting under different circumstances. He looked at Preegar. "I am very sorry that we have to meet this way Sir. I admire your people greatly."

Jewbee translated for Preegar by mind touch, she then spoke for him. "We thank you for your kindness. Do not concern yourself over much. We have always known that our home world was a dead planet." Roeman put his hand on Pregger's arm. He touched his mind and Preegar stiffened. "I must see this thing." Jewbee said out loud for Preegar.

"Yes," said Duvale. "If you will follow me, you can be fitted with AECS's. There is no atmosphere on the planets surface."

The trip to the surface was spent in complete silence. As the shuttle came in over the land mass they could see dwellings, land transports, everything one would expect to see on a populated world except life. With no atmosphere on the planet everything was perfectly preserved, including the corpses of the now mummified population, the bodies lay or sat everywhere.

The group stood just outside the shuttle on the biggest space port they had ever seen. Countless ships, just like New Home, lay cradled in their launching stanchions. Their numbers went on right into the horizon, the mass and volume were almost incomprehensible. It was Sebastian who broke the silence of the group.

"I believe I know what happened here." The others looked at him. "These ships are to large to be launched into space. Their regular engines could never produce enough thrust to brake away from the gravity pull of the planet. These ships should have been built in space."

"Then how did New Home get off this world?" asked Jewbee.

"The original crew must have used the fold engines on the planets surface. That created an open vortex into space which sucked the atmosphere away from the planet." Sebastian shook his head. "It must have been horrible for the Catsman crew when they realized what had happened. Their launch of New Home had killed everyone on this world."

"Perhaps this is why we have no record of our history." Preegar spoke through Jewbee. Roeman asked if he wanted the others to know of this. [{"Yes, they have a right to know everything."}]

"Do we want to use these other ships?" asked Duvale. Roeman looked at Preegar who nodded his consent.

"It will take a lot of work to get even one of them ready. The first thing we need to do is see to the dead." Roeman looked around them. There were a number of bodies laying on the tarmac. Everything was covered in a fine dust perhaps one quarter of an inch thick. Dust was still settling back down from the disturbance of the shuttles landing on the tarmac.

[{I believe my people will want to help with the dead.}]

said Preegar. [{After all, it was our ancestors who caused this. It is fitting that we should be the ones to bring this to an end by honoring the dead."}]

[{I understand Preegar, but you are so few. I will ask my people to join yours in this endeavor. We will make the arrangements when we return to the ship. First lets have a look at one of those ships and see if its like New Home on the inside as well as the outside."}] Jewbee didn't want to go with them so Duvale stayed with her on the shuttle while the others went to have a look at the closest ship. Roeman had hoped that there was a cryo chamber on the ship to match the one on New Home, complete with embryos and gestation tanks. Unfortunately the power cells that powered the chamber had failed.

✶

"I am sorry for Preegar and his people." said Sinsee, as she looked at her screen and the image of her husband. "How many ships have you checked?"

"Just the one for now." Roeman scratched his chin. "I don't know about the other ships and their cryo chambers."

"It is possible that there still are some with working power cells. I know you said that we should see to the dead first, but we should check all those chambers first. There still might be a chance no mater how slim." said Sinsee. "I take it you have already got the word out about the hazard of using a fold engine in an atmosphere."

"Bad news travels faster then folding space. Now I am really glad we didn't let the Tec's put fold engines in the shuttles." said Roeman. "Sinsee, do you remember what you said about history. Those who forget history are bound to repeat it. This is one part of history we don't want to repeat."

"No one will forget this. I will see to that." said Sinsee. "When are you coming home?"

"I will stay here until the relief ships get here. Then I have one more stop to make. I want a good look at Lightenglow's ship." said Roeman.

"Yes, I was wondering about that myself. How did he get all the way out there?" Sinsee's eyebrows dipped.

"Did the Tec's locate the position of Antella in reference to the known galaxy?" asked Roeman as she perked his interest.

"Brace yourself Roeman. You are no longer in our arm of the galaxy. In fact, you are on the other side in the outer rim." She waited for this information to sink in. "I have had the Tec's recheck their calculations and they are very surprised with the results. They didn't think their communications system was that powerful. So, I guess you could say this is the longest communication we have ever had." Her sense of humor was not lost on Roeman.

"Just goes to show you the length I will go to just to hear your voice." He watched the smile cross her face but it did not stay there long. Duvale signaled for his attention. "Looks like help has just arrived. I'll talk to Preegar and see how he feels about checking the ships before they see to the dead. I want to have one more look myself. Maybe we can use the ships and their atmosphere scrubber to rejuvenate the planets atmosphere. Bring it back to life."

"It is a nice thought Roeman, but is it really worth the effort?" she asked him.

"Maybe not. This was once a beautiful world. I have to wonder why they wanted to leave it." Roeman had recorded their flight to the space port and intended to study that recording further. "I will see you in the morning." Sinsee turned her screen off and went to see what the kids were up to.

Roeman told Captain Lane that he wanted to make one more stop before returning to Home Station. Sebastian not only folded the ship to Antella but he accompanied Roeman to Lightenglow's little Island. From the beach line there now ran a stone walkway into the jungle all the way to the ship. As they came upon the ship they could see that a small monolith had been erected and had been inscribed in the memory of Dr. Lightenglow.

While they were going over the engine compartment they were interrupted by a man who had been stationed there to keep an eye on things and keep the path from being over grown by the encroaching jungle. The rest of his team were out in the jungle collecting samples of the many plants that covered the island. When he saw that it was Lord Roeman in the ship he put his laser pistol back into its holster. While Sebastian continued to look over the engine Roeman had a talk with the man who had been left in charge of the area.

"Found it," said Sebastian. "It is not completely like the ones we are using but Dr. Lightenglow used a fold engine. There is no doubt about it."

"There is only one group of humans who could have developed a fold engine." Roeman looked at Sebastian. "So his first children on ZENTEX were smarter then we thought. They had to be, to avoid the government agents from earth and then later on from their own government." Roeman dismissed the man who had interrupted them and he turned back to Sebastian. "I have something I want you to do for me. After you drop me off at Home Station I want you to go to ZENTEX. I think that the government there is still trying to pull the strings of the Tec's that remained on ZENTEX. We sent them Dr. Lightenglow's medical notes and journals. They have had more then enough time to brake the codes. Tell them that we already know where the Tec's came from. Let them know that I am tired of them stone walling me. I want those translations on my desk in three days or I will do to Them what was done to the Catsman home world."

Sebastian looked at Roeman with opened mouth. "Sir, you wouldn't take a fold engine down onto ZENTEX would you?"

"I have taken a lot from the ZENTEX government for the sake of the Tec's. You and I both know that all the telampathices are ZENTEX Tec's. I doubt that any of them would do such a thing. No matter what order I would give them. But remember Sebastian, I am both telepathic and Telampathic." He sent Sebastian a vision of what he looked like just then. "Tell them no more games. Remind them that I have held nothing back from them, that I have given freely to them and have called them brothers. Ask them if this is the right way to treat a brother. I know that you are true Sebastian. I do not distrust you because of the love Destiny has for you. But your leaders are a different matter."

"If what you say about the notes and journals is true, I will get to the bottom of this." Sebastian stood tall before Roeman. "This one thing you should know. You and the High Chandler are my Leaders. I owe no allegiance to the ZENTEX government." Sebastian turned and walked out of the engine room. Roeman, wearing a big smile, walked out behind him.

Sebastian was nobodies fool, so when he went to ZENTEX to visit his former government he took half the ships crew with him, armed to the teeth.

When he had to force his way into the chambers of the ruling government, there were a large number of people who ended up needing a stay in the Medical Unit's the government had hoarded for so many years.

The ZENTEX Leaders started to threaten Sebastian, telling him that he and his brother would spend the rest of their lives in prison. Sebastian shoved one of them back down into his chair and told the rest of them to shut up. One by one they took their seats.

"Times change!" he told them. "My Lord Roeman had been more then fair with you. He has even shared the wealth of the Belt with you. Something he has not done for any of the other worlds. Shall I tell you why?" Sebastian told them how the Lord Roeman had kept the secret of the ZENYEX Tec's origin. Brothers of the same father creator. "And how is it you repay this Lord, you deceive him with your lies and deception. Now let me tell you of a discovery that the Lord Roeman has just made, and what he intends to do should you ever try to deceive him again."

By the time Sebastian was finished with this meeting, he had more cooperation then he knew what to do with. He also arranged for his brother to join him back at Home Station. Just in case.

When Sebastian returned to Home Station he presented Roeman with a full translation of all of Dr. Lightenglow's work, including an encrypted diary that had been hidden inside one of the Medical Journals.

Chapter Nine

Sɪɴsᴇᴇ ʜᴀᴅ ʙᴇᴇɴ ᴍᴏʀᴇ interested in the encrypted diary then the medical data. Parry and his team on the other hand were delighted to have codes that finally made sense to them. At least for a while. They ran into an enigma that would take some time to work through. Parry was in his element and happy as a clam.

Sinsee on the other hand spent hours going over Lightenglow's personal diary. She found that if she took only certain passages from his entries a very interesting story began to emerge. Inside Lightenglow's diary, Sinsee found her own enigma.

2918ADH

Day241

My work with the unsuspecting mothers is progressing well. Brain wave activity of the fetuses is reading over 310 entering third trimester. I will start the bio feedback tomorrow to reduce stress.

2918ADH
Day253
We lost a mother and twins to a freak accident on the transport underground. 278 people were killed when the train derailed.

2918ADH
Day310
Twenty nine sets of twins all born within a two week time frame. Brain wave activity stabilizing between 460 and 500.

2922ADH
Day47
I am taking the twins and their parents into the back lands with me. There have been to many questions about the twins. I recognized the Earth agent leaving the home of subjects 19. Fortunately he did not see me.

2933ADH
Day182
The twins have far exceeded my own expectations. Their ability to over come any scientific problem is amazing. They have even developed their own language.

2938ADH
Day10
There was a stranger in the settlement to the south of us last week. He was asking questions of the locals. I have kept the twins isolated from any contact with the local people. Who ever the stranger was, he did not get any information from the locals.

2938ADH
Day57
The stranger was back again. The twins believe he is

looking for me. They are working on a plan to get me off world and make everyone think I have died in one of my own experiments.

2938ADH
Day110
The twins have presented me with a small artificial womb. They have also supplied me with frozen ovi and sperm. I did not ask them where they got it from. The ship is almost ready for me to take off. I keep looking over my shoulder for that agent from Earth.

2938ADH
Day128
We have got people headed this way. I am going to launch the ship and drew their attention away from the others as they make good their escape. I am going to miss my children.

2938ADH
Day129
The new jump engine worked just fine. I am sending out the remote probe ahead of the ship. If I can get a clear reading from the probe, I will make my next jump.

2939ADH
Day37
I have found a new world that is uninhabited. I am going to start my work all over again and this time no one will interfere with it.

2961ADH
Day271
I am afraid that my ship will be seen from space if this world is ever discovered. I have decided to leave here and let my perfect children remain hidden. They understand about

humans. I am sure that if this world is found by the humans that my children will remain out of sight. I have not got to many more years left in me. All I need is some small place where I can just rest.

2963ADH
Day unknown
Old habits are hard to brake. I have been altering the genetic codes of a small life form on the island. I have managed to increase its IQ levels to the sentient level. They may not be able to speak my language, but they understand me well enough. They fly around the little garden I planted and keep it free of what bugs there are here. I am so tired. I think I will go out and take a nap in the shade. First good weather we have had sense I got here and it is hotter then all get out.

Sinsee put down the file and looked at Roeman who sat across from her. "So he went to Antella to protect his perfect children. If he didn't think of the twins as being perfect, just what would he have considered to be perfect?"

"Who knows." said Roeman. "Parry and Patrick are going over his DNA file codes right now, trying to get an idea as to what these perfect children might be capable of doing. If we ever do find them, I don't want any surprises."

"Do we have any information on his field of study when he first started his work, other then genetics, I mean?" she asked him.

"No, the only other things he ever had any interest in was gardening and fly fishing." Roeman smiled at her.

"What?" she asked him.

"It is just when I heard about the fly fishing I thought it had something to do with fish that fly. Patrick had to explain it to me." Roeman squinted at her. Sinsee had to bite her lip to keep from laughing at Roeman, but when he started to laugh at himself she joined him.

"Roeman, if you would like, I could teach you how to fly fish on our next vacation." That made him laugh even more.

✳

Sector Marshal Dee invited Roeman to a small gathering of some of the older Captains. "Sort of a for old time sake party." said Dee. "Just a few of us old timers. Lane, Duvale, Burton, Tank and myself. If you join us that will make six. We can brake out a deck of cards and I can take everyone's credits away from them, just like old times."

"Oh Ya!" said Roeman. He wondered if he could use his new talents to find out what everyone's cards were. "We will just see about that. Where is this party going to be held?" Roeman told Sinsee where he was going and that he might not be back for a while. He took the Halley's Rail over to the third sphere and arrived at Dee's quarters the same time as Lane and Duvale. Tank and Burton were late, same as always. Tank had a bottle of his personal stock with him. He and Burton had already cracked the seal on the bottle.

Dee broke out a new deck of cards and dealt the first hand. Talk around the table varied from subject to subject. Burton had trouble at first with his telampathices, but they were working it out now. "Every time they would talk to me I used to get dizzy trying to see which one was talking. Now I just look at their hands." He turned to Roeman. "Did you know they can carry on two different conversations at the same time? You should have seen the look on their faces when I used that hand language of theirs to give them an order while I was talking to Jessup at the same time. It really set them off."

"Are you telling us that you actually understand that hand code of theirs?" Tank didn't believe Burton so he gave them a demonstration. They all watched him as he hand signed what he was speaking out loud.

"This really isn't that hard to learn. I can articulate most anything I want to say using my hands alone. What is hard is speaking and signing something else at the same time." At this point he stopped signing. "I spent long hours practicing before I tried it out on the twins."

"Can you teach others this language?" asked Roeman. Burton said that he could. He would make a film recording of what he knew so far and send it to Roeman. "Send it to Sinsee, she has more time to study it then I do."

Lane changed the subject and asked Tank about the new colony worlds. She had not had a chance to get out that way yet and wanted to know what they looked like. He told them about Talbit's reaction as he came up on the system. "He was still shaking when he joined me". Tank did not bother to tell them that he and Talbit had gotten stinking drunk. He did describe, in order of the farthest planet out from the G type star right down to the closest to that star each planet in full detail. When he described the third planet and what they saw from the probes, Roeman became very interested and listened intently, that was when he missed Dee slipping a card out of the deck. Dee won that hand and Roeman could not figure out how.

When Roeman stumbled back to their quarters in the late hours of the night, Sinsee and the kids were sound asleep. He undressed, tossing his clothes into a corner and climbed into bed, trying his best not to wake Sinsee. She was having morning sickness again so they knew that she was going to have another boy. The moment Roeman's head hit the pillow he was asleep. Sinsee rolled over and draped her arm around him without waking up.

The next morning Sinsee woke up first and picked up his discarded clothes and put them into the laundry bin. She made sure the kids got off to their classes on time and then she went to have a shower. While she was in the shower Roeman came in and joined her.

After the shower they went into the dinning room and had a light breakfast and coffee. Sinsee asked him how the game went. He told her that at least this time he had broken even with Dee.

"Burton will be sending you a film. He broke the hand code of the twins on his ship. Maybe you can teach it to others. It would come in handy with the Catsman and those who can't mind touch with them. I think that is why most of the Catsman are living on New Home now." Roeman could not blame them, there were times he wished that he was back on the Antiack himself. Even Sinsee had had to order the majority of the back doors of so many of the offices in the center sphere sealed off from access to her private corridor. Home Station was beginning to feel rather cramped.

"I agree with you there. A common language would be of tremendous help." Sinsee pored more coffee for them both. "Did Burton say when he was going to have this film for me?"

"No, but you might want to contact him and work something out with him. I told him you were better at this kind of thing then I was." Roeman picked up a small piece of fruit out of the glass bowl on the table. With one bite half the fruit was gone, then he popped the other half into his mouth and it to was gone. "There is something else that has been nagging me at the back of my mind. Something that Tank said." Roeman described the third world of Tank's new worlds and Sinsee eyes blinked rapidly. Roeman knew that she was thinking at a rate that put him to shame. He sat there watching her for over ten minutes. When she did move it was the spread of a smile that filled her face and that smile told Roeman she had figured something out.

"He wanted to create the most perfect beings. Perfection. I know who they are. The most perfect beings are those who have no reason to lie or cheat or cause harm to any other living thing. They would fear nothing because they could go where others can not. Lightenglow was creating the Millally when the government took over his project. Terra Two's doctors used that same program and took it a few steps further. Telepathic! That was what Lightenglow was doing. Creating the perfect society" said Sinsee. "Perfection!"

"So where are they?" Roeman looked at his wife as she began to shake with excitement.

"I think we need to go see Parry and Patrick today. If I am right, and I know that I am. I think we just found Lightenglow's perfect children." said Sinsee.

"You still have not told me where they are!" Roeman followed Sinsee out of their quarters. She would not answer him until she had talked to Dr. Parry and Patrick.

They entered the lab in the research section of the hospital where Patrick and his father were working.

"Hi. What brings you here?" Patrick got to his feet when they came in, a pile of papers fell off his work area onto the floor. He bent down to pick them up and Sinsee walked right past him without acknowledging that he was even there. Patrick looked at Roeman who just shrugged his shoulders as if to say, you have got me.

Sinsee stood before Parry and for the first time in his life Parry felt uncomfortable. "Doctor, that encrypted DNA code you have been working on. Is there or is there not an aquatic signature in it?"

Parry was taken back by her question. "How did you…but I just now found… Are you reading my mind?"

"Of course!" roared Roeman. "Any sensor readings would discount them as just another aquatic life form and ignore them."

Sinsee turned to Roeman, pleased that he had finally figured it out. "Yes, a telepathic aquatic life form. The perfect beings."

"I think I am missing something here." Patrick said as he looked at Roeman with a perplexed look on his face. Roeman started to laugh and he looked at the expression on Parry's face which sent him into a side splitting roar. When he got himself under control, he and Sinsee sat down and explained how she had come to this logical conclusion.

"So now what do we do?" asked Parry.

"We make first contact." Sinsee told them. "I think I should be the one to do this. I still am the strongest telepath so far. Bethany has a strong mind voice but it still does not match mine."

[{Give her some time and I believe she will surprise you.}] Roeman touched her mind and there was a sense of humor in that touch.

Before Roeman and Sinsee set out for Tank's third world, word came in from the Catsman home world. Twenty ships had been found so far with their cryo chambers still operational. Back up power cells had been set up to augment the older power cells on these ships. Crews on sight were requesting additional help so Roeman put the word out and he was surprised when more then half the fleet wanted to go and help out. Many of the senators offered teams of engineers to help with power supplemental work needed to keep the chambers from shutting down. The Tec's who had remained on ZENTEX offered to lend their skills in this endeavor. Roeman had to remind them that there was no atmosphere on that world and the workers had to be in AECS's at all times. At that point most of the senators backed down, but those who did not were granted the chance to see what they could do.

Roeman talked to the Tec's and told them about his idea of using the gigantic ships atmosphere scrubbers to rejuvenate the planet. They told him that it could be done if there were enough ships to be placed around the planet. Roeman enjoyed telling them about the vast number of ships, so many that you could not see them all as they went from horizon to horizon. The Tec's could not wait to get to the Catsman home world.

Sinsee checked with the kids to see if they wanted to join her and their father on this trip. Bethany said that she had her final exams to study for and Danny was just starting his new job for Sector Marshal Dee. Sinsee had to resign herself that her kids were no longer kids. Bethany was now at the same age she was when she had been brought onto the Antiack for the first time. Danny had already moved into his own quarters in the forth sphere and Sinsee suspected that he had a friend who would stay with him on occasion. Her children were grown up now. She put her hand on her stomach. "Well I still have you." she said to the fetus now growing within her. Sinsee loved being a mother and if it were up to her she would have as many children as she could. Right now she had to pack an overnight bag and join up with Roeman.

Once again Captain Lane was making her ship available for them. As Sinsee, along with Abby by her side, walked up the ramp and into Destiny which was now dock in Bay Eighty, she wondered if this trip would have any effect on her unborn child.

Lane had a standing berth in that bay now and even when her ship was out no one was allowed to dock at her berth. She had bullied the docking control saying that sense her ship was the one that the Lord Roeman made use of more then any other she had more then enough right to her own personal berth. Sector Marshal Dee agreed with her and she got her berth.

While Abby took their things to their cabins Sinsee made her way to the bridge. As she entered the bridge Sebastian was talking to Roeman. Lane walked over to her and gave her a little hug. "Congratulations, Roeman tells me that you are going to have another child." She stepped back and took a good look at Sinsee. "You don't show at all. How far along are you?"

"Just a little over a month." Sinsee looked over to where Roeman and Sebastian were so deep in conversation that they had not even noticed her entry onto the bridge. "What are they so wrapped up in?"

"More word came in from the Catsman home world. Seems that the Tec's want to use almost all the big ships but before they can bring them on line to generate an atmosphere they need to clean out the scrubbers and the algae tanks. The problem is that there is no algae to replace what was destroyed." said Lane. "Sebastian says that there isn't enough algae anywhere to fill all those ships."

Sinsee went over to join them. "I can't believe the two of you. You want everything now. I knew that this was a bad idea." She got some sour looks from both of them. "If you are so dead set on this project I suggest that you change your time line. It is not as if you have to have this thing done by the end of this year. You are not fighting a clock here. There are no lives at stake. Take your time and cultivate the algae tanks. And before you say anything Sebastian, I am well aware of the growth rate of algae. Even the type needed for the oxygen production. We may never see that world brought back to life, but that does not mean that our grandchildren wont."

"She is right." said Sebastian. "I guess you can call them back and give them the bad news." He was looking right at Roeman.

"At least they can move those ships to where they will be needed." said Roeman. "But after they get to where they are going I want those fold engines removed from them. There will be no repeat of a fold on planet."

"What did you just say?" asked Sebastian.

"I said there will be no repeat of a fold on planet. Why are you looking at me like that?" asked Roeman.

"Atmosphere, Place, Place, Same, Same." Sebastian was so excited that he had returned to speaking in Tec's syntax.

"Hold up there boy! We can't understand a word you are saying." Roeman turned to Sinsee. "Don't just stand there, get inside his head or something."

"I don't need to." she looked at Roeman with a smile on her face. "He is broadcasting all over the place. Open up Roeman, you can see it in his mind." The three of them stood there on the bridge and sent views back and forth for a good ten minutes until Lane had had just about enough of this.

"Hay! When are you three going to let the rest of us in on this. It really isn't fare that you leave me out." Lane was pouting, she did not like being on the out side on her own bridge.

"I am sorry Captain." said Sebastian, who now had control of himself. "It's the fold engines. I never thought of it before. We can move from one vacuum point to another, right? What we can't do is move from a vacuum into an atmosphere. What if we can move from an atmosphere into an atmosphere?"

"What? You have got to be kidding! How the hell can you test something like that? And what world would let you even attempt such a thing knowing what we know now." Lane was shaking her head.

"We have one world that we could launch from, and there are the two new colony worlds. We have only started colonizing one of them at the moment." said Roeman.

"You want to risk a new colony world on this hair brained idea!" Lane tossed up her hands.

"We don't have to move from planet to planet." said Sinsee. "Antella is the perfect place for the test." Sinsee had to duck as a small bird zipped down from somewhere in the ceiling to tap her on the head. "You have a butterfly bird! Where did you get it?"

"We were the ones who found Antella, remember." said Lane. "I don't think she likes the thought of you using her home world for your experiment any more then I do."

Sinsee looked at the bird now perched on Lane's shoulder. "She is beautiful. Can I hold her?"

"That is up to her." said Lane. "She is mad at you right now."

"She is one of Lightenglow's little life forms. He said that they were very smart. Jewbee took the pair that came in from Antella. Alright sweet thing, we will find some where else to test Sebastian theory." When Sinsee said that the little bird zipped over to land on her out stretched hand. "Maybe we should stop over at Antella so that I can get one of these little darlings for myself."

"No need to do that. She has five eggs in her nest right now and all of them are fertile. My cook has a male and the two of them seem to get along real well. They don't sing or anything like that, but they do buzz in a patter." said Lane.

"Are you sure she will let me have one of her eggs?" asked Sinsee.

"We should wait until they are hatched and at least are eating right." Lane put out her hand and the bird zipped over to her. "She has had six hatchings so far and all of her young have survived."

"Survived?" asked Sinsee.

"Most of the young on Lightenglow's Island don't survive the storms that rake the island." said Lane as she held up her hand and the bird zipped up to a small box that Sinsee now saw hanging from the ceiling. "Being as intelligent as they are, they greave the same as we would at the loss of a child."

"Such is the curse for eating the fruit of the tree of knowledge." said Sinsee. Lane looked at her with a puzzled look on her face. "It comes from a very old book that has its roots going all the way back to Earth. I can get you a copy of one if you are interested." said Sinsee.

"No thank you." said Lane. "Old Earth has never been one of my favorite places and if you had ever been there, you would not want to return anytime soon."

Now that Sinsee thought about it, there was no Senator at Home Station from Earth. They had made no petition to join the Union of Worlds. She wondered about that and made a note to herself to check into it.

"Well we have a destination to go to, so lets get this show on the road." said Roeman. "Sebastian, you have a film of Tank's new worlds?" Sebastian nodded. "Well lets get going."

✶

Roeman set the shuttle down near one of the landings that stretched out into a fairly large waterway. He opened the hatch and extended the step ramp. Holding out his hand for Sinsee, they walked out to the beginning of the landing.

"I should go out there by myself." She looked at Roeman and smiled softly at him. "I am going to have to use my big voice. We don't know how far out they are and I want them to hear me."

Roeman lifted her chin with his right hand and kissed her. "You will reach them, there is no way that they could not hear your mind. I will keep the shuttle engines on just incase they don't want us here, so you be ready to jump into the hatch for a quick get away."

"I hope that it does not come to that." She turned and started to walk out onto the landing and Roeman went back to the shuttle. The landing was longer then it looked from the air, specially if one had to walk the full length. It took her a while to reach the end of the landing. Now that she was there she just stood there wondering if this was really a good idea. She cleared her mind of any negative thoughts, took a deep breath and opened her mind.

[{"Hello, are you there? If you can hear me, I just wanted you to know that the Humans no longer rule the Stars. We, The Millally, the first of Lightenglow's children now rule. You are now safe from the agents of Earth or any other planet as far as that goes. No one will come to your world unless you want them to. I just wanted you to know this. I will go now and leave you in peace."}] Sinsee turned and started to walk back the way she had come. Behind her there was a big splash in the water and the sound of something thudding onto the landing. Sinsee turned slowly, she did not want to frighten who ever it was.

His skin was a tight shade of gray. He wore a modesty wrap of cloth about his hips, water dripped onto the landing. His hands and feet were webbed between the fingers and toes. Sinsee could see the gill slits on the sides of his neck. His hair had a green tint to it. Other then that the only thing that made him different was his height, he stood over seven feet tall.

[{"Hello my brother. I am called Sinsee. I am also known as The High Chandler of The Millally. I have much to tell you. I will sit here by the waters edge and tell you the truth of my life and how I came to be here."}] Sinsee sat down, taking her shoes off and dangled her feet in the water. The tall gray man came and sat down next to her, he tilted his head, a look of curiosity on his face.

Sinsee told him about the slaves of space and how a brave woman who had found her power, had set them free. She told him about her life as a child on Terra Two and about her brother Seenan. All the things that they had done as children. She spoke of her life at the Foundation. The story of how she had found Kit, and how together they had hunted and killed the big dog. She told him about the mock battle at Ben and Mam's farm. How badly it had made her feel to have to lie to those who had come to her rescue. How she had helped to save Kreeote and his people. The battle for Home Station and how she had killed a man gone mad, who had caused the death of so many children. She told him how she and Roeman were trying to join all the worlds under one rule, and about their brothers and sisters on ZENTEX. About the ships that could fold space, and the dead Catsman home world that they were going to bring back to life one day. She told him everything, even about the little butterfly birds their father creator had made on Antella. She told him how she knew to find him.

Sinsee looked out over the water and saw the many bobbing heads of other aquatic men and women, some with small children, others with older children. The sun was setting and the water shimmered in the failing light. She turned back to look at the man sitting next to her. He got to his feet and looked down at her. [{"Come here tomorrow. We will know by then."}] He dived back into the water and was gone, so were all of the others. Sinsee had not heard them leave and she was a little disappointed that no one had said any more to her then to tell her to come again. She got to her feet and began the long walk back to the shuttle.

As Roeman helped her into the shuttle she looked back down the landing, the intake of her breath caused Roeman to turn around and look in the same direction. Small lights were coming on under the water and the surface took on a soft blue glow. They could now see domes under the water that had looked like mounds of coral in the daylight. "Now we know where all the building are." said Roeman. "They are a lovely sight aren't they."

For some reason Sinsee was thinking about a story by a man named Anderson, it was about a little mermaid and a sea witch. "We will come back tomorrow at the same time. He said that they would know by then."

"Know what?" asked Roeman as he followed her into the shuttle.

"Whether or not they want to be a part of the rest of the Universe or not." She sighed, and then took her seat behind his.

"You sound as if you don't want them in the Union of Worlds." said Roeman as he took the pilots seat.

"They have such a perfect life here that it seems wrong to come in and muck it all up for them." She was silent for their trip back up to the ship. Lane and Sebastian wanted to know what had happened but Sinsee left Roeman to explain things to them while she went to their cabin to get some rest. She had never felt so tired before and she put it down to the fact that she was unable to keep any food down. Why did they call it morning sickness when it lasted all day long?

Abby was there to see to her needs as always, and Sinsee was glad that Abby rambled on about the crew members and the little birds that seemed to be everywhere. The sound of her voice had a calming effect on Sinsee now a days, it took her mind away from the hard decisions she had to make on a daily bases and reminded her of the every day lives of every day people.

The next day at about the same time they had arrived the day before, Roeman and Sinsee walked out onto the landing together. The aquatic man from the other day was waiting for them along with two others, an elderly man and a woman of middle age.

[{"It has been decided. We will allow only those of the mind to come to this world. We have no reason to leave here and go to the stars as you have done. All that we need is here."}] The tall man made this very clear as he swept his arms before him.

[{"Our world is perfect."}] said the woman to his right.

[{"We will welcome these Catsman you spoke of. There is much good land in the interior of this world that we do not make use of. They can grow good crops there. The water from the little rivers is sweet and good."}] offered the elderly man. [{"I have seen the land myself, many years ago."}]

[{"Is this acceptable to you?"}] asked the tall man.

[{"More then acceptable. I will make sure that only those of my kind with telepathic talents will ever set foot on this world. To all others this will be a closed world. You have lifted a great burden from my mind, for I did not want to bring harm to you or yours. I am glad that you will stay here where life is perfect. Where Lightenglow intended you to stay and be happy."}] Sinsee walked to the edge of the landing and put her hand into the water. [{"Perfection is such a hard thing to create let alone achieve, yet it would be so easy to destroy such a thing."}] She looked back at the three of them standing there.

[{" I pledge to you that I and my children will give our lives to protect this world."}] She stood up and put her hand on her stomach. [{"Do you hear me my son, I give you a great charge. You will not fail these wonderful people."}]

The woman gave some kind of signal and aquatic men and women leaped out of the water and onto the landing, they carried with them mats and containers filled with food. They unrolled the mats and placed the containers of food before their guests and sat down for a feast.

Roeman and Sinsee sat down and the others gathered around them on the mats. Sinsee sampled the different foods and found them to her liking. There was no meat among the many dishes that were passed around, that also explained the many cultivated fields and the groves of fruit trees. The aquatic men and women were vegetarians. The food was very good and this time Sinsee was able to keep it down. She wondered if it could be that simple, could it be that all she needed to do was take meat out of her diet or was it this food. She asked if she could have some of the food to take home with her. The women were more then happy to wrap up some of the food for her.

Later in the shuttle on their way back to the ship, their stomachs full, Roeman asked Sinsee what was next.

"I don't know Roeman, But it is out there somewhere, just waiting for us." said Sinsee as she snuggled down in her seat and fell fast asleep.

"Out there somewhere it is then." said Roeman, but Sinsee did not hear him. Her steady breathing told Roeman that she would sleep for a long time. Once back onboard the ship Roeman carried Sinsee to their cabin and made sure that no one would disturb Sinsee until she had slept away her fatigue.

So it was that Sinsee slept for three days. Roeman became concerned on the second day and called Jewbee. She wanted to know exactly what Sinsee had done, everything. When Roeman told her about the feast with the aquatic humans,

Jewbee wanted a sample of the food just to make sure that it was nothing in the food, seeing that Roeman had eaten the same food and seemed unaffected by it. It turned out that Sinsee was lacking vital minerals in her body from being sick to her stomach all the time. The food she had eaten at the feast was so loaded with all the minerals and vitamins that she needed, that her body did the best thing it could have done. While she slept she metabolized the minerals and vitamins at a faster rate then she would have had she been awake. Jewbee suggested that Roeman acquire more of this food for Sinsee.

"I know that it makes her sleep a lot, but it is also the fastest way to build up her strength. Why didn't you tell me that she was going through a bad bout of morning sickness before now. I could have prevented her from becoming so weak." said Jewbee.

"She never had this kind of problem before." said Roeman.

"Yes she has. Don't you remember how sick she was with Danny." Jewbee reminded him. "The reason it never went this far then is because we had her in the hospital under constant watch. How much of the food did she bring back with her?" There was just enough to last for a week, but Jewbee still wanted Roeman to get more from the aquatic humans. This time he sent one of the Catsman to deal with the aquatics.

It was one of their females who got up enough courage to walk out onto the landing and call to the aquatics. She explained the situation to one of their females who understood, She also said that Sinsee should not eat any meat until the birth was over, it was bad for the baby. The Catsman female agreed with her and said that she could not understand how the humans could eat meat in the first place. It gave her the willies to watch them wolf down the flesh of those creatures they called cows. She refrained from saying that humans also ate fish and birds.

That was how and why Sinsee became a vegetarian.

Chapter Ten

Sinsee was looking at herself in her mirror, she kept turning from side to side. "This is not right," she thought to herself. She reached out with her mind and contacted Jewbee. [{"Jewbee, are you busy right now?"}] Jewbee said that she was not too busy at the moment so Sinsee asked her to please stop by her quarters and to bring her med scanner with her. Jewbee asked if she was feeling alright, when she said yes, Jewbee wanted to know why Sinsee wanted her to bring the med scanner with her. [{"If I explain it now, you just might say that I was over reacting. So you will just have to humor me for now."}] That alone got Jewbee's attention.

Jewbee arrived ten minutes later and Sinsee took her into the bedroom where she took off the robe she was wearing and turned sideways. "I know that I am only two months into this pregnancy but I will swear that I was never this big with Danny or Bethany." Jewbee could see that she was right, Sinsee was showing her pregnancy early on alright. She took out her scanner and ran it over Sinsee's belly. She looked at the read out, reset the scanner and took another reading, just to make sure that there was no mistake. The reading was the same. She looked at Sinsee.

"Where is Roeman right now?" Sinsee told her that he was with the Senators in a meeting about the colony quotas. "Tell Him to leave the room." Sinsee did as she asked.

"Why did you want me to do that Jewbee?" asked Sinsee with anxiety showing on her face. Jewbee led her over to the bed and made her sit dawn, then she sat down next to her and patted her hand.

"There is nothing wrong with you physically. You are right about the size of your belly though. The reason you are so big right now is because there are three separate fetuses growing in there." Jewbee braced herself for the mental scream she knew was coming, and she was not disappointed.

Just outside the Senators Hall Roeman was having his own reaction. Between the two of them the entire Station became aware of Sinsee's condition in a matter of moments. Roeman headed for their quarter at a dead run, tripping over his own feet as he went. As he entered the main room he was breathing hard, his hair was out of place and his shirt had been torn on the side from where he had collided with someone who could not get out of his way fast enough.

"Sinsee!" He called to her. Jewbee came out of the bedroom first followed by Sinsee who was fastening her robe. Roeman went to his wife and picked her up in his arms, spinning her around then putting her down again. He placed his hand on her belly and looked over at Jewbee who nodded her head once.

Jewbee left them for a few minutes and went into the kitchen to make some coffee. She had more news to tell them, but right now she needed a cup of coffee. Bringing the coffee back into the main room on a tray with cups and condiments, she poured coffee for Roeman and Sinsee, black, she then poured some for herself and added sugar and cream to hers. She sat down in one of the stuffed chairs.

"I am afraid that Sinsee is not the only one to be having a multiple birth. There are a number of women who are having twins. Sinsee however is the only one with triplets, so far as I know." She looked at the two of them, to make sure that they were listening to her. "I am not sure, but I think it may have something to do with the Fold engines. The twins are all identical, which means they are the same sex." Before Roeman could ask her she told them that their triplets were boys. Roeman said that he already knew that.

Sinsee leaned back and put her hands on her belly. "Just how big am I going to get?" she asked no one in particular.

"BIG." said Jewbee. "I suggest that you spend as much time as possible in the zero gravity chamber during your third trimester. You are going to be very uncomfortable during that phase of your pregnancy."

The next Catsman competition was only two weeks away. Jewbee admonished Sinsee, she was not to do any showboating at the competition.

"She doesn't have to." said Roeman. "The kids and I will do it. We have gotten pretty good at it." Sinsee gave him a look. "Anyway, with the three of us working together we can almost put on as good a show as you can yourself." he admitted.

"Well at least that is settled." said Jewbee as she got to her feet. "I'll have to send you a stronger supplement Sinsee. You are going to need it, so take them. If you need me, just call." She tapped the side of her head. "I will always make myself available for you." She made her good bys and returned to the hospital.

*

As it turned out, Roeman had been right about himself and the kids. They did put on a great skills show for the Catsman youth. Sinsee was proud of her two eldest children and their performance. Roeman had handled the rings almost as well as Sinsee could herself.

But it was how Bethany had mounted the rings that had impressed everyone the most. Danny had climbed onto his father's shoulders, Bethany then climbed up both of them and taking Danny's hands in hers, she did a hand stand, balancing above her father and brother. Very carefully, Roeman moved under the rings and Bethany slipped her legs through the rings and Roeman moved away. Danny jumped from his father's shoulders and took up position to one side of the rings while Roeman took the other side. Bethany's routine on the rings was not as impressive as her father's or mother's routines had been but no one seemed to notice that.

For this batch of Catsman youth, the competition had to be changed because there was an odd number to their sexes this time.

Roeman had asked Patrick if he could control the ratio of male to female in the tanks. Patrick told him that it was the luck of the draw. "We have been taking them out in rows of ten, the same way they went in."

"Yes, but you are only using thirty of the five hundred gestation tanks." said Roeman. "Humm." was the only reply that Roeman got out of Patrick.

Jewbee complained to Roeman when Patrick started to set up the other Four hundred and seventy gestation tanks. "Between the humans, the Lions, and now this! Roeman, we are running out of room. Not to mention the number of people it is going to take to care for all these infants! Granted, the humans can take care of their own babies, but there are simply not enough Catsman or humans to handle that many infant Catsman. And what about when they reach the change?

Roeman assured her that he would come up with a solution for this situation even if he had to work around the clock for the next seven days, he would find an answer for her.

Later with Sinsee, Roeman was forced to admit that Jewbee was right. "I have been doing some checking, and our people are spread real thin with everything that is going on. Even with the Station crammed to capacity, we are short handed."

Roeman was pacing back and forth in the living room and stubbed his foot on a package. "What is this?"

"Just another gift for the baby's room. This one is from Chronus Three." Sinsee sneezed, and a little butterfly bird came up to her holding a tissue in her little feet. "Thank you." said Sinsee as she took the tissue and wiped her nose. The bird zipped back to her perch at the corner of the room. "I have been swamped with gifts just like this from all over. We really don't have the room for all of it so I have been sharing the gifts with the other expectant mothers on the Station" She sneezed again.

Sinsee, are you getting sick?" Roeman asked her as he came over to sit next to her and feel her forehead for any signs of a fever. "When did you start sneezing?"

"Come to think of it, right after that package arrived." she pointed to the box on the floor.

"Come on, we're getting out of here. Where is Bethany?" She told him that she was at her evening classes in the second sphere. He took Sinsee by the hand and pulled her off the couch. "You too Flit!" said Roeman as he held out his hand for the little bird, who zipped over to Him.

Jewbee was surprised when Roeman contacted her, she was not accustom to his mind touch under normal circumstances, but right now Roeman was both mad and worried at the same time. He told her that they were on their way to the hospital. When he told her why, it became Jewbee's turn to get mad.

Decontamination teams were sent to retrieve the package and seal off their quarters. Then Sinsee remembered the other gifts she had shared with the other mothers to be. She used her big voice and ordered all of them to leave their quarters, to take nothing with them, and to report to the hospital with their families and pet companions.

Chronus Three had been one of the worlds denied entry into the Union of Worlds. Inside the package they found hidden inside a stuffed doll a very nasty contaminant. Had the triplets come in direct contact with it they could have died. Sinsee turned out to be sensitive to the presence of the air born esters of the organic compound. A fact that Chronus Three had not counted on in their assassination attempt.

With the other quarters evacuated the decontamination teams went in and found four other gifts with the same compound, but these gifts had not come from Chronus Three.

While her mother and father were at the hospital, Bethany called an emergency meeting of the Senate. When they were told of the assassination attempt all hell broke loose and they got into a shouting match like nothing else. Bethany had no choice but to let them vent their outrage and anger.

It was the replacement senator from Colvert's World that got everyone's attention. "We must not rush into this blindly. I want the reports on all the gifts and a list of the worlds from where they came. We need to learn just where this poison came from."

"What if other products have been contaminated!" someone yelled from the back.

"That is a good point." said Bethany. "Right now our people on the station are working as hard as they can on that. Some of them are working three to four jobs just to keep this place running. What we need is more help. But right now the station is over crowded as it is."

"What if we bring in a few of those big ships from the Catsman home world. We could incorporate them into the station the same way New Home was. That would take care of the over crowding." the same voice spoke up.

"Yes, but that doesn't take care of the manning problem." someone else said.

"My planet can supply some strong young men and women to handle the heavy work." said Senator Jole from one of the mining worlds.

"What about the cargo!"

"Our people are scanning everything that is coming off the 'ships right now, but that still leaves what we have in storage. I am sure that you will agree with me that everything that is in storage right now should stay there until it can be checked for tampering." Bethany turned to look at the Senator from the mining world. "Senator Jole, how soon can you set up a recruitment program on Your world?" she asked him.

"I can do it today if you like." he puffed his chest foreword. She nodded to him and he left the Senate Hall.

Bethany looked to the other Senators. "We also need ships crews and medical personal. If you have people who are specialized in the care of infants, we need them as well. I will inform my Mother and Father about the Big Ships. If you have anything else that can be of help to us at this time, see either myself or my Brother. I do not want my parents bothered at this time. I am sure that you are all aware of the High Chandlers condition and with this attempt on her life and that of her unborn sons, you will honor my request for the time being. Talk to your Home Worlds, then get back to me. I will be at the Hospital for the next four hours but you can reach my Brother at the Sector Marshal's Office in the outer sphere. Thank you Gentlemen for all you have done and for all that I know you will do."

The Senate broke up and everyone went to contact their Home Worlds. Bethany went to the hospital to tell her folks what she had done.

"I know how you feel about space belonging to the Millally, but times change." She was looking at her mother and did not see the way Roeman's eyebrows raised. "It does not take a telepath to move cargo, clean floors, or feed and care for an infant. We can free up a lot of our people from mundane jobs and put them where they will do the most good."

"She is right Sinsee. Besides, she has already got a good start on this thing." Sinsee look at Roeman, she could see the pride he felt for Bethany in his eyes, Sinsee relented. "Good." said Roeman. "I will have two of the big ships brought in. We can have one of them refitted to accommodate the new hospital. The other one can be living quarters and recreational. We will keep Government and Fleet here on Home Station." He turned to his son. "Danny, arrange for the big ships to be moved. Bethany, ask Senator Jole if he or any of the others have people who can do the refitting on those ships. And Danny, tell Dee to recall our people and ships from Chronus Three. Nothing comes off that world or onto it." Danny nodded and headed out the door with Bethany right behind him.

Roeman put his arm around Sinsee. "I never noticed until now just how grown up Bethany is. Both of our kids take to responsibility well enough. But the way Bethany maneuvered the Senators, she got them to do just what she wanted them to do and made them think it was their idea. Danny has been doing well under Dee, coordinating the Fleet movements. He is quite a boy."

Sinsee looked up into Roeman's eyes. "I am not surprised at that. After all, they have a great Father."

Senator Chase from Colvert's World had her people working around the clock, categorizing the gifts and learning where they had come from. She had learned the identity of the other four worlds who were involved in the plot to assassinate the Millally First Family. Roeman ordered that the ships and personal be remove from those planets as well. He was not surprised to learn that every one of them had been denied entry into the Union of Worlds.

Sinsee was glad when their quarters were declared clean of any contaminate residue and she could leave the hospital, which was over crowded even before the evacuation from quarters.

Senator Jole's word was as good as gold, by the time the big ships arrived he had work crews ready to go and within two weeks medical personnel started to take up residence on the hospital ship. The work crews started on the next ship within the month. When the work was done many of the work crews offered to stay on as maintenance personnel, while still others offer to go to the Catsman home world to help bring even more ships online.

Fleet enlistment was a different matter all together. They needed personnel who could work sensitive equipment and handle themselves in zero gravity. Even though the ships now ran under full gravity, there were still those rare occasions when the gravity fields would malfunction and you would find yourself floating away from your work station, or worse.

Potential recruits were put through a rigorous physical and academic screening on their home worlds. When the first reports came in for medical to go over and choose the best recruits, Jewbee got a surprise and contacted Roeman and Sinsee right away. She told them that she had something to show them and she was on her way to Roeman's office right then and there. The excitement Sinsee felt in her mind told her that this was going to be good, so Sinsee did not pressure her for any information, instead she headed for Roman's office via her private corridor. She arrived before Jewbee just long enough for her and Roeman to speculate what this new thing was all about.

Jewbee showed up with a box full of file disks and a smile so huge her face looked like it was going to crack. She put the box down on Roeman's desk, pushing some of his own files out of the way. "Wait till you get a load of this!" She took out one of the disks and slipped it into the reader. The screen came up and the medical profile of a young recruit scrolled across the screen. Roeman and Sinsee looked at the screen, Roeman's eyebrows raised and he reached for another disk, replacing the one in the reader, then he did it again and again. "There all like that, every one of them."

"Do we know what the rate of exception is to those who applied?" asked Sinsee.

"It is standing at about seventy to eighty percent, depending on the planet of origin." said Jewbee. "It looks like Jayson was right. We have got Millally every where."

"Have you shown this to Dee yet?" asked Roeman.

"I thought I would leave that up to you." smiled Jewbee. "Would you mind if I sit in when you show him this. Not to many things throw Dee off balance, but I have a feeling this is going to be one of those things."

"I'll call him now. It would be a shame to leave him out of this." said Sinsee as she reached for the com link. While they waited for Dee to show up they went through more of the files. "Have you noticed the age groups? They all seem to be within seventeen to twenty five years of age."

"That is not surprising. Most people are still looking for career choices at that age. Any older then that, they have already settled into a career." said Jewbee.

"Then we can assume that the percentage is stable through out the populations. The question now is do we make this public or keep it to ourselves?" Roeman looked at Sinsee. "It is your call."

"Wait a minute, Why Me? Take it before the Senate. That is why they are there aren't they?" said Sinsee, trying to back away from such a task.

"So how do we explain to them that seventy percent of their populations are actually Millally." said Roeman.

"Jayson had a good idea a while back. And now that we have Dr. Lightenglow's notes, we have the perfect answer." said Jewbee. "Dr. Lightenglow was trying to enhance humans to their full potential. Now nature has done it for him. Human kind has advanced up the evolutionary chain and now the human race has caught up to a point where the Millally were when space was being explored and new worlds colonized. This way we still give the Millally a jump on the rest of humanity."

"Back to lies and half truths, Jewbee." Sinsee looked at her. "I can't condone that. No. If we are to release this to the worlds, then let it be the truth. All of the truth."

"Even the cryo tanks being turned off deliberately?" asked Roeman. Sinsee nodded. "I guess I could speak to some of the Senators. Get a feel as to how the news will be excepted. We could end up with a real mess on our hands, you do know that, don't you?"

"Not if we handle it right. What we have done is bring Lightenglow's dream of perfect humans to light. Lets use Lightenglow's own words to bring the truth out. That way the Millally will not be seen as criminals but as victims of the old governments. That is the truth. That is how we tell the worlds that they are Millally and we are The Millally Spacing Guild." Sinsee looked at Roeman and then at Jewbee, who nodded her agreement with Sinsee.

"Well I am no story teller." said Roeman. "I wouldn't even know where to begin."

"I know someone who is a great story teller." said Sinsee. "If she is willing, I'll bet she could tell it in such a way that no one would blame us for turning off those tanks."

Jewbee looked at Sinsee with a puzzled look on her face. She knew that Sinsee was not talking about Allison, because the old Chandler had passed away just last year. "Who could do this for us?" she asked Sinsee.

"Why Abby, of course. The woman can spin a yarn like you have never heard before." smiled Sinsee. "She is going to need a secretary."

"She is going to need four secretaries and ten interpreters." laughed Roeman.

"Roeman, she is not that bad, is she? I am rather used to her myself. Well maybe you are right. I will have to see to it myself." smiled Sinsee.

"What is keeping Dee?" said Roeman. Just as he said that, there was a knock at the door and Dee let himself in.

Jewbee sat up straighter in her chair, this was going to be fun she thought.

Roeman sat Dee down in front of his screen and began to put file after file into the reader for Dee's benefit. They were not disappointed in his reaction to the news that he now had more then enough personnel to man the ships and more.

"But I don't have a training center large enough to handle all these people. What the void am I going to do? There is no way I am going to put untrained personnel on a ship. Gees Roeman, what the hell do you think I am anyway, some kink of god." Dee was losing it, and Jewbee was enjoying every minute of it.

"That is not all of it." said Roeman. He explained what they were going to do about the Millally populations.

"I'm not even going to ask you if you are nuts, because it is plain that you are." He looked from one to the other. "OK, what do you want me to do?"

It became Sector Marshal Dee's job to set up training centers on the different worlds. Before any recruit got the chance to see space they first had to go back to the classroom. There they would learn everything they would need to know about the new ships and also be evaluated to determine in which field they would excel in. Only after a cram course of six weeks would they then be brought to Home Station for their final training in zero gravity.

Roeman had insisted that this training take place on Home Station for two reasons. One, the zero gravity chamber on Home Station was the very best and there was no chance of a malfunction. Two, every ship made port at Home Station and it would be a simple matter for the new recruits to board their new ships at this point.

It was during one of these training sessions that one of the trainers happened to notice two recruits standing in line just outside of the zero gravity chamber, they were scratching their heads as hard as they could. The trainer turned around to see a pair of Lions at the other end of the Hall. He pulled the two out of line and marched them down to where the Lions were standing. He had to continuously pull their hands away from their heads. Then all of a sudden their eyes got huge and the boy fainted.

Later, in Dee's office. "We got one of each. I thought only the Tec's could be telampathic." said Rivor, the zero gravity trainer.

"Nope. Even The Lord Roeman is a telampathic plus a telepathic. He's lucky that way." said Dee.

"I wish the Lions weren't so picky about who they chose. I would love it if one would choose me for a change." Rivor rubbed the back of his neck.

"You and me both. I haven't won a poker hand with Roeman sense his talent was activated. It's darn right depressing." said Dee.

"So I guess it all depends on how honest a person is, is that it?" asked Rivor.

"For the moment, I am going to ignore that statement. But you might be right about that. It would explain a lot about the Lion Riders but it also doesn't explain the Lord Roeman." said Dee. "I have known him all my life, and I never thought of him as some kind of puritan."

"Maybe some of the High Chandler rubbed off on him." suggested Rivor.

"And to think that she was once a woman of my house and I let her go to that big lug. I wonder.." Dee had that look on his face that said he was in deep thought.

"It wont work, Sir." said Rivor. "She can't do it. The Lions have to be willing and you know that."

"Don't go taking away my dreams so fast." Dee gave him a look of disgust. "Well one thing we can do, is to have the recruits exposed to those Lions who have not yet chosen their riders. Who knows, we might get lucky and find more telampathices. The ship yards have eight new ships ready to go on line. We are going to need fold pilots for those new ships." Dee ran a scan on what ships were due in. "Looks like Rosy is due in today. I'll check with her and see if she can take our new recruit on as a pilot in training." He looked up at Rivor. "On your way out would you ask Danny to come in here."

"Sure, I know when I'm not wanted." said Rivor as he got to his feet. "I think I'll just take a little trip over to New Home and see how many young cubs there are over there. Who knows, I just might get lucky."

"Dream on." said Dee, secretly wishing he could join Rivor.

Danny filled his parents in on the new telampath and also about Rivor trying to get one of the cubs to choose him. Later that day Sinsee was telling Jewbee about it while she was getting her physical.

"I had almost forgotten about that." said Jewbee. "Jayson was so disappointed when none of the cubs chose him. You know, I really didn't think they would, given his age and all." She looked at her scanner. "Sinsee, you haven't been taking your supplements regularly enough. Flit, I want you to remind her every day to take her supplements."

Flit hovered around Sinsee's head and buzzed as if to say I told you so. Sinsee put out her hand and Flit settled on her finger. To Jewbee's trained eye the little bird looked bigger then normal, so she took her scanner and ran it over the bird. "Just what I thought. You are going to have to get Flit some nesting material. I would say you have about a week before she drops those eggs of hers."

"Eggs! Really!" said Sinsee. "Why Flit, and to think I never even noticed. I am so sorry dearest. Can you ever forgive me."

"It is amazing how fast these little birds mature isn't it. From shell to adult in only a few months. I'll send you a package of the nesting material that Jinxy likes so much along with a nesting box that will hang on her perch." Jewbee was putting her scanner away and heard Flit give a big buzz of gratitude. "You are welcome Flit." she said.

Sinsee opened a little box on the table that held tiny little meal worms. Flit buzzed with excitement. The meal worms were a special treat for the little Butterfly Birds. They thrived on seeds and nutrient rich sweet water, but what they loved best were meal worms.

Chapter Eleven

SECTOR MARSHAL DEE REQUESTED a meeting with Roeman, which surprised Roeman because it was such a formal request. Dee also wanted to have some of the ships Captains at the meeting as well. Considering the number of ships that were docked at the station, Roeman knew that he would have to find some other place to have this meeting, his office was not big enough. Sinsee suggested that they use the Great Hall. She had long tables and chairs set up and also a coffee bar.

The Hall filled up rather fast and people were milling around talking to each other in small groups. Some were speculating what all this was about, and some one suggested that perhaps the Sector Marshal wanted to have a huge poker party, which elicited a round of laughter around the one making that comment. The only one not laughing was Captain Lane.

Earlier that day Dee had come to Roeman's office to go over what he considered to be a real problem. "I still don't know how we missed it." said Dee.

"We were so wrapped up with the Fold Engines that we never bothered about it." said Roeman. "The ship yards were going on the old contracts and I never changed that part in the new ones. This was my mistake."

"What good are the new ships with out weapons?" Dee was thinking about the attempt on Sinsee and the triplets. "We may be at peace with most of the worlds, but there are still those other five. I for one would feel a lot safer if we fitted those ships with weapons."

"We can take the weapons from the old ships and refit them to the new ships." said Roeman. "Put Danny on that job, and have him trained in weapons control so he can train the recruits."

"Roeman, have you ever wondered what would happen if one of those bad boy worlds ever got their hands on the specs to one of our ships. I mean, there have been a lot of new personnel around here lately, and not only here on the station. The ship yards are full of new workers as well." Roeman had not thought about that. Even if they took steps to prevent the theft of vital information now, it might be to late. He would have the Senators recheck their lists, to make sure of the origins of their people. It is possible that spies from Chronus Three and the other blockaded worlds had managed to infiltrate the other worlds before the blockades were put into effect.

Now as they entered the Great Hall, Roeman could see that the refitting of the ships was the most important priority. He also knew that he had to set up his ships into different formats. Civilian transports and cargo ships, and armed military ships. The problem here was that he knew all these Captains, and not one of them would want to be considered a mere civilian captain. Roeman was not looking foreword to this meeting at all. He took a deep breath and called for every ones attention.

By the end of the meeting Roeman had relented, he would have all the ships refitted with weapons. Dee made sure that their best Captains were the first to have their ships refitted.

✳

It was Bethany who came up with a way to make any new personnel loyal to the Millally. "We have all that wealth from the Belt. If we spread it around, some of it that is." she corrected herself when she was the look on her Father's face. "They can even send some of their new pay home to their families. We pay them more then they need along with their regular credit points. We could end up converting any bad seeds to our side. If they are out there, this may even get them to turn on each other. Which ever way you look at it, we win."

"OK, adding to their credits sounds good to me." said Roeman.

"That is not what I meant. We need to give them something that they can hold in their hands. I was thinking that we could use some of the small diamonds and rubies. They can exchange them for more credits or send them home to their families." said Bethany, standing up to her Father in defiance of his attempt to keep the pay rate on a credit base only.

"Yes," said Sinsee. "Give them something they can hold in their hands. How about taking some of the gold and making coins out of it."

"What is a coins?" Roeman and Bethany asked at the same time.

"A coin is a small disk that has an imprint on both sides. They come in different sizes and values. The larger the coin the more it is worth." She took out a piece of paper and drew different size circles. "There should be a face on one side and a symbol on the other. Something that represents the Millally."

"I'll take this to the boys in fabrication along with a hundred bars of gold." said Roeman as he took Sinsee's drawing. He would rather use the gold then the gems any day. Gold they had in abundance. Bethany asked if she could join him and he said she could. Sinsee told them that she would be over in the zero gravity chamber. Roeman made a mental note to have a zero gravity room installed in there quarters. As Sinsee got closer to her due date Roeman worried about her going over to the next sphere all the time and he really didn't like it when she took that Rail of Halley's.

The fabrication foreman understood what Roeman was asking him to do. "We can melt the gold into rods and cut the disks from that. Gold is a softer metal, so we can stamp a design onto both sides at the same time. What do you want the designs to be?"

Bethany answered that question before Roeman had the chance to. "The face of the coin should be the outline of a Terra Two Lion with my Mother's image impressed over that. The back should be a replica of one of the ships, no, make that a shuttle and put a planet under it."

"The planet should be Terra Two." said Roeman. The foreman was writing all that down on the back of Sinsee's paper.

"Do you want the weight of the coin to be on it as well?" he asked them. "You do understand that even the smallest of these coins is going to be worth a lot of credits?" They knew that. "OK, I'll get my boys on this right now. Is it alright if I take one of the coins for myself?"

"You can give one to each of your boys who work on this project." said Roeman. "After that I will distribute them as I see fit." Roeman and Bethany left the very happy fabrication foreman to his work and to get his crew together.

On their way back to their quarters they made a pact not to tell Sinsee what the coins would look like. "We can let it be a surprise." said Roeman. "By the way, what made you think of that design for the coins?"

"It felt right. It represents what we are because of Mother, and You going in to rescue her in that shuttle of yours. It was really rather romantic when you think about it." She smiled up at her father.

"Believe me, it did not feel romantic at the time. And what would you know about romance in the first place?" He was teasing her and she knew it.

"Nothing yet." she teased right back at him. "Do you want

me to make lunch now or do you want to wait for Mother to get back?"

Roeman remembered that he had forgotten about the zero gravity room for Sinsee. "You go ahead and fix something for yourself. I have got to go back to fabrication. Something I forgot to tell the foreman. I will eat with your Mother later."

Five days later twelve bags of gold coins were sent to Roeman's office for his inspection. He sent word to the foreman to expect an additional shipment of gold. The foreman almost had a heart attack when crate after crate after crate of gold was brought into his shop. The first thing he did was to order armed guards posted inside and outside of every entry into his shop then he went to his quarters and got stinking drunk.

Sinsee just sat there looking at the one ounce coin she held in her hand. Tears rolled down her face as she kept turning the coin over and over. Finally she put it down and wiped her tears away with the tissue Bethany handed her. She didn't know what to say so she reached out and hugged Bethany to her. She started to cry all over again.

"I have sent a small bag of coins to the senate. I have also ordered more of the smaller coins to be produced in mass quantities." Roeman told her. "The larger coins are to be made sparingly. I figure we could use them as rewords for special services."

"Yes, yes of course." Sinsee said between sniffles. "We will start with the small coins first. How soon will it be before they are ready?"

"The boys down in fabrication are chinking them out as fast as they can. I am hoping that we will have enough coins to give at least one to every person by next week." Roeman picked up the coin on the table and turned it over in his hand. The image of Sinsee was a good one. Roeman hadn't known that there were such artists among the Millally.

"Roeman, I would like to go and see the coins being

made." Sinsee put her hand on Roeman's arm. He nodded and told her that she would have to cover her ears, the noise in fabrication was enough to make one deaf.

✹

The moment Sinsee entered the fabrication shop her ears were assaulted by the most horrendous noise she had ever heard. Someone handed her a pair of hearing protection guards. She put them on and they did help some but not by much.

She walked over to one of the stamping presses. Ten coins at a time were being stamped and dropped into a catch bin. She was about to reach into the bin when the operator stopped her by grabbing her hand. He shook his head then took a small wooden doll and stuck it into the bin. The moment the doll passed by a sensor it was cut in two. The operator made the hand sign for (security protection.) (I understand.) She signed back at him. (Thank you.) (Don't mention it.) He pointed to a counting machine that was counting and wrapping the coins in rolls of twenty per roll. The rolls then dropped down a shoot that went through the floor. (Storage is down there.) signed the man. He pointed to the guards around the shop. (More guards down there. You want to see?) he asked her. (No thank you. I think I have seen enough and heard enough. How can you stand this noise?) she signed to the man. (I have been deaf from birth. It is good to have others understand me for a change with out having to write all the time. I understand that I have you and one of the Captains to thank for this sign language.) (Sign language?) "Well I'll be damn." she said out loud.

✹

The coins did the trick. Soon they had a number of individuals in custody. The ones who were turned in were under heavy guard, and the ones who did the turning in went through screening again and were placed in other jobs that they were more qualified for or else they were placed in jobs that were less sensitive then the jobs they held.

The refitting of the ships was going along just fine until someone came up with the idea to fit lasers and short range missiles on the shuttles as well. Roeman asked Dee if that had been his idea.

"I can't take credit for this one, but I will give you three guesses as to who's idea it was." Dee was smiling at Roeman and chuckling under his breath. Roeman didn't need three guesses, he got it right on his first pick. It had been the coins that had given Danny the idea. A shuttle could fight in space or in an atmosphere. They could maneuver faster then a ship as well and trying to fire on a shuttle as it zipped from one vector to the next in the blink of an eye was impossible. Roeman felt a swelling of pride in his son. He knew that Danny would make an excellent Captain one day.

To keep an eye on the five blockaded worlds Dee had set up a string of motion satellites around each system far enough out from the planets that they would go undetected. It was a good thing too, because not long after the last ship was refitted the alarms went off in the Chronus System. Chronus Three was breaking out. Then the alarms for the world of Tolly went off next, followed by Muddy Gulch. Roeman did not wait for the other two, blockaded worlds, satellites to go off. He ordered his Fleet into action.

They folded space to come out just out side of the Chronus System. Checking the scanners, they locked onto fifty ships headed their way. "Now where the hell do you think they got all those ships?" asked Dee as he looked at the screen. "Give me a close up on those ships." The screen changed and they got a better look at the ships headed their way. "They must have cannibalized every piece of equipment on the planet to come up with that many ship."

"It doesn't matter where they got the material from. What does matter is weather or not they have fold capability." said Roeman. "Can we get a reading on those engines from this distance?"

"Yes Sir!" said the ops coordinator, as he took the reading. "They are regular drive engines Sir. I am not getting any readings on fold capabilities. I also don't think they have seen us yet."

Roeman looked at Dee. "What do you think, should we let them know we are here?"

"It would be a shame to come all this way and not say hello." chuckled Dee. "Recorders on, give us an open channel com."

Roeman leaned foreword in his seat. "Chronus Three, this is Lord Roeman of The Millally Battle Fleet. You don't want to do this. Surrender your ships now and you will be returned to Chronus Three unharmed. We do not want to destroy you."

"GO TO HELL!" came their reply. Roeman signaled the link cut.

"We gave them fair warning." said Roeman as he looked at the screen. He preferred it this way anyhow. With only one fifth of his fleet with him, Chronus Three felt that they had the upper hand. Anyone would feel the same way if they had fifty ships and their opponents only had fourteen ships and one battle cruiser.

What Chronus Three did not know was that each one of Roeman's ships carried thirty shuttles each and each shuttle carried an average of 200 one hundred pound missiles with the destruction power of a one kiloton blast each. Laser cannons were mounted just under the nose of the shuttles, they would work at close range in space and long range in an atmosphere.

Roeman's own ship housed sixty shuttles. The ship had been a last minute gift from Senator Jole and his home world. Roeman had given her the name Queen's Pride. This portion of Roeman's Fleet was comprised of four squadrons plus the Queen's Pride and four hundred and eighty fighting shuttles. Someone had given the shuttles the nick name of (Hornets), and it stuck.

Roeman had learned that the planet of origin for the poison that had been hidden inside the gifts had been Chronus Three. That alone was reason enough for him to be with this part of his Fleet at Chronus Three. The rest of his Fleet was taking up their positions at the remaining blockaded worlds.

Roeman wanted everyone to witness first hand the outcome of this confrontation. He had arranged for visual broadcasts from each of his ships to be transmitted to all the worlds. Every Captain had strict orders not to fire first. Roeman did not care which one of the Chronus Three ships fired first, so long as everyone understood that they were the aggressors and not the Millally.

Captain Duvale on the bridge of The White Dove was in charge of Lancer Squadron. Along with his own ship he had Long Neck and Wishful Thinking. Both of their Captains were young but they were also at the top of their class when they had come out of training.

Captain Tankfull on The Upper Class, had Darts Squadron, his ships were The Black Hand and The Cross, both of their Captains were new to their rank as well.

Captain Lane on the Miss Destiny, had Kicker Squadron, with her were ships Turn Key and Step Up. There Captains, Rosy and Jewel, went way back with Lane and she knew exactly what she could expect from these two women.

Captain Burton on Lady Fair, had the Stallion Squadron. One of his ships was the Bucking Bronco, Captain Cody in charge. Cody was older then dirt but he would not leave the Ships. Captain Trace on the ship Standing Tall, was the only person known to have bested Sector Marshal Dee at cards, three times in a row. Dee swore up and down that she was cheating, but after she leaned over and whispered into his ear he stopped complaining. He also never played cards with her again.

Roeman's own Queen's Pride had Talon Squadron. There was Captain Bobbie on The Cats Claw, and on Baby Sis was

Captain Danny. Dee and Danny had kept his captains training a secret until the day he was certified. Roeman was very proud of his son and all Sinsee could do was cry. She never got her captains certificate and when her son got his all she could do was cry and hug him every chance she got.

Sitting in a higher seat then Sector Marshal Dee and just behind him, Roeman had a clear view of all the screens on the bridge. "Open a channel to the Squadron Leaders." Roeman put his hand on Dee's shoulder. "Here we go old friend." Then to all the ships he said, "Just like we planned it people. On my mark, box them in and pull that formation apart. Tease them if you have too, but under no circumstances are you to get to close to them or fire the first shot. Standby to Fold. Mark!"

The Fleet folded space and reappeared on top of, behind, under, on both sides, and in front of Chronus Three's fifty ships with more then enough room to evade any missiles they might send their way. Queen's Pride faced down the front of those ships alone, Baby Sis and Cats Claw had folded to the underside of the Chronus Fleet.

Roeman leaned foreword in his seat. "Come on you sack of shit. Take the bait." There was movement and Roeman placed his hand back on Dee's shoulder. He tapped once.

"Twins, set your mark." said Dee. Roeman caught the glint of missile fire, he waited then tapped Dee Twice. "Fold Now!" yelled Dee. Queen's Pride vanished just as the missiles past where they had been only seconds before. Now they were with Baby Sis and Cats Claw under the Chronus Fleet. The ships were starting to break into smaller groups.

Danny's voice could be heard coming from the speaker designated for Baby Sis. "Gees Dad. Could you cut it any closer!"

"Their coming apart aren't they." said Roeman. "Lane you got—Never mind. Come on People, pull them apart some more, we need room for those Hornets to get out there."

"Lancer break right! That was close."

"THAT A WAY KICKER! You go girls!"

"SHUT UP AND DO YOUR JOB!"

"Take it easy Lane, there is plenty to go around."

"Stallion, you have got room now, send out your Hornets."

"HORNETS AWAY!"

"Talon's first wave, GO!"

"Gees! Did anyone see that!"

"They have got guidance missiles! Shit!"

"HORNETS INCREES YOUR SPEEDS"

"CROSS! YOU HAVE GOT ONE COMING UP YOUR BACK SIDE! FOLD!"

"Where did she go?"

"There she is!"

"Jane! Are you alright?"

"Lower decks took a hit. We're still functional."

"Forget this! Hornets, see if you can drag some of those missiles back to their own ships! Lets see how they like it for a change!"

"Cats Claw! You are to close!"

"Not close enough! FIRE!"

Up to this point the Fleet had only been playing cat and mouse with the Chronus ships in an attempt to pull them out of their formation. When Cross took a hit in her lower decks not one of the Millally ships had fired off a missile yet. Cats Claw had fired the first return shot. That is when all hell broke loose, literally.

A Hornet zipped across the screen in front of Queen's Pride, a missile hot on her tail. She pulled up hard and came around to come up behind the missile, a laser beam reached out and struck the missile. The shock wave barely rocked the Queen's Pride. The Hornets were not so lucky. Their pilots fought to regain control of their small ships.

One of the Hornets had managed to guide a missile back to the ship that had fired it. The pilot waited until the last moment to pull out, the underside of his shuttle scrapping against the hull of the Chronus ship. The missile coming in hot and fast, striking the ship dead center. The explosion ripping the ship apart.

"DAMN! HE CUT IT IN HALF!

"THEIR HULL PLATES AREN"T STRONG ENOUGH!"

"They didn't have the ship grade metals to build their ships."

"Don't they realize the danger they are in?"

"I don't think they care! Watch it Jewel! You got one coming after you!"

"Hornets, target their mid ships with your lasers. Hopefully they are smart enough to keep their hatches closed. If we can cut those ships in half, we can bring this conflict to a safe end." Roeman didn't like this business. It was to easy. Why would Chronus Three send these ships out knowing that they could not possibly survive with such flimsy hulls. Then it dawned on him. "Damn it! All ships! Back off!"

"Dad!" came Danny's voice over the speaker. "Those ships are death ships." Just as he said that one of the young Captains had gotten his ship to close to a Chronus ship. The Chronus ship exploded taking The Black Hand with it.

Roman had not wanted this, but here it was. He had no choice now. Dee turned around in his chair. "They are not going to surrender Roeman. Those are suicide ships."

"I know. Transmit to the rest of the Fleet. Tell them what to expect." Roeman reluctantly order his ships to open full batteries. "Take them out from a safe distance. Hornets, take out any missiles headed your way. I had hoped …"

It was like shooting fish in a barrel. Roeman did not stop until all Fifty ships had been destroyed.

"Has any body been keeping count?"

"Later!"

"Lady Fair, look to your right."

"I got it. Thanks Baby Sis."

"Any body seen any missiles being launched?"

"Hey! I think they stopped fighting!"

"Squadron Leaders, bring your Hornets home. Captain Jane, do you need any help? Can you retrieve your Hornets?" Roeman asked her.

"Sir, my port bays are a total loss. I think my Hornets would be better off with someone else." She coughed. "We are filling up with smoke on the lower levels and some of it has gotten into the ventilation system. We're trying to vent it now."

"How bad is it?" asked Roeman. She told him and he made the decision to have her and her crew abandon her ship for the time being. A tether line was run from her upper hatch to Baby Sis and the crew made their way over in AECS's. Their wounded were tethered to those who could hold onto the line. Jane was the last one over, she had made sure that all the hatchways in her ship were opened to space. It was the best way to put out any fires.

Jane's Hornets along with those of The Black Hand clamped onto the hulls of the other ships in the Fleet for now. Roeman called in the hospital ship, New Hope, there was enough room in her bays to take on those Hornets who now found themselves homeless.

New Hope folded in close enough but not too close. Small craft expelled from her bays, they went to any damaged ship to render assistance, weather that ship was Millally or Chronus, it did not matter.

Roeman made sure that this too was broadcasted to all the worlds. This one act proved beyond a shadow of a doubt that the Millally had earned the right to rule space.

It took forty two hours to go through all the ships, bringing out the living only. When this was done The Millally Fleet towed the wreckage of the Chronus ships onto a course that would send them directly into the sun of the Chronus system.

New Hope folded to the next battle field, Taking with it the crew of the Cross and her Hornets and the Hornets of The Black Hand.

Roeman made ready to make planet fall. He was trying to come up with a reason why he should not use his fold engine in their atmosphere. He couldn't find a reason, yet he did not use his fold engine. Instead he took the leaders of Chronus into custody, even the mayors of the small towns and villages. He left his own people in key positions on the planet with enough fire power to back them up should anyone object. Then he folded to Muddy Gulch, where the next battle was still taking place.

With each victory, Roeman became more and more depressed. How could they send their young so willingly to their deaths is such rat traps that couldn't even qualify as real ships.

Back on Home Station, people were in a state of shock. They had watched as hundreds of their friends had died on The Black Hand. Both men and women trying to hold back the tears and going on with their work.

Chapter Twelve

SINSEE SAT IN JUDGMENT over the Leaders of the five worlds, Chronus Three, Tolly, Muddy Gulch, Kearney, and Norvox. She wanted no mistakes made here. The defendants had the right to choose their own defense person. To everyone's surprise they chose to have the ZENTEX Tec's defend them, knowing the meticulousness of the Tec's, Sinsee was aware that this was going to take a long time.

The record of the many space battles were replayed, leaving no room for doubt that they had sent their youngest and bravest to their death in ships designed to never leave an atmosphere. There defense was to accuse the Millally of leaving them no choice. Of stopping all shipment to them from off world. How the Millally denied them entry into the Union Of Worlds for no reason. That the Millally were taking everything from the other worlds and not giving anything in return.

Witnesses were called from a number of worlds. The first witness to refute the defendants claim that the Millally took everything without giving back was Jeffery Cane. He testified how the High Chandler of the Millally had helped the miners by finding the loop hole in their law that was returning their claims to the real miners from that of their government. He told them how now the miners were actually working harder then they had ever worked before because they were now working for themselves. "The Millally take no profits from their gold mine claim. Instead those profits have been funneled back to the miners themselves in the form of advanced medical care, housing, and profit shares for each miner who works in the Millally claim. Because of the new management policy of the Millally Mine many other Mines have also adapted a similar policy. The standard of living has improved dramatically on my world."

Next to testify was a woman from Burner One. The story she told was one of horror. There were many listeners who turned away from their view screens and many more who lost the contents of their stomachs. "Yes," she said. "It is true that they destroyed half of the city. But you have to understand, we have tried so many times to destroy those freaks and each time their retribution was worse then the first." She held up her right arm that up to this point had been concealed under her wrap. Her wrist was a stub, her hand gone. "They made me kneel before them and forced me to eat my own hand off, then they made me watch as they feasted on my three year old son. I am glad the Millally took out half the city to get those bastards. I can also tell you that those who died that day gladly gave their lives knowing that their tormenters would die with them." She turned to face Sinsee. "Thank you my Lady, for giving us our lives back." Sinsee nodded her head at the woman and waved for a medical aid to come foreword.

"We can not return your son to you, but we can give you back your hand. Please go with this gentleman and he will take you to our hospital." Sinsee watched as the woman left with the aid, then she turned back to the proceedings.

It was the same with all the witnesses who testified for the Millally. When it came to the poison inside the baby gifts and the fact that this was done before the blockade of the five worlds was put into place the defendants claimed that they knew nothing about the gifts until after the battle. The fact that each poisoned gift had come from their worlds was still no proof that it was sent by the governments of the five worlds. True, the poison had its origin from Chronus Three, but again that did not prove that it was sent by the Chronus Three Government or that they had any knowledge of the act. It was at this point that those present at the Judgment started chanting.

"Stand and be Judged! Stand and be Judged!"

The leader from Chronus Three demanded to know what was happening. Sinsee looked at him with no emotion showing on her face what so ever. "They are demanding that you be judged as a Millally is judged. Let me explain this to you. I am a mind reader. Not the kind that you may remember from childhood tails. I am a telepath. I can enter your mind and strip from it your entire life as if it were my own. In doing so, I can learn the real truth. There is one drawback. If you are not truthful, you die. Not by what I do to you but rather by what you have done to your self. Do you still hold that you knew nothing about the poison?"

The Man turned to the other defendants, he had a half smirk on his face, it was obvious that he did not believe her about reading his mind. The others were not so sure. He turned back to face Sinsee. "Sure, I'll play this little game of yours." he said with a smug look on his face. He stepped out from behind the defense table and stepped up to where Sinsee sat. "Now what?" He asked in a snide manner.

It was not Sinsee's intention to make a martyr out of this man, so without touching him physically she reached out with her mind to his. [{Prepare Yourself, this could hurt.}] The moment she thought those words he backed away and stumbled down the few stairs, back to the main floor.

"She's in may head! She's in my head!" The man went to his knees on the floor before everyone. "Don't kill me!. Please don't kill me! Yes! Yes! We knew about the poison. We all knew about it and we all agreed to it." He pointed to the leader of Kearney. "It was his idea. He said there was room for only one God, that you were setting yourself and the Millally up as Gods. He said that you had no right to rule."

The Leader from Kearney stood up and pointed his finger at Sinsee. "You are an abomination to God! You must die!" From some where on his body he produced a throwing knife and sent it hurtling towards Sinsee. Even in the finale stage of her pregnancy Sinsee was still a Millally, and her speed and quick movement were as sharp as ever. A wave of astonishment went through the Hall as Sinsee reached out and caught the blade in her bare hand. It was made out of clear plexy glass, and it was no wonder that it had gone undetected. It had laid hidden just under the skin of Kearney's Leader. Blood now flowed from where he had used his own ring on his flesh to free the blade. Sinsee looked on as he was now struggling in the arms of the guards. The Hall was in a state of uproar. Now the call for Judgment was even louder.

Sinsee raised her hand holding the blade, she left it there until the Hall was once again silent. She looked at the defendants, lowered her head for a moment then raised it again only this time she would not look at anyone. "You have foolishly and wastefully cost the lives of hundreds of thousands of young men and woman from your worlds. Some of them had evolved on their own to match the greatness of even our pure blood Millally. I am sure that this fact comes as a surprise to you. To only now learn that we are in some forms, equals. This is true of many of the populations on all the Worlds, not just those of the Union. In time, you will learn how this came about. Right now I am ordering that your governments be dismantled and your worlds will go under the rule of what ever governments I so choose. Your citizens will pay the fines for your deeds. You want the slaves of space back under control so badly? So be it. You and your citizens are now indentured slaves. The fines that are now levied against you are so great that it will take you generations to pay them off."

When the sentence was passed, everyone knew that they had gotten what they deserved. What no one expected was what Sinsee did next.

"Because I am putting your worlds under the control of other worlds it is not my intention to saddle them with your debts. So I here and now suspend the fines levied against your worlds. You on the other hand will be placed into service under strict control. You will obey all rules and regulations of your chosen handlers. I already know that the mayors and leaders of your smaller cities and villages were not party to your conspiracy. They will be returned to their planets and you will now be taken to service." Sinsee, with the help of her husband, waddled out of the Great Hall.

The lesser of the defendants were taken to the ships that waited to return them to their own planets. No Millally would speak to them as they were led away. They whispered among themselves, wondering how the High Chandler could be so generous to them after what their Leaders had tried to do. It would take them years to learn that Sinsee was revolted by the thought of punishing the innocent along with the guilty. That for her, truth was the God of her choice and that in her eyes all mankind was equal in that they had the capacity to do good as well as evil. It just so happened that she chose the path of good.

Sinsee went directly into her zero gravity room. The moment the fields went on she relaxed. She had been in gravity far to long for her condition. The trial had lasted for days, and today had been the longest of all. She had sat through all the evidence and had listened to the defense arguments. All of it had been presented before the public. The truth could not be hidden from anyone who tuned into the broadcast. The way Sinsee had handled herself in the Hall left no doubt that the Millally were a great people. Great enough to forgive even those who had tried to assassinate her and her unborn sons, but right now Sinsee did not feel well at all. She reached out with her mind and touched Jewbee. [{"I need you my friend. I think it is time."}] [{"I am coming right now."}] came Jewbee's reply.

✹

It had been a difficult birth, Sinsee now lay in a portable Med Unit that had been wheeled into her Zero gravity room. There was a nurse on duty at all times, monitoring her vital signs. In the other room, the triplets were being looked after by two Nannies. Roeman looked in on Sinsee every hour until Jewbee told him that he was making the nurses nervous. "Relax Roeman. Sinsee will be out in two days, tops. Now go spend some time with your sons." Even though Jewbee said that everything was alright, it didn't stop Roeman from worrying or checking on Sinsee. Though he did stop coming in every hour on the hour.

Flowers and cards were coming in from everywhere. The flowers lined the corridors and passageways through out the Station. The Butterfly Birds were flitting from one bunch of flowers to the next. There friends had never seen them so happy before. It was a buzzing, zipping frenzy out there. People were ducking all over the place.

Bethany decided that what the birds needed was a year round botanical garden. Now that there was more room on the Station she ordered that the whole third sphere be converted into a botanical garden, complete with trees that thrived in large pots. She had them section out the sphere so that gardens from all the worlds could be represented, each with its own climate control. In the years to come, travelers from all over the Union would be able to see a bit of home here on Home Station. There would be those who made the trip just to see the gardens.

A replica of Lightenglow's Island was recreated on a smaller scale and every day the Butterfly Birds would come to this garden to exchange gossip on the days events.

✸

Just as Jewbee had promised, Sinsee was up and about in a few days. The first thing she did was fuss over the triplets then she spent a quiet evening with Roeman. The next day was back to business as always.

Sinsee ordered a complete survey and assessments of the five worlds. What was found appalled even the most hard minded members of the senate. Conditions on those worlds had not been seen sense the early 19th and 20th centuries back on old Earth. Poverty was so wide spread that it affected almost ninety five percent of the populations. The infant death rate was so high it was surprising that they had a population at all.

Given all the evidence, the Senate didn't take long to vote and approve of emergency relief shipments and medical supplies to be sent to all five worlds. Because Sinsee had not yet chosen under who's control the worlds would be given the jurisdiction fell under the control of the Senate of Worlds. Sinsee saw no reason to alter that jurisdiction.

In private Roeman confessed that if he had known of the conditions on those worlds he would not have been so eager to destroy those ships and their crews. The loss of life had been staggering.

"I understand how you feel Roeman. They didn't leave you much choice in the matter." She reached out and squeezed his hand. "Those governments were corrupted to the core. We could not interfere with out good cause. It is not our way. There has to be reason behind any action we take."

"I know, but when they threatened you and the boys, they brought their politics off world. It provided us with a reason to act against them." Roeman looked over to the play pen where his sons were trying to reach for the plastic mobile that hung over their heads. "Should they be doing that so soon?"

Sinsee laughed. "Roeman, where have you been? Your sons are rolling over on their own now. I expect them to be sitting up on their own within the week." Roeman walked over to stand next to the play pen. Sinsee moved to his side and he put his arm around her. He stood there smiling down at his sons. The boys smiled up at their parents and began waving arms and legs at them. Roeman started to chuckle which sent little Tenco into a squealing laughter, his brothers joined him.

✴

Roeman was going over the latest reports from the exploration ships when he came across one report that he almost took for a joke. If it had been anyone other then Captain Lane he would have dismissed it as just that, a joke. He reached out with his mind and touched Sinsee. [{"You need to come to my office. Bring Bethany with you."}] Roeman continued to scan through the photo files just to make sure he was really looking at what he thought he was looking at.

Sinsee and Bethany entered his office a few minutes later. "What's up?" asked Bethany. Roeman stood up from his chair and offered it to Sinsee. She sat down and with Roeman standing at her right and Bethany on her left they all looked at the screen. Roeman gave them enough time to go through the whole report. "Well, what do you think? Could this be more of Lightenglow's work?"

"There is no reference to this kind of stuff in his files. Besides, there are too many variations from one to the other." said Sinsee. "Has Parry seen this file?"

"Not yet. I wanted to get your take on this first. So what do you think?" he asked them again.

"I don't know about the two of you," said Bethany, "but I want to see one of these things up close and personal."

"So do I." said Roeman. "Shall we take a little trip and join Captain Lane? Yes? Bethany, I want you to tell Parry to gather his best teams, and I mean all of them." Roeman removed the file disk from the reader and handed it to her. "Show this to Parry, it should be enough to motivate him."

"Dad, some times I think you have a mean streak in you." She took the disk and headed out.

It took a few days to prepare for the journey. Parry insisted on bringing in teams from all over the Union. By the time he had everything he wanted Roeman had to call in another three ships to transport all of Parry's people and equipment.

"I never thought it took so much stuff and staff just to research a new world." said Duvale as the last of the crates were being loaded into his holds. "What is so special about this new world anyway?" Patrick reached into his pocket and pulled out a photo copy of one of the file reports. He handed it to Duvale, who looked closely at the photo. Patrick was not disappointed when Duvale's jaw dropped. Duvale started to stutter then was silent, he looked at Patrick.

"Yes Duvale, it is real." was all Patrick would say.

"Then what the hell are we doing standing around here for! You there! Get that hold sealed! We haven't got all day you know!" Duvale went to speed things up and Patrick just chuckled to himself, picking up his duffle bag, he walked onboard The White Dave.

Their small group, consisting of only key personnel at the moment, along with the triplets, stood on a small knoll off to one side of the blue green valley. The trees which lined the opposite side of the valley were in bloom with tiny velvet flowers the color of sapphires. The two shuttles were parked behind the knoll, out of sight from the valley. The group had been there for almost three hours now.

"There they are." someone whispered. "Just coming out of that grove of trees by the brook."

"Look Seenan." said Sinsee to the boy she held in her arms. "Look at the pretty ponies, look, can you see them."

The boy squirmed in his mothers arms and smiled trying to get a better look.

"It feels rather odd standing here looking at them like this. I keep expecting to wake up at any minute now and find that it has all been nothing more then a dream." said Captain Lane.

"If this is a dream, I don't want to wake up." replied Bethany.

"Maybe this is a sign that everything is going to be alright now." Sinsee looked up at her daughter who was holding Tenco in her arms. Roeman was holding Jayson and pointing to the small heard that was now grazing in the valley. They had not heard her words, but Captain Lane had.

"Do you want to bring one of them back to the Station with us Chandler?" she asked.

"No. This is their home. I don't want them to be stressed in any way." said Sinsee.

"You do know that people are going to want to come and see them. I have been here for some time now and each time I see them it invokes a different feeling in me. It sounds silly to say it out loud, but it is magical." said Lane.

"Yes, you are right on both counts. I will have to designate this world as a National Park. At least that way people can come and see for themselves, but no one is to touch any of those creatures." Sinsee looked over at Parry. "Do you understand me Parry. You can study any of the many life forms on this world, but you leave those," she pointed to the small heard below, "ALONE. You got me Parry?"

"My dear girl, only a mad man would want to harm a real live unicorn. I am a scientist, not a fool." he smiled at her.

"Look! There is a little foal coming out of the trees." That got every one's attention.

"Has any one thought of a mane for this world yet?" asked Duvale. "What about it Lane, you found this place, so what do you want to call it?"

"How does Magic in The Dreaming sound?" she smiled at him.

"A bit long in the tooth, don't you think?" Duvale smiled so much that she could count all of his teeth.

"It does sound just like it feels." said Sinsee. "I like it. From this day on this world will be known as Magic in The Dreaming. I feel that it will become a bright star for all of us. The kids are getting hungry, but I am not ready to go in just yet."

"Why don't we have a picnic right here? We can enjoy the rest of the day and watch the heard from right here." said Bethany.

"That sounds like a great idea. Come on Duvale, we can get the food and drinks for everyone." Lane grabbed Duvale by the hand and pulled him towards the shuttles. Parry offered to lend a hand and that was how they spent their first day with the unicorns. No one really wanted to work that day anyway. They were quite content to just lay or sit on the sweet smelling grass that covered the knoll. The boys were crawling all over the place. Every now and then an adult would get up and retrieve one or the other of the boys who would manage to wander a little too far out from the group.

The unicorns were watching the antics of the humans just as much as the humans were watching them. Little Tenco managed to get far enough away from the adults that the unicorn foal dared to come up to him. An adult unicorn called to the foal and it returned to the heard. Roeman went to retrieve his son. "That is enough of that young man."

"It is time to go." said Sinsee. The sun was just beginning to set and the color of the sky changed and spread out from the horizon in bands of gold and crimson. "Bed time now." Sinsee picked up Seenan while Bethany carried Jayson. "We can see the pretty ponies again tomorrow."

"Come to think of it, I am rather tired myself." said Roeman. He followed his words with a yawn, which started a chain reaction all the way around. They all laughed as they gathered up their belongings and headed back to the shuttles.

✸

Upon returning to Home station Roeman and Sinsee set about setting restriction for any visitors to Magic in The Dreaming. They did not want the planet to be contaminated in any way. All waste had to be removed when the visitors left the planet. It was Parry's job to discover the time frame for the breeding and foaling seasons of the unicorns. During this time no visitors would be allowed on Magic in The Dreaming. All housing had to be temporary with the ability to be removed at a moments notice. Only one structure would be allowed that was to be a permanent research facility.

While these preparations were put into effect Sinsee decided to visit Third World, where her new friends lived. She had not been to see them sense before the boys were born. Roeman thought it was a good idea. He wanted to see the Gill men's reaction to his three sons. And it was a good idea for his sons to see the world that they were going to be protecting in the future.

As They walked out onto the landing Sinsee called a greeting and the aquatic men and women came leaping up out of the water. They were happy to see their new friends again and even more astounded to see the three boys. The women made a huge fuss over them and asked Sinsee how she had managed to have three sons at the same time. [{"Your man must be very powerful."}] Laughter in the mind has a different feel then when someone laughs out loud. It is more like a ringing and tingling sensation. One that Sinsee wished she could share with everyone.

They spent a full week on Third World. Roeman was surprised when his sons went into the water with some of the aquatic women and actually started to swim even before they could walk. Sinsee took to the water as if she were an aquatic herself. When she tried to get Roeman into the water he shook his head and said that he could not swim so he stayed on the landing and just watched.

When it came time for them to return to Home Station the Aquatics presented Sinsee with a fan of deep blue coral a good three feet tall with a spread of almost six feet. She had never seen anything like it before.

The boys started to cry when they were taken onto the shuttle. Roeman and Sinsee got another shock when Jayson gave a mental cry. [{"Swim!"}] Roeman looked at Sinsee. "Now why couldn't he say Daddy or even Mommy? Why does his first word have to be Swim?" Sinsee put both her hands over her mouth and tried to stop herself from laughing. Then she abruptly stopped. The look on her face was one of pure wonder.

"Roeman, Jayson is telepathic. He didn't speak that word, he thought it." She looked down at her son who was now sucking his thumb.

"But how can that be? He is only what, eighteen months old? What a minute, are you thinking that exposure to the aquatics may have triggered his talent?" Roeman knelt dawn to get Jayson's attention. [{"Say Daddy. Come on, be a good boy and say Daddy, Daddy."}]

[{"Swim Daddy."}] came Jayson's reply.

"Well at least he said Daddy." laughed Sinsee.

Sector Marshal Dee sat in the chair across from Roeman and watched the expression on his face as he read the new file from the terraforming team on the Catsman Home World. Roeman shook his head in disbelief as he put his hand on the viewing screen. He looked up from the screen at Dee. "How did we miss this?" he asked as a rhetorical question.

"We have been working there now for a few years. The size of that port is so massive, not to mention the number of ships that we still have not entered yet. The original empty cradles were on opposite ends of the port. When we started to take the ships off planet we opened up more cradles and it just got lost in the crowd. What do we do now?" Dee leaned back in his chair and crossed his legs.

Roeman contacted Sinsee by gently touching her mind, he warned her to control her reaction before he told her what was going on. She said that she would be joining him and that she would send Pregger to his office as well. She also might be a few minutes late, Bethany was not yet back from her meeting with the senator from Colvert's World.

Dee waited patiently while Roeman communicated with Sinsee. He had recognized the expression on Roeman's face that told him Roeman was using his telepathic talent. Dee's mouth formed a half smile as he thought of Rivor, the zero gravity trainer, he finally got a lion cub to accept him and that fact encouraged Dee to continue to visit the lion nursery on a daily basis. If a lion would pick Rivor then there had to be one out there who would pick him, and the new birthing season was about to begin.

"Sinsee and Pregger will be joining us soon. Bethany is still in a meeting, but she says she will join us as soon as she gets out of the meeting with Senator Trace. She also says that Trace has told her something very interesting, but she wont say what it is." Roeman smiled. "She is more and more like her mother."

"If you ask me, she is more like you then she is Sinsee." said Dee. "She looks like Sinsee but she acts like you."

"How so?" asked Roeman.

"Well for one, Sinsee doesn't play cards, doesn't drink with the boys, and doesn't have more then one lover." said Dee.

"What!" Shouted Roeman. He had no idea that his daughter even had one lover let alone a number of them. He would have to have a talk with her about that. [{"You leave her alone Roeman. Her love life is none of our business!"}] came Sinsee's voice in his head.

"You just got chewed out, didn't you?" asked Dee.

"Shut up!" Roeman sneered at Dee. "How is it you know so much about Bethany and I don't? And for your information, Sinsee is the only woman I have ever been with."

Dee's mouth dropped. After all those years of card playing and drinking, he never knew that Roeman had never been with a woman before. That meant that he had never partaken in the first pairing rites. That also meant that when he and Sinsee... Oh Shit!

"Oh shut-up!" Roeman said once again. Dee couldn't help himself and he started to laugh. Roeman just sneered at him until he got himself under control. "Are you done now? Do you think we can get back to the business at hand?"

"I'm sorry Roeman, it is just that I thought I knew you. I promise that I wont laugh at you anymore." said Dee with a straight face, but inside he was laughing up a storm.

"You better get yourself under control before Sinsee gets here or she will have you hanging by your heels." said Roeman. "Your broadcasting that laughter of yours. Shit! You are Broadcasting!" Roeman got up from his seat and went to the main door of his office and opened it to have a look out into the hall. Just outside of his office was a young male Lion pacing up and down in the corridor. "Hay Dee! I think there is someone out here who is looking for you."

[{"There you are. I have been looking all over for you."}] said the Lion as he walked into Roeman's office. Dee reached up and scratched the hell out of his head. Now it was Roeman's turn to laugh at Dee.

By the time Sinsee arrived Dee was getting to know his new friend. His name was given to him by the others from his litter. They called him Greedy Boy, though he did not understand why. He had been the largest cub in his litter and naturally he needed more food then the others, but the name stuck.

Pregger arrived and Roeman showed him the report. "

This means that one other ship made it off your world. Was there any information handed down to your generation about another ship that left your world?"

[{"I don't remember being told of another ship. Perhaps one of the others remembers something. We must remember that if that information was passed down, it might have been passed from Captain to Captain. Our original Captain died of the sickness."}] said Pregger.

"What about personal records of the former captain?" asked Sinsee. "Did your captain keep records other then ships business?"

"Not that I know of." replied Pregger.

"Then the only thing we can do is keep an eye out for any signs of the other ship." said Roeman. "I'll send the word out to all the search ships. We may never know what happened to that other ship."

"I don't know about that Roeman. It seems that we have had pretty good luck up to this point." said Dee.

"Are you sure its luck and not just hard work?" Roeman looked at him.

"Fair enough." said Dee, as he rubbed the back of his new friend, Greedy Boy. "Well, there is nothing we can do about it right now other then notify the ships, so if this is all, I think I would like to take Greedy Boy and show him his new home." Roeman smiled as he watched his old time friend lead the way out of the office. He laughed as he heard Greedy Boy tell Dee that he liked milk and wanted to know if Dee had any milk where they were going. Roeman could just see the expression on the supply manager's face when he got an order for milk from Sector Marshal Dee.

Bethany had a late night meeting with her father. He agreed with her that Sinsee should not be told the news from the Senate just yet. He wanted a chance to check with Senator Trace himself to verify her intentions.

Sinsee spent as much of her free time as she could in the third sphere in the garden that resembled the one at the Foundation on Terra Two. She could of coarse name every plant and tree there. Now that the triplets were in school she found that she had more time on her hands. Danny was out somewhere with his Fleet and Bethany now chaired the Senate. She had been spending long hours in closed conferences with the Senate and Roeman had joined his daughter with the Senate today.

Sinsee sat next to the small pond and ran her fingers over the surface of the water where tiny fish darted away from her hand. It was here that Roeman and Bethany found her. She looked up as they approached her.

"You are out early today." she said as they reached her. She saw the look on Roeman's face. "What has happened?" she asked as she started to get to her feet.

"No don't get up." said Roeman as he sat down next to her, he took her hand in his. "The Senate and the Union of Worlds have cast their vote."

"Cast their vote on what?" asked Sinsee. "What do they want now?"

"Sinsee, they have voted You, The Empress of The Empire of Worlds." He squeezed her hand.

"NO!" She looked at Bethany who nodded her head. "OH GOD! WHY ME!" Sinsee closed her eyes and shook her head, when she opened her eyes she was smiling. "I had just gotten used to all this free time too."

Roeman laughed at her. "You could never just sit around for long. I know you to well. But at least now you have all the help you could possibly need."

Sinsee looked into Roeman's eyes. "If I am the Empress doesn't that make you the Emperor?"

"No. It is a right that can only pass from Mother to Daughter." Roeman looked up at Bethany. "And it would seem that we now have three generations of women in the family."

Sinsee looked up at her daughter who put her hands on her stomach and nodded. Sinsee jumped to her feet and hugged Bethany to her.

Bethany leaned in to whisper into her mother's ear. "The Empire lives on."

"Yes my Beth. It does." laughed Sinsee.